To Kill the

MARK JOSEPH grew up beside the Mare Island Naval Shipyard in Vallejo, California, where many of the American nuclear submarines were built, and this early familiarity gave him a lifelong interest in them. He read Political Science at the University of California, spending a year at the University of Sussex where he wrote his first short story. He has been writing ever since, primarily for magazines. *To Kill the Potemkin* took five years in all to complete, including three years of research. Although it is a first novel, Gerald A. Browne, author of *11 Harrowhouse*, has said: 'Mark Joseph is that rare first novelist who seems to have mastered his craft and subject overnight. Remarkable!'

'More thrilling than THE HUNT FOR RED OCTOBER' *Kirkus Reviews*

'A winner of a story . . . for readers of DAS BOOT' *Publishers Weeekly*

MARK JOSEPH

To Kill the Potemkin

FONTANA/Collins

First published in Great Britain by Souvenir Press Ltd 1987
First issued in Fontana Paperbacks 1988

Printed and bound in Great Britain by
William Collins Sons & Co. Ltd, Glasgow

FOR MY FATHER

War is a game.
CLAUSEWITZ

All war is deception.
SUN TZU

PROLOGUE

On May 27, 1968, at one o'clock in the afternoon, the USS *Scorpion*, a nuclear submarine with ninety-nine men aboard, was due to arrive at her home port of Norfolk, Virginia, after a ninety-day patrol. The families of the crew were waiting on the dock.

At about three o'clock a navy public affairs officer announced that *Scorpion* was overdue. She had failed to request her berthing assignment and tug services.

Scorpion had last communicated on May 21, when she filed a routine position report from fifty miles off the Azores in the mid-Atlantic.

After several more hours of continued silence, the navy undertook a massive search of the waters around Norfolk. Over the next few days the search was widened into deep Atlantic. On June 5, the navy declared *Scorpion* presumed lost with all hands, and on June 30 her name was struck from the navy list.

The loss of *Scorpion* was the worst disaster to befall a fully armed United States Navy warship on patrol since the end of World War Two.

The USS *Scorpion*, SSN 589, one of six Skipjack class submarines, was 252 feet long and 31 feet wide. She was built by the Electric Boat Division of General Dynamics Corporation in Groton, Connecticut, and commissioned July 29, 1960, at a cost of forty million dollars. Her S5W nuclear reactor, built by Westinghouse, was capable of lighting a small city. An attack submarine, a hunter-killer, she carried no ballistic missiles. She was armed with torpedoes of various types, including several with nuclear warheads designed to destroy enemy submarines and other capital ships. Her crew of ninety-nine represented the highest level of training and achievement of any military unit in the Armed Forces of the United States. They were the navy's elite.

Their loss went largely unnoticed. In May 1968 American soldiers and sailors died every day in Viet Nam. France endured a general strike. Students at Columbia and elsewhere laid siege to their universities. The battle of Khe San, the cultural revolution in China, the civil war in Nigeria, and the death the previous month of Dr Martin Luther King, Jr, crowded the front pages of America's newspapers. Unlike the *Thresher*, which sank in April 1963 during a time of relative tranquility, the *Scorpion* has been all but forgotten.

On June 5, 1968, a Navy Court of Inquiry convened in Norfolk and took testimony in secret from more than ninety witnesses. On August 5 *The New York Times*, in a two-paragraph article in the back pages, reported that technicians at a US Navy SOSUS (Sound Surveillance System) listening station in Greece made a tape recording of an implosion in the mid-Atlantic on May 21.

Meanwhile, the search in the deep Atlantic began in earnest. The USS *Mizar*, an oceanographic research vessel, was assigned the task of finding the wreck. *Mizar* towed a sled over the bottom, more than ten thousand feet down, and searched with sonars, magnometers, lights, and television and still cameras.

In August the Court adjourned with no conclusive evidence as to the cause of the disaster. On October 29 *Mizar* found the wreck of *Scorpion* four hundred miles from her last reported position, under 11,235 feet of water, and took twelve thousand photographs of the debris field.

The Court reconvened in November, examined the evidence gathered by *Mizar* and issued a Findings of Fact on January 31, 1969. Most of that document remains classified today. In the declassified portions the Court declared that 'the certain cause of the loss of *Scorpion* cannot be ascertained from any evidence now available.' The death of SSN 589 became an official mystery.

During the early months of 1968 multiple submarine disasters were reported in the public press. On February 25 the Israeli sub *Dakar* disappeared in the Mediterranean. In the same month, the French sub *Minerve* also sank in the Mediterranean. On April 11 a Soviet Navy Golf II class submarine sank in the Pacific. Several months later parts of that sub were raised by the *Glomar Explorer*. *Scorpion* exploded and sank on May 21. Were all these events coincidence? Answers may lie deep in the archives of all the navies involved. The essence of submarine warfare is secrecy and stealth, and submarine operations rank among the most carefully guarded secrets of all military powers. In the US Navy, submariners are said to belong to the Silent Service. The boats are quiet, but the men are mute.

Nevertheless, as in all navies, there is scuttlebutt. Rumours circulate for years, become exaggerated and inflated, but never lose their fascination. Was there a sub war in the late 1960s, when the Soviet Navy was making frantic efforts to catch and technologically surpass the US Navy?

The story that follows is fiction. The ships and the men who sailed them are imaginary, but their time and the nature of their struggle were real. Then, as now, twenty-four hours a day, 365 days a year, the submarine forces of the United States Navy and Soviet Navy confronted one another under all the oceans of earth, playing a deadly game of nuclear war. What happened then, if it happened at all, may happen again . . .

MAY, 1968

___

1

SILVER DOLPHINS

Twin dolphins faced each other across Sorensen's chest. Sailors called them dolphins, but the strange creatures inked into Sorensen's skin scarcely resembled the small singing whales that live in the sea. Their eyes bulged and their mouths gaped, as if they were about to devour the submarine making way between them. The sub, an old-fashioned diesel-electric with knife-edged prow, crude sonar dome and archaic anchor, appeared to drive straight out of Sorensen's heart.

Over the years the tattoo had faded to a bluish grey. Tufts of blond hair obscured some of the intricate detail, but the legend that curved over the sub was still legible: SSN 593.

Sorensen was a big man. Even in his present condition, drunk, stoned, sprawled naked on a whore's bed, his wide shoulders and lean swimmer's muscles spent and exhausted, he radiated tension like a sheathed sword.

Almost asleep, he closed his eyes and listened to the girl breathing softly beside him.

Ordinarily, Lorraine took little notice of her tricks, most of whom came from the navy base. Sorensen was different. He spent a lot of money, he knew what he wanted and he treated her right. She was enjoying herself. She liked the way his lopsided smile slanted across his face when he grinned. Dark rings surrounded his eyes, but whether they were a permanent feature, she didn't know. His hair was longer than regulation and slicked back over large ears. His skin was tan and healthy.

Lazily, she traced her fingers over the tattoo. She had been in Norfolk long enough to recognize the insignia of the Submarine Service, and long enough to know which questions not to ask a submariner. No, they didn't get claustrophobic. Yes, they got insanely horny on a long patrol. Yes, they worried about the radiation, but not too much. They all said the asbestos was worse.

'How long you been in the navy, Jack?'

Without opening his eyes, Sorensen mumbled, 'Too long.'

'I bet you're a lifer. Otherwise you wouldn't have this tattoo.'

'Yeah, well, one night in Tokyo I had too much to drink. So it goes, so it goes.'

She giggled. 'You submarine guys are all a little crazy, you know? But you're the only one I ever saw with a tan.'

He smiled. 'You like that?'

'You look like one of them California surfers.'

'Hardly likely. I'm from Oakland. That's California, but the only beach is a mudflat where people shoot ducks and watch bodies float by. That's my home town, but I've never been back.'

'Wait. Let me guess. Now your address is on your chest, right?'

'Right.'

'SSN 593. That your ship?'

'USS *Barracuda*. The one and only.'

'You're a lifer, Sorensen. Admit it.'

He opened his eyes and looked at her. 'We're all lifers, every last one of us. You, too.' He closed his eyes again. 'What time is it?'

'Three a.m.'

'Listen, be a good girl and let me sleep for an hour. Wake me up at four.'

'Sure, sailor.'

He listened to her slide out of bed, walk across the room and pour herself a drink. Ice, whiskey, water. From outside came insect noises and the grinding and whirring of a garbage truck. Sorensen pulled a pillow over his ears.

Lorraine sipped her drink and gazed at the naked man on her bed. He fidgeted in his sleep as if he were disturbed by his dreams.

Suzy had told her that Sorensen visited the house once or twice a year, usually the night before *Barracuda* went on patrol. That evening he had presented Suzy with a silk kimono, explaining that he had just returned from a two-day round trip to Japan. Upstairs he had a drink and relaxed. To Lorraine's delight, he had demonstrated a novel miniature tape recorder he had brought back from Tokyo. The machine fit into his jumper pocket, and he had dozens of tiny reels of ultrathin tape. During the night they had listened to Fats Domino, Mose Allison, Beethoven, Hoyt Axton and the Grateful Dead.

While Sorensen slept she found the Hoyt Axton tape and listened to him sing about junkies and cowboys, wondering lazily what life was like under a city block of ocean.

Sorensen listened to the night. A toilet flushed on the floor above, and he followed the water as it gurgled down through the pipes on its way to Chesapeake Bay. He strained to hear the sounds of the harbor, ships and buoys, but they were too far away, lost in the shore sounds of trucks and trains and the low rumble of a sleeping city. Gradually the sounds of Norfolk were replaced by the ocean sounds inside his head. Submarine sounds, underwater sounds, whales, snapping shrimp, sonar beacons.

Just before passing out, the last thing Sorensen heard was the sound of engine-room machinery pounding in his head. Steam throttled through valves and pumps, pushing turbines and turning gears. It was as if he were listening to his own blood rushing through his arteries. He fell asleep and dreamed he was a steel fish with a nuclear

17

heart, swimming effortlessly through the vast blackness of the sea.

He had surrendered to the dream long ago. Asleep, he became *Barracuda*. The ship's technology became an extension of his senses; her sonars were as his own ears, plunging him into a world of pure sound. The open sea is a noisy place. Whales signal across thousands of miles. Fish chatter and croak. Surface ships clutter up the medium with their struggle against wind, waves and turbulence. As *Barracuda*, perfect and invulnerable lord of the deep, Sorensen ignored them all. He was searching for one sound, one unforgettable sound. It was another sub, sometimes far away, sometimes nearby, but always moving and elusive. The sound faded in and out, one moment barely audible, an instant later roaring in his ear. The sound was deeper in pitch than that of any other sub in Sorensen's experience, and conveyed a sense of raw power and terrible menace. Though he taxed his remarkable hearing to the limit, he could never establish its identity.

This time it was closer than ever before, so close he could hear men breathing inside. They wore black uniforms. One of them was the sonar operator, sitting at a console. Sorensen listened to his beating heart, and when the man turned around, Sorensen saw his own face.

After an hour Lorraine gently shook his shoulder.

'Jack, wake up.'

'Go 'way.'

'Listen, you told me to wake you up at four. It's a quarter after.'

She heard him sigh. 'Okay. Give me a minute. Turn off the light.'

Awake, he realized the dream would never end. It was too deeply rooted in his psyche to disappear completely. Sorensen wasn't sure what it meant. Perhaps he had lived underwater too long. On each patrol *Barracuda* seemed to get closer to the Russians. Or maybe the Russians were getting closer to him.

Lorraine was standing next to the bed, her dressing-gown parted in the middle. Between the wine-red folds of satin, a streak of creamy flesh was visible from her neck to her blond pubic hair. Sorensen kissed her thigh. She smelled of strawberries.

'Did you have a bad dream?'

'Why? Did I say anything?'

'You said, "It's a Russian," but the rest was mumbo jumbo.'

He slapped himself in the cheek. 'Shut up, Sorensen. You talk too much.'

She lay down beside him and fondled him until he grew hard. He ran his hand over her rump and stroked the back of her legs. She was a bit overweight, which was why he had chosen her from the line-up in Suzy's parlour. Skinny women reminded him of his ex-wife.

She rolled over and straddled him.

'This one's for free,' she said, and leaned over to lick his chest.

It had been a steamy night. After eight years of living on a submarine, Sorensen knew how to get his money's worth. Expensive, but worth it. Blowing his brains out with sex and booze made as much sense as anything else. Nothing he did ashore made any difference because nothing ashore was real. Life ashore was layer after layer of illusion, like the TV news. Nothing important ever got on TV. Anything important was classified. Reality was top secret.

'Can I turn on the light?'

'Sure.'

Sorensen shaded his eyes with his hands and looked at Lorraine. She was pretty. At Suzy's they were always pretty. She slipped off and lit a cigarette.

'Is there any beer left?' he asked.

'It's warm.'

'That's okay.'

He stood up and teetered. 'Christ almighty.' He grinned his off-center grin. 'I must be getting old.'

He found a bottle of beer, opened it and sat back down on the bed. The room was decorated in a Victorian style with paisley wallpaper and velour couches. Suzy's was the best whorehouse in Norfolk, and he was comfortable there. He liked the whores. They didn't complain when he babbled nonsense about the navy, the nucs, the officers or even the Russians. They didn't try to pry secrets out of him, or ask him to explain what he did or why he did it. They just fucked him and laughed at his jokes. Sometimes they gave him the clap.

Through an open window he heard trucks passing on a highway. Norfolk droned, a city asleep. The ocean never slept. Underwater there was neither night nor day, only the passing of the watches and blinking numbers on a digital chronometer.

It was time to go. *Barracuda* sailed at dawn. The reactor in his mind was critical. The chain reaction had started.

While he was putting on his uniform, there was a knock on the door. 'Sorensen, you *pinche cabron*, are you in there?'

The voice was pure East Los Angeles.

'Who's that?' Lorraine asked.

'Open it up,' Sorensen said.

Jesus Manuel Lopez y Corona stood in the corridor, two hundred fifty pounds of Mexican torpedoman dressed in the full regalia of a chief petty officer.

'I ain't gonna let you screw up, Ace. Come on outta there. You're late.'

'Want a beer, Chief? Meet my friend, Lorraine.'

'Pleased to make your acquaintance. You'll excuse me,

but it's a little early in the day for breakfast. The shore patrol has kindly lent me a car and driver. He's waiting downstairs.'

'How'd you know I was here?' Sorensen wasn't angry, merely curious.

'I'm chief of the boat, Sorensen. It's my job to know where every one of you *cabrones* is every minute. Besides' – Lopez lowered his voice and winked – 'me and Suzy are old pals. She called the ship and told me you were here. Let's go.'

Sorensen looked at himself in the mirror. His eyes were bloodshot and he needed a shave. His uniform was rumpled. He drew himself to attention, placed his hat two fingers above his eyebrows and saluted.

'Listen, Lorraine, did I pay you?'

'You paid Suzy.'

Sorensen picked up his kit bag, checked to make sure he had his recorder and tapes, and pulled out a fifty dollar bill.

'Here's a little extra. For truth, justice and the American way. See ya later, baby.'

2

BARRACUDA

Sorensen sat in the back of the jeep, peering with underwater eyes at the shabby streets and rotting Victorians of Norfolk. He felt as though a sheet of water was between him and *Barracuda*'s home port. To him, Norfolk was a target, a blip on a Soviet attack console, and when he was there, he felt naked and exposed, like a sub on the surface.

The jeep turned a corner and he caught a glimpse of lights on the river and the darkness of the Atlantic beyond.

'What's the word, Chief?' We got us a Russkie out there?'

Lopez shook his head. 'Nah. There was one sub that tried to get in yesterday, but Ivan hasn't figured out yet that we can track him anywhere in the Atlantic. We let this November class get in as far as fifty miles offshore, but *Mako* flushed her last night. She won't be back. She's heading for the ice pack.'

'Why didn't they leave it for us?'

'You're nuts, Sorensen, you know that? All you ever want to do is chase the Russians around the ocean. Me, I like a nice quiet patrol with no excitement.'

'That's because you're a torpedoman, Lopez. It makes you nervous to think that someday you may even have to blow off one of your fish.'

'This is my last patrol, Sorensen. I been down below for twenty years and I've never fired a war shot yet. I want to go out the same way.'

'I'm gonna miss you, Chief.'

'You won't miss me, Ace. You'll be a thousand feet down, worrying about a saltwater pipe bursting and a jet of water cutting you in half. You'll be eating radiation and turning in your film badge. While you're trying to get into the Gulf of Finland, waiting for the Russians to drop sonic depth bombs all over the place, I'll be in LA lyin' around the pool sippin' a cold beer.'

'Sure, Lopez. And what about your seven kids? You gonna buy them a beer, too?'

Lopez laughed, his heavy jaw hanging open and his gold teeth glinting in the street light. 'My kids don't drink beer. They smoke reefer and drink mescal.'

Traffic picked up as they neared the navy base. The day shift was going to work in the dark. The shore patrol driver stopped at the gate, and the Marine guard waved them through.

Sorensen said, 'I heard a nasty rumor, Chief. I heard they assigned thirteen apprentice seamen to the ship yesterday.'

Lopez turned around to face the back seat. 'You heard wrong. They're not all apprentices. Yours is a third class.'

'Mine? What do you mean, mine?' Sorensen groaned.

'That's the way it is. You get Sonarman Third Class Michael Fogarty.'

'I don't suppose he's qualified in subs.'

'You suppose right. But he's supposed to be another hotshot, just like you, Ace. He's your baby, you keep him in line.'

The first red splashes of dawn appeared over Hampton Roads, turning the Elizabeth River to blood. The jeep wound its way through the base, past shops guarded by marines, past the quonset hut that served as headquarters for Submarine Squadron Six.

Two hundred people lined the submarine pier. Families clustered around their sailors, touching them in little ways. Mothers patted flat their sons' collars, fingering the white piping. Little boys saluted their fathers. One by one the sailors kissed their wives and children and

23

disappeared down the hatch.

There was a commotion as the crowd parted before the jeep. Lopez and the driver sat in front, faces impassive, eyes straight ahead. From the back seat Sorensen waved his hat to the crowd like an astronaut on parade. 'I love ya, I love ya,' he shouted to the kids.

Out of the side of his mouth Lopez growled, 'Shut up, Sorensen. You ain't no movie star.'

Sorensen smiled at the crowd and continued to wave. The kids waved back.

The jeep stopped at the gangway. Straining at her lines, *Barracuda* rode low in the water with little more than her sail and rudder above the surface. She had the look of a great black shark, a predator of the deep come momentarily into the light. Bunting hung from the gangway, and for a moment the white stars in the fabric shimmered red.

Sorensen smartly squared his hat and climbed out of the jeep. Reaching inside his jumper pocket, he extracted a five dollar bill and dropped it in the shore patrolman's lap. 'Thanks for the lift, pal. This is my stop.'

From his perch on the bridge Captain John Springfield watched the proceedings on the pier. He enjoyed the pomp, if only because it meant a brief respite from the tension of preparing his ship for patrol.

The tall, slender Texan had been in command of *Barracuda* for eighteen months, long enough, he thought, to have become intimately acquainted with the ship and her crew. He scrutinized the sailors as they went aboard. Torpedomen, yeomen, reactor technicians, the quartermaster. The eldest was the steward, forty-three-year-old Jimmy 'Cakes' Colby. The youngest was an eighteen-year-old seaman apprentice, Duane Hicks. Springfield was thirty-five.

He watched Sorensen come aboard. At sea Sorensen

was perfectly disciplined. Ashore, well, at least this time they didn't have to salvage him from the drunk tank at Newport News.

The ship tugged gently at her lines. The tide had peaked, stopped for an instant and now was ebbing back to the sea. A flurry of butterflies churned up his stomach. A navy band struck up *The Stars and Stripes Forever*.

In the control room the executive officer, Lt Commander Leo Pisaro, was going through the departure checklist when Sorensen came through the hatch. Pisaro held up his hand for Sorensen to wait and went on with his list. He spoke into a headset with division heads throughout the ship.

'Reactor control, report.'

'Steam, thirty-one percent.'

'Very well. Engine room, report.'

'Engine room standing by on number one turbine.'

'Very well. Helm, report.'

'Helm standing by.'

'Very well. Stern planes, report.'

'Stern planes standing by.'

'Good afternoon, Sorensen, good of you to join us.'

Sorensen snapped to attention. 'Petty Officer First Class Sorensen reporting for duty, sir.'

Starkly bald, swarthy, tenacious, Pisaro was the only officer aboard who was not an Annapolis graduate. His jumpsuit was covered with patches and insignia, a quilt of blazing lightning bolts, missiles, guns, swords and antique engines of destruction. The newest and most prominent patch was a sub whose bow tapered into the snout of a great barracuda. 'SSN 593,' it read. 'Shipkiller.'

He snapped open a heavy Zippo and lit a Pall Mall.

'You're four hours late, Sorensen.'

'Yes, sir.'

'It's a good thing Chief Lopez knew where to find you.'

25

'Yes, sir.'

'You drunk?'

'No, sir. Hung over.' Sorensen tugged at his crotch.

Pisaro shook his head, smiling to himself. Every cruise was the same. Either the shore patrol or the civilian police would drag Sorensen back to the ship, and he would stand in the control room with a shit-eating grin on his face and scratch his balls. His uniform was a mess. His hat was dirty. He smelled.

One thing was certain: drunk or hung over, Sorensen could go into the sonar room right now, sit down at his console and drive the ship to Naples.

'All right. Get out of your blues. I want you in sonar in fifteen minutes.'

'Yes, sir.'

'You're a disgusting mess, man. Take a shower.'

'Aye aye, Commander.'

Sorensen descended two decks to the forward crews quarters. The compartment was crowded with boisterous sailors changing from blues into shipboard uniforms, dark-blue nylon jumpsuits and rubber-soled shoes.

'What say, Ace? Where the hell you been?'

Sorensen searched the upper tier of bunks for the owner of the bayou drawl. A freckle-faced redhead peeked out from behind a technical manual.

'Hey, Willie Joe.'

'Where you been, man?'

'Tokyo.'

'Tokyo, Japan?'

'That's the one.'

'You're puttin' me on. Lopez was pissed. You ain't never on time.'

'It's a long ride back from Tokyo. Don't worry about the chief. We kissed and made up.'

Sonarman Second Class Willie Joe Black lay down his booklet and yellow felt-tipped pen. 'Tell me something,

Ace. I know I shouldn't ask, but why the hell did you go to Japan with just three days' liberty?'

'I got a friend over there.'

'That's a long way to go to get laid.'

'Not that kind of friend,' Sorensen laughed. 'I know this guy, an old pal from sub school who lives over there. He's what you might call an advanced gadget freak. He likes to make toys a few years before anybody else.'

'So what did he make for you?'

'This,' Sorensen replied, tossing the tape recorder on Willie Joe's bunk.

'What is it?'

'What's it look like?'

'I dunno. I never seen anything like it.'

Sorensen pushed a button and out came the Beatles' 'Can't Buy Me Love'. Throughout the compartment, heads swiveled toward the music. A half-dozen sailors crowded around Willie Joe's bunk, all talking at once.

'What is that?'

'Whereja git that thing?'

'Is it a radio?'

'I hate the Beatles, ain't you got the Stones?'

'It's a tape recorder, the smallest in the world. Rechargeable battery, the works.'

Shaking his head in amazement, Willie Joe asked, 'Transistors?'

'Yeah, nothin' to it, really, except the heads.'

Willie Joe picked up his pen and resumed his study of advanced hydraulics. Sorensen peeked at the cover of the manual. 'You looking for a promotion, Willie Joe?'

'Yeah. My old lady wants a new Bonneville. If I make first class, I guess she can have it.'

'You spend your liberty with her and your kids?'

'Sure did. I think I spent all three days buying carloads of crap in the Navy Exchange.'

'You love it,' Sorensen said.

'*You* went to Japan.'

'For six hours.'

The Beatles went into 'Back in the USSR'. Sorensen looked around at the faces shining in the bright fluorescent lights. The music seemed to pop the bubble of pressure that surrounded departure. He recognized all but one of the sailors.

'Willie Joe,' he said, 'I hear we got a green pea.'

'That's right.'

'Did you check him out?'

'No, he just got here. He's a good-lookin' kid, and he'd better watch his ass.' Willie Joe grinned and nodded his head in the direction of a young sailor standing in the passageway, hands stuffed in the pockets of his jumpsuit, staring at the maze of piping and cables that ran through the top of the compartment. He didn't appear shy but he hung back from the crowd around Willie Joe's bunk and the little tape recorder. He had a pretty face and a look that wasn't so much cocky as confident.

Fogarty felt Sorensen's eyes looking him up and down. He lit a Lucky Strike and turned to meet Sorensen's stare.

Sorensen walked over to him. 'Got another smoke, kid?'

'Sure.' Fogarty held out his pack and offered his cigarette as a light. Sorensen noticed that Fogarty had not torn the aluminium foil away from the pack but had carefully folded it over the tobacco to keep it fresh. Sorensen took a cigarette and replaced the foil as he found it.

'Fogarty, right?'

'Right.' Fogarty smiled. 'You must be Sorensen.'

'That's me.'

'I heard about you in sonar school.'

Sorensen waited.

'They played us tapes of all the different Soviet subs and told us you're the guy who made the tapes. They said you've collected more signatures of Soviet subs than

28

anyone else.'

'That's what they told you? It wasn't me, kid. It was *Barracuda*. Whatever we do here, we do together. Willie Joe there, he's done his share, too. It's the luck of the draw.'

Fogarty nodded. 'That makes me the luckiest guy in the navy. I asked for this ship.'

'You must believe in miracles. I'll tell you straight, kid. *Barracuda* is going to get a special assignment in Naples, and they put you and all these other apprentices on this ship to foul us up and get in our way.'

Sorensen was a good four inches taller than Fogarty, and his narrowed, unsmiling eyes bore down on Fogarty. When he saw that Fogarty didn't flinch, kept cool, he relaxed.

'Well, you're here,' he said. 'We'll make the best of it. You stow your gear?'

'I did.'

'Tell me something, Fogarty. Why'd you ask for this ship?'

'Because of you, Sorensen. I wanted to learn from the best.'

'You mean you don't know everything yet?'

Fogarty seemed to blush and shook his head. Sorensen punched him in the shoulder and was surprised to find the muscle hard as steel. 'All right, kid. Welcome aboard.'

'Thanks.'

'Thanks for the smoke. Catch you later.'

Sorensen retrieved his tape recorder, switched off the music, and put the machine and tapes in his locker. 'Show's over for today, gents. Tune in tomorrow.'

Willie Joe leaned over the edge of his bunk. 'We muster in ten minutes, Ace.'

'Okay. Where's Davic?'

'Where do you think?'

'In the galley stuffing his face. Who's the sonar officer

this trip?'

'Hoek. He's been made weapons officer, too.'

'Oh, that's ducky. We'll have a regular fat guys' convention,' Sorensen said. 'You know something, Willie Joe? The navy's got its head up its ass.'

He stripped off his blues and stashed them in his locker. In jockey shorts he paraded through the compartment, flexing his muscles and displaying his tattoo. Whistling, *We all live in a yellow submarine*, he headed for the showers.

A year out of Annapolis and fresh from Nuclear Power School, Lt Fred Hoek was making his second patrol. Twenty-three years old, gung-ho, overweight and plagued by zits, Hoek was the ninth sonar officer to serve on *Barracuda* in eight years.

He was standing at attention in the executive officer's tiny cabin, watching Pisaro shuffle papers. Pisaro's thick lips and large teeth made Hoek nervous.

'You squared away, Lieutenant?'

'Yes, sir.'

'At ease. Sit down.'

'Thank you, sir.'

Hoek sat at attention. Pisaro stacked his papers in a neat pile. 'You're wearing two hats this cruise, Lieutenant, weapons and sonar. Did you go down to the torpedo room and have a chat with the boys down there?'

'Yes, sir.'

'You run a check on the weapons console?'

'Yes, sir.'

'All right, have you looked through the sonarmen's records?'

'Yes, sir.'

'Well?'

'Davic and Black are solid, hard-working men. Davic is, ah, unusual.'

'He wants to go to work for the CIA when his enlistment is up. He knows quite a lot about the Russians. You might learn something from him.'

'Yes, sir. Black is up for first class, so he's going to be a bookworm this cruise.'

'Willie Joe is a top-notch technician. On any other ship he'd be the leading sonarman. I expect him to get his promotion and move on. We're lucky to have him here.'

'Yes, sir.'

Pisaro lit a cigarette. 'That brings us to Petty Officer Sorensen.'

'Yes, sir.'

'Did you go through his records carefully?'

'Yes, sir.'

'And what do you think, Lieutenant?'

'Well, Commander, he's clearly a genius at sonar, but otherwise he's somewhat unconventional.'

'Somewhat? He's a fucking maniac.'

'I was trying to maintain decorum, Commander.'

Pisaro burst out laughing. 'Okay, Lieutenant. You're very young, and I'll give you the benefit of the doubt. A short lecture: The strength of the navy is our senior petty officers. You don't see many of them around the Naval Academy. They're called men.'

'Yes, sir.'

'Petty Officer Sorensen is the kind of man who puts to shame computer projections. He knows more about sonar than you or I ever will. Sonar is an art. Every sound is a question of interpretation, and Sorensen has an uncanny feel for it. Don't ask me how. I doubt if he can explain it himself. If he is, as you say, unconventional, we tolerate that down here. As long as a man does his job, we leave him alone.'

'Yes, sir.'

'All right, did you meet the new man? What's his name?' Pisaro looked at his papers.

31

'Fogarty, sir. Yes, sir, briefly. He did very well in sub school.'

'School's over, Lieutenant. Sorensen will look after him. Here's one more short lecture: This is an experienced crew. They've been through a lot together, the Cuban missile crisis and more than one dangerous patrol in unfriendly waters. When we close the hatch and dive, we're all alone. We're at war with the sea every second, and not far from same with the Russians. Under those conditions there is no such thing as a routine patrol. That's all. Dismissed.'

Hoek found the sonarmen waiting in the control room.

'Good morning, sir,' Sorensen said.

'Good morning.' Hoek cleared his throat, realizing that nothing he had learned at the academy had prepared him adequately for this moment. He felt the steel deck vibrating slightly under his feet. He heard the white noise of air conditioners and the background chatter of the command intercom. He saw Sorensen's eyes, still bloodshot but testing him. Next to Sorensen, Willie Joe looked like a puppy dog, anxious to please. Then came Davic, a scowl firmly etched across his plump face. At the end of the line was Fogarty, looking straight ahead.

Hoek cleared his throat again. 'Our transit time to Naples will be ten days. We don't expect to encounter any problems, but let's keep our ears alert and our eyes on the screen.'

Sorensen rolled his eyes. It was a tradition in the Submarine Service for the most junior officer on a ship to be assigned the duties of sonar officer. Over the years Sorensen had learned that the only things these young lieutenants had in common were a bad complexion and a drive to become admirals.

Hoek continued, 'There is one thing to note. Crossing the Atlantic, we will be participating in a test of a new

SOSUS deep-water submarine detection system. As you know, the bottom of our coastal waters has been seeded with passive sonars for ten years. This new extension of the system will enable us to track any sub in the North Atlantic. The hydrophones are laid out in a grid centered in the Azores. It's similar to the system we've been operating in the Caribbean for the last year. As far as we know, the Russians don't know anything about it. Any questions?'

Sorensen asked, 'Do we have to give position reports to Norfolk?'

'Not until we get to Gibraltar. We pretend it's not there. Anything else?'

Sorensen shook his head.

'Okay, Chief Lopez has assigned the watches. Sorensen, you take the first watch, Willie Joe the second, Davic the third. The watches will be four hours, so you'll all be four on, eight off. Sorensen, you will be responsible for training the new man, Third Class Fogarty.'

'Yes, sir.'

Throughout the ship, division heads were making similar speeches. Pisaro, who also served as navigation officer, stood before the assembled helmsmen, planesmen and quartermaster, and spoke out for the benefit of the entire control room. 'Set the maneuvering watch and let's haul ass.'

'You heard the man,' Hoek said. 'Sorensen, you and Fogarty take us out. Dismissed.'

The sonar room was amidships, next to the control room and flush against the pressure hull. A tiny chamber, it contained a cabinet for tools and parts and three operators' consoles, each with a keyboard and CRT screen.

Fogarty followed Sorensen into the small chamber and looked closely at the banks of loudspeakers and tape

33

recorders mounted on the bulkheads. Layers of acoustic tile and cork insulated the compartment from noise in the control room and the machinery aft.

'Welcome to Sorensen's Sound Effects. Sit down.'

The colors were drab military. The overworked air conditioner never completely cleaned out the smell of cigarette smoke and sweat. In 1962 during the Cuban missile crisis Sorensen had taped up a newspaper photo of his hero, John Kennedy. It was still there, yellow and ragged, partially obscured by fleshy pinups and a photograph of Sergei Gorshkov, Admiral of the Fleet of the Soviet Union. A large chart displayed line drawings of the several classes of Soviet submarines: Whiskey, Hotel, Echo, Golf, November and the new Viktor.

Sorensen put on his earphones, and the last effects of his hangover disappeared. His fingers danced over the keyboard and activated the array of sixteen hydrophones, each a foot in diameter, mounted on the hull around the bow and down the sides of the ship. The hydrophones – the passive 'listening' sonars – were sensitive microphones that collected sounds that traveled through the water, sometimes across great distances.

He listened to the familiar sounds of *Barracuda*'s machinery, the pulse of pumps and the throttling steam. He heard the underwater beacons, fixed to the bottom of Chesapeake Bay, that would guide the ship through the channel and into the Atlantic. Satisfied that all was in order, he took off his earphones and looked at Fogarty.

To his surprise, Fogarty's eyes were closed. He was literally all ears. 'What do you hear?' Sorensen asked.

'*Barracuda*.'

'And what does she sound like?'

Fogarty opened his eyes and smiled. His eyes were dark brown, almost black. At first glance they were relaxed, but on closer inspection there was a hint of controlled tension.

'She sounds like World War Three.'

Sorensen blinked, then laughed. 'Okay, wiseguy, switch on the fathometer.'

'Switching on fathometer.' Fogarty's hands played over his keyboard.

'What's our depth?'

'Thirty feet under the keel.'

'Test BQR-2, passive array.'

'Testing BQR-2, passive array.' Fogarty checked the circuits which connected the hydrophones to his console. 'Test positive. All circuits functioning.'

'Test active array.'

Fogarty punched more buttons, activating in turn the transducers mounted in the center of each hydrophone. The transducers created the familiar sonar 'pings' that radiated through the water and, if they struck an object, returned as an echo heard by the hydrophones. The 'echo ranger' was rarely used, only in special circumstances, since each time it was activated it revealed the sub's location.

'Testing active array, test positive.'

'Test weapons guidance.'

'Testing weapons guidance. Weapons guidance locked on. Test positive.'

'Test target-seeking frequency.' In combat the target-seeking frequency was created by a special transducer to locate and pinpoint a target. To the target it was the sound of doom, followed immediately by a torpedo.

'Testing target-seeking frequency. Test positive.'

Sorensen lit a Lucky Strike. 'How'd you do in sonar school, kid?'

Fogarty flushed. It seemed he did that easily. 'I was first in the class.'

'No foolin'? Good for you. You look like a smart kid. Why didn't you go to nuclear power school? How come you're not a nuc?'

'I'm not that fond of radiation.'

Sorensen blew smoke at the air-conditioning vent. 'Can't say I blame you for that. Where you from?'

'Minnesota.'

'Oh yeah? A child of the frozen north. You don't look like an Eskimo.'

Fogarty grinned. 'I'm from Minneapolis, and I hate snow.'

'Well, at least you've got some sense, you left.'

'At the first chance.'

Sorensen said, 'Okay, read the notice on the door. Read it out loud.'

Fogarty twisted around in his seat and read, '"WARNING! This Is A Secure Area. Any Unauthorized Use Of Classified Material Will Result In Imprisonment And Forfeiture Of Pay. Removal Of Classified Material Is A Violation Of The National Security Act."'

'That's not all,' Sorensen said.

At the bottom, scribbled in large block letters, Fogarty read, '"LEAVE YOUR MIND BEHIND."'

'That's what you do when you come in here,' Sorensen said.

On the bridge the captain told the lookouts to be sharp. Two tugs stood off the bow, but Springfield intended to take his ship into the channel without assistance. The wind was in his favor, blowing from the south.

'Deck party, stand by to cast off lines,' he shouted to the sailors fore and aft. He watched the shore as the ship drifted with the wind and current, then spoke quietly into his microphone, 'Bridge to navigation, how's our tide?'

'Navigation to bridge, the tide is running with us.'

'Very well. Cast off the stern line.'

'Stern line away.'

Some people on the pier began to cheer and wave. The band played *The Star Spangled Banner*

'Cast off the bow line.'

'Bow line away.'

'Steer right ten degrees.'

'Right ten degrees.'

When *Barracuda* cleared the dock and there was no danger of fouling her huge propeller, he ordered, 'All ahead slow.'

Sorensen and Fogarty listened intently to the sounds coming through their earphones. With infinite smoothness, sixteen thousand horsepower surged out of number one turbine, passed through the reduction gears, and the five blades of the massive propeller began to turn. They heard the whoosh of water as it began to wash over the hull, and the cavitation of the prop, the chunk chunk chunk of every revolution that would be audible until they submerged to four hundred feet. Sorensen punched several buttons on his console and the computer began to filter out the sounds of *Barracuda*'s machinery. Ungainly on the surface, the ship rolled and pitched slightly as they headed for the channel.

'Sonar to control. Do you have the beacon on the repeater?'

The repeater was the sonar console in the control room that duplicated what the sonarmen saw and heard. Hoek sat at the repeater, but it was Pisaro who replied, 'Control to sonar, we have it.'

Twenty minutes after leaving the pier the captain and the lookouts came down from the sail. Springfield closed the hatch.

'Prepare to dive,' said the captain. 'Take her down, Leo.'

Pisaro gave orders to retract the radars and systematically went through his diving panel.

'Mark two degrees down bubble.'

'Mark two degrees down bubble, aye.'

'Flood forward ballast tanks.'

37

'Flood forward ballast tanks, aye.'
'Half speed.'
'All ahead half, aye.'
'Stern planes down three degrees.'
'Three degrees down, aye.'
Barracuda angled over and slid silently beneath the sea.

3

CHAIN REACTION

Barracuda steamed through the Atlantic at twenty-four knots, four hundred feet beneath the surface. There was no wind, no waves, no turbulence. At four hundred feet the water pressure was so great there was no cavitation behind the prop. No bubbles, no energy lost to drag. As the screw turned, the ship moved ahead with maximum efficiency. Three precise inertial navigation gyroscopes recorded every movement of the ship in three dimensions. Without contacting the surface, the navigation computer determined *Barracuda's* exact position.

The crew settled into the patrol routine of repetitious drills – damage control drill, collision drill, atmosphere systems failure drill, weapons drill. When not practicing for calamity or battle, they were kept busy continuously maintaining machinery and studying technical journals for rating exams and promotions.

Muzak wafted through the ship. Two days out of Norfolk *Cool Hand Luke* was rolling in the mess. Air conditioners maintained a comfortable seventy-two degrees.

From the conning station the captain looked around the brilliantly illuminated control room. The green hue of fluorescent lighting, accented by the CRTs, gave the compartment an unearthly glow.

Springfield was not a religious man, but he often thought the control room had the solemn atmosphere of a church – an inner sanctum of high technology. Men watched their instruments with the faith of true-believers. Every act was a ritual prescribed by regulations, perfected by repetition. *Barracuda* represented the highest order of human artifice, and Springfield thought it ironic that such engineering genius was devoted to a man-o'-war. If *Barracuda* resembled a church, it was the church militant.

'Lieutenant Hoek,' the captain was now saying to the weapons officer, 'you have the conn.'

Fred Hoek felt as if he had just stuck his finger into an electric socket. As he moved his heavy frame up a step to the conning station, his heart was palpitating and his face was white. He put on a headset.

'Aye aye, sir. I relieve you of the conn.'

Lt Hoek scanned the displays in the conning station. Sweat began to collect on his upper lip. He was in heaven. He was radioactive. He had the conn.

Springfield strolled over to the reactor displays that monitored the chain reaction taking place at six hundred degrees fifteen feet away. Instinctively, he fondled his film badge, a strip of sensitive celluloid that measured the amount of radiation he was receiving. Like everyone else, the captain turned in his badge once a month to a hospital corpsman, who processed the film in the darkroom and determined how much radiation each crew member was receiving.

In the stern of the ship, in the steering machinery room, Machinist's Mate Barnes was standing his watch amid the jungle of pipes and compressors that moved the rudder and stern planes. Barnes worked at an exquisitely compact lathe, turning parts for the constant maintenance and repair of the ship's intricate machinery. From the engine room came the high whine of turbines and the throttling noises of high pressure steam.

'Howdy, Barnes.'

It was Sorensen, standing in the hatch in a pair of red Bermuda shorts, thongs and wraparound sunglasses. He held out a set of schematic diagrams. 'I'll need this in Naples.'

Barnes shifted his goggles to his forehead and looked at the diagrams. 'No sweat, Ace. Throw it on the bench.' He turned back to his lathe.

'Barnes.'

'Yeah.'

'Dont fuck it up.'

Portside was a small door with a brass plaque that shone brilliantly amid the flat navy gray of the compartment: WELCOME TO SORENSEN'S BEACH. NO VOLLEYBALL ALLOWED. PLEASE KNOCK.' Sorensen went in without knocking.

Designated in the ship's plans as storage space for electronic parts, Sorensen's Beach was barely six and a half feet long by four feet wide. Stooping under the low tapered ceiling, he switched on a pair of bright sunlamps and pulled a plastic mat and wooden beach chair from a cabinet. Taped to the door was a travel poster. Santa Cruz, California. Sun, surf, pier, golden bodies.

'Surf's up.'

He turned on the tape recorder and out flowed the mellow tones of Dave Brubeck's *Home at Last*.

From a pile of magazines he grabbed the one on top, a dogeared *Playboy*. Tapping his feet, he flipped through the pages to the centerfold.

After a while the same old tits and ass became monotonous. He dropped *Playboy* and picked up *Newsweek*. Bad news. Riot, revolution, war, assassination. A general strike in France. He liked the naked women better.

The chaos of life ashore made him crazy. Millions of half-wits running around in confusion, like an ant colony gone amok. Greed, selfishness, corruption, lives without passion, without purpose.

Underwater, the madness disappeared. Inside *Barracuda*'s pressure hull Sorensen had found a purpose and an identity. On the ship life was orderly, pure, simple, and defined only by the implacable laws of physics. The sub demanded total discipline and absolute dedication. Every man had a job to do and did it with his whole being or not at all.

Few could give that much, but certain men blossomed and thrived in the artificial environment of a submarine. For Sorensen it was liberation. He had joined the navy on his eighteenth birthday and never looked back, never wondered what his life might have been like under open skies. Now, after ten years, he realized that he couldn't stay below forever. For one thing, navy regulations were against it and eventually he would be promoted to chief and stuck in a sonar school where he'd probably drink himself to death . . .

He dropped the magazine and put on a whale tape. He liked whales and recorded them frequently. On this tape the whales were hooting up a storm. What could interest a bunch of whales so much, he wondered. Lunch? Whale sex?

In the torpedo room Chief Lopez was feeding a fly to his pet, a brown Mexican scorpion named Zapata. The scorpion lived in a glass cage mounted over the firing console and was the subject of many whispered rumors and legends.

Lopez dimmed the lights in the compartment and switched on an ultraviolet bulb in the cage. The scorpion glowed an iridescent blue. Lopez leaned his full face closer to the cage, sweat running into his heavy beard, eyes flaring like an *aficionado de toros* awaiting the kill. The fly buzzed around, banged into the glass and finally dropped to the sand. The scorpion moved. Lopez imagined he could see a drop of venom leaking from its tail.

The rest of the watch stood around quietly while Lopez acted out the ceremonial feeding. The torpedomen knew better than to make smart remarks about Lopez and his bug.

In the galley the Filipino cook, Stanley Real, had worked for hours on a *sauce demi-glace*. Stanley fancied himself a *chef de cuisine* rather than a navy cook. He was trying to explain the difference to Cakes Colby, the steward.

'This sauce it is cook for three days.'

Cakes thought Stanley's fuss over the sauce was ludicrous.

'It looks like gravy to me, Stanley.'

The cook waved a slotted spoon in Cake's face. 'Once, they say to me, cook for the President Marcos. On the *Andrew Jackson* in Subic Bay the President Marcos eat his dinner on the ship. Big missile sub, yes, the *Andrew Jackson*. The President Marcos he come and he run his hand all up and down the missile, like he love it, then he eat. He like what he eat. He call me from the galley to the officers' mess and he say come cook for me in the palace of the president. No no, I say, I am loyal to the US Navy. I am qualified as a submarine, first class, I say. I am citizen of the USA.'

Cakes was making his last cruise. The only member of the crew to have served in World War Two, he had seen a lot of cooks in twenty-five years, but never one like Stanley Real.

'Good God, Stanley. Where do they find guys like you?' Cakes muttered as he locked away the officers' flatwear in a cabinet. 'Whatever happened to white beans and ham hocks?'

In the forward crew quarters, in a bunk on the third tier, Fogarty lay sleepless, all in a sweat. In two days his world had changed so completely that he seemed to have forgotten who he was. The discipline of the sub often required him to react without thinking, as if he were a robot, and he lay now in his bunk pretending that his brain had been replaced by a reactor. Someone pulled the control rod a little ways out of his head, and he speeded up. Pull it all the way out and he speeds up so much, he melts. Push it all the way in and he stops, he scrams.

Fogarty understood that on a submarine there was no margin for error. A moment's hesitation could mean disaster. Fogarty knew that in time the discipline would become automatic, but the learning was painful. Two hours out of Norfolk, as the crew raced through their first damage-control drill, he had banged his knee on a bulkhead while scrambling through a hatch, and it still hurt. Yet the bruises to his body were nothing compared to what was being done to his brain. He was being bombarded by information. A whole new world was being revealed to him in the sonar room – the sea and all its multifarious sounds – and he was close to overload. Sitting watches with Sorensen was an exacting experience. In his casual way, Sorensen was a perfectionist who never tolerated mistakes. Off watch, Fogarty frequently found himself running from one end of the ship to the other during endlessly repeated drills. Not a single watch had passed without a drill, and he felt as if he had a terminal case of jet lag. Night and day had been replaced by the rotation of the watches; his circadian rhythm was off. He knew it was five o'clock in the morning – four hundred feet up there was weather, a sunrise, a sky – but on *Barracuda* there was only machinery, a handful of radioactive metal and one hundred men.

The compartment was dark. His bunk was a tidy cocoon. To his right he could feel the acoustic rubber insulation that lined the pressure hull. To his left a flimsy gray curtain gave him a sense of seclusion. He heard the whir of air conditioners, and the sounds of sleeping men packed together as carefully as the

44

uranium pellets in the reactor.

His mind refused to shut down. Electrical circuits popped like flashcards into his imagination, demanding recognition. When those were exhausted he started going through the signatures of Soviet submarines, retrieving the sounds from memory. The Russian ships were noisy, but he had had no real idea how loud they were until Sorensen played a tape of a Hotel-class fleet ballistic missile submarine. Fogarty thought it was the most frightening thing he had ever heard.

Fogarty could hardly believe that he was lying in a bunk with the sound of Soviet machinery running through his head. All his life he had waited to get on a nuclear-powered sub. When he was eight years old he had been electrified by the news that *Nautilus*, the world's first nuclear-propelled submarine, had put to sea. When *Nautilus* went under the polar icecap and surfaced at the North Pole, Fogarty made up his mind that he was going to become a submariner. He read *20,000 Leagues Under the Sea* and *Run Silent, Run Deep* so many times his paperback copies fell apart. His father, who had served on a submarine in World War Two, encouraged both his sons to join the navy, but it was young Mike who fell in love with subs. In high school Fogarty had puzzled over the mysteries of nuclear reactors and spent hours in the library buried in *Jane's Fighting Ships*. He built model submarines, marvelous, handcrafted working miniatures with radio control that struck terror into the hearts of toy sailboaters on Lake Minnetonka.

At first Fogarty had been impressed by the enormous power and fabulous mystique of the nuclear sub. *Nautilus* and the ships that followed her had conquered the great ocean and opened a new frontier. He very much wanted to be part of it.

At an early age he had learned to distinguish the different types of submarines. First, there were the SSNs, fast attack subs, hunter-killers like *Nautilus* and *Barracuda*. Then there were the FBMs, the Fleet Ballistic Missile subs, the city-killers that had captured the public's imagination after the first one, the USS *George Washington*, was launched in 1960.

The missile subs had frightened him. The idea of a ship that by itself could destroy a civilization drove a wedge into his adolescent mind. It seemed crazy to him that such a wonderful device could be turned to such a terrible purpose. Though he never wavered from his ambition to join the Submarine Service, he grew increasingly haunted by dark visions of nuclear war with the Russians. In the end World War Three would be resolved by submarines. If and when the war occurred, the primary function of attack submarines like *Barracuda* would be to find and sink enemy missile subs. If they succeeded and sank the enemy 'boomers' before they could fire their missiles, at least something might be preserved. In effect the SSN was a defensive weapon, an anti-ballistic missile system. Fogarty wanted very much to believe that serving on such a ship was a decent if not noble endeavor, but a little corner of his mind remained unconvinced. When he was old enough to enlist, he argued with himself. In the years he had spent studying submarines and naval warfare he had developed an understanding of the consequences of nuclear war, in particular nuclear war at sea. He realized that if the American and Soviet navies started sinking each other's ships with nuclear torpedoes, rockets, depth charges and mines, they also could very likely kill all marine life and thereby doom life on earth.

Such questions bothered Fogarty, but in the end he realized there was only one place to find the answers. Besides, no matter what, nothing was going to keep him off a sub.

Boot camp, sub school, sonar school, and here he was, breathing air-conditioned air, listening to Muzak and sitting watches with the great Sorensen himself. In sonar school the scuttlebutt had been that Sorensen was the only American enlisted man whose name was known to the Russians. He doubted that, but who could be sure? In any case he didn't have to deal with Sorensen the legend but Sorensen the taskmaster, who had no intention of making Fogarty's life easy.

Leave your mind behind.

In the maneuvering room Master Chief Alexander Wong, the head nuc, and the three men on watch were discussing the high-paying civilian jobs waiting for them when they got out of the navy. Surrounded by the maze of instrumentation that accompanied controlled nuclear fission, the nucs – nuclear engineers who had completed a course at one of the navy's nuclear power schools – figured they had it made.

When the captain walked in, though, they stopped talking and stared at their displays. Springfield stood for several minutes in silence, hands on hips, watching the engineers. Without warning he reached over Wong's shoulder to the main control panel and flipped a bright red switch. The control rods dropped into the reactor vessel and the reactor scrammed. The neutron chain reaction came to a complete stop.

With no chain reaction, no more heat was created in the reactor. If the engineers continued to use the residual heat to make steam the reactor would cool too quickly and crack, spewing radioactive material all over the compartment.

The reactor control team responded instantly.

'Close main steam feed,' ordered Wong.

The technician sitting at the steam panel spun a wheel and the steam supply to the engine room was cut off. With no steam, no power was delivered to the turbines. The ship was now without main propulsion power. As the prop stopped turning, the ship lost way and began to sink. The trim was off and the ship slowly sank at an angle, stern down.

Wong grabbed the intercom. 'This is a drill, this is a drill. Reactor scram, reactor scram. All hands to damage-control stations. All hands to damage-control stations. This is a drill. This is a drill.'

Sorensen felt a shudder run through the ship and was out the door and past Barnes before alarms began sounding in every compartment.

In the torpedo room the alarm burst in on Lopez and his ritual. Leaving the fly untouched, the scorpion retreated to a corner of its cage. 'Son of a bitch,' Lopez said, 'what is it this time?'

In the mess Strother Martin had Paul Newman trapped inside a church. 'What we have here is a failure to —' and the film stopped dead.

In the forward crew quarters Pisaro stood in the hatch. 'This is a drill. Off your asses and hit the deck.'

Sleepy sailors stumbled out of their bunks and into their shoes. Like firemen, many slept in their clothes, ready for such a moment. Fogarty delayed long enough to zip up his jumpsuit. Pisaro swatted him on the butt as he rushed out.

The passageway was jammed. The new seamen collided with one another in the hatches and banged into hard steel at the turns. Grunts and howls of pain rattled around in the dim light.

Fogarty was dizzy. More than anything on the ship, the reactor terrified him. Every minute aboard he knew he was being irradiated. Yet now he was rushing through the ship because the reactor was shut down.

Throughout the ship, damage-control teams put on asbestos suits and checked fire extinguishers. Everything loose was fastened down. Everything already fastened

48

down was double-checked.

In the galley Stanley was indignant. The cook could not have explained the physics of a reactor scram, but he knew that with no power to his stove his sauce was ruined. He slopped the brown fluid into a plastic bag and swore in Tagalog.

Sorensen moved rapidly through the ship on bare feet, one step ahead of the confusion. In the control room Lt Hoek still had the conn. As Sorensen passed through he noticed the blissful look on the young officer's face as he gave the commands to recover from the scram.

'Engineering, rig for battery power.'

'Batteries on line and ready to go.'

'Very well, switch to batteries.'

'Batteries engaged.'

'Very well. Blow forward trim tanks.'

A sailor spun a valve and compressed air was forced into the tanks, expelling the water into the sea. The rate of descent slackened.

'Blow after tanks. Slowly, very slowly. Let's not spill the coffee.'

Willie Joe was on duty in the sonar room when Sorensen burst in. The screens were clear. There was nothing around them but ocean, nine thousand feet of it under the keel.

'Okay, go,' Sorensen said. Willie Joe quickly changed into a white asbestos suit and hurried to his damage-control station.

Fogarty came in, eyes red and swollen. Sorensen frowned.

'You have to get in here quicker than that, Fogarty. Much quicker.'

'The passageway was blocked.'

'No excuses. If people are in your way, jump over them, run through them. I don't care, just get in here.'

'Aye aye.'

The ship was still going down. Fogarty stared at the digital fathomer: six hundred fifty, seven hundred, seven hundred fifty feet. His face remained impassive. The sea didn't frighten him.

Sorensen liked his nerve.

At eight hundred feet the ship leveled off and stopped. The sea was quiet.

'Tell me what you hear,' Sorensen said.

'The Atlantic Ocean,' Fogarty replied. 'The turbogenerator,' he added quickly.

'That's all?'

Sorensen punched a button and the overhead loudspeakers came on. An intermittent scratching sound came from the sea.

'What's that?' Sorensen asked.

Fogarty listened. 'I don't know.'

'Turtles,' Sorensen said cheerfully. 'Fishing at one hundred fifty feet. Unusual for them to be so far north, but it sounds like they've struck it rich.'

Still in shorts and wearing sunglasses in the darkened room, Sorensen scrunched up his face and contorted his voice, trying to reproduce turtle noises. He glanced up to make sure a tape was rolling.

'Attention all hands,' Hoek's voice came through the intercom. 'Prepare for slow speed.'

Fogarty stared at the screen and fiddled with his film badge.

The ship began to move, making just enough way to maneuver. The turtle sounds faded. A moment later weird beeps and hoots came through the speakers.

'Right whales,' Sorensen said, and began to hoot and beep himself. Every few seconds his fingers reached for the keyboard as he altered the combination of arrays, filters and enhancers, playing the sea like a vast water organ.

Fascinated, Fogarty asked, 'What are you doing?'

Sorensen only tweaked and buzzed a little louder.

A minute later the whales went silent.

Fogarty said, 'You turned the whales up, Sorensen. In sonar school they told us to filter them out.'

Sorensen grinned. 'I like whales.' He flashed a smile. 'Ever watch *Star Trek*?'

'A couple times. So?'

'Well, think of me as Mr Spock, the Vulcan, all right? I'm not human, Fogarty, I'm an alien. I'm weird. When we're on watch, just keep your eyes on the screen and your ears on the big phone. And watch out for them Klingons, boy. They bad dudes.'

Fogarty persisted. 'In sonar school they called all marine noises signal interference. They said to filter them out.'

Sorensen took off his glasses. 'Listen, Fogarty. Forget school. Forget the navy. Read the sign: Leave your mind behind. This is the real ocean. If you're going to be a good sonarman, you listen to everything, and you think about everything you hear. Are you following me?'

'I am.'

'All right. I'm going to keep you on the first watch until you qualify. If you're any good that will be in about thirty days, just before we get back to Norfolk. If you aren't, I'll keep you just to make your life miserable. We're in for the duration, Fogarty. We're watchmates . . . Tell me, Fogarty, how come you volunteered for subs?'

'I quit school. I was going to be drafted, I was at loose ends.'

'But why volunteer for subs? Why not the Coast Guard?'

'I looked around. The Submarine Service had the best deal. Best food, best pay, most interesting working conditions—'

'Don't feed me a line of shit.'

Fogarty shrugged. 'Okay. I've wanted to get on one of these things since I was a little kid. That's the truth. I must have built fifty models of *Nautilus* when I was a kid.'

'So what? Every kid in America builds models.'

'Yeah' – Fogarty grinned – 'but mine worked. Servos, radio control, watertight seals, the works.'

Sorensen nodded. 'I see. I suppose you were first in your class in sub school, too.'

Fogarty shook his head. 'No. Second.'

'Shame on you. Where'd you screw up?'

Fogarty smiled. 'Navigation. In the simulator I drove the sub right up onto the beach.'

'Yeah, navigation is a bitch. That's why I like computers. When we fuck up we can blame it on them.'

'That's what I told my instructor. He didn't buy it.'

'So you came out second out of how many?'

'Four hundred.'

Sorensen raised his eyebrows.

'Four hundred twenty-seven.'

'Ah ha! Okay, you're a genuine sub freak. How come?'

'During the war my dad was a radioman on *Yellowtail*.'

'No shit?'

'He's a very proud man. He always wanted my brother and me to join the Submarine Service.'

'So where's your brother now?'

'He joined the Marines. It broke my dad's heart. He hates jarheads.'

Sorensen chuckled, 'Oh, boy, a tough guy.'

Fogarty grinned. 'What about you, Sorensen? Why are you here?'

'Me? I'm a native. I was born here.'

'C'mon, tell me. Why did you join the navy?'

'You want to hear the story of my life, kid?'

'Yeah. Where's your home town?'

'Oakland, California.'

'Home of the Raiders.'

'That's right. Also the home of Fast Eddie, the pool shark in *The Hustler*, of Sonny Barger and the Hell's

Angels, Reggie Jackson, Huey Newton and the Black Panthers, former home of Jack London, noted oyster pirate and liar, to mention a few illustrious citizens. Ever been there?'

'No.'

'Well, it's California, but it ain't Hollywood.' Sorensen swallowed a long draught of coffee. 'I had no sense, no real education, although I read a lot. I got married when I was seventeen. There I was with no job, nothing but an old lady who thought life was driving up and down East Fourteenth Street showing off your new car. Her brain was lost in the wrong decade. I needed a job, so on my eighteenth birthday I walked into a navy recruiter's office and said, "Man, I built my first sonar when I was twelve out of a microphone, a plastic bag and a tube of rubber cement." He said, "Son, sign on the dotted line." I signed. I was fresh meat for the fleet.'

Sorensen paused to light a cigarette, and Fogarty asked, 'Where's your wife?'

'She divorced me when I reenlisted. She hated the navy. A few years ago, the night before the ship was leaving for a sixty-day cruise, she told me she'd be gone when I got back. I didn't blame her. She was looking at two months of lonely nights in crummy bars in another crummy navy town, getting hit on by horny sailors, horny civilians, horny WAVE dykes. She didn't have much use for submarines, either. I think she went back to California. She still gets a piece of my check.'

They continued at slow speed for two hours. Springfield stopped once to transmit a position report as part of the SOSUS deep submergence detection test.

Sorensen assigned Fogarty the elaborate, time-consuming task of checking all the circuits that ran from the sonar room through cables to the torpedo room in the bow. The sonars were mounted on the hull all around the

53

bow and Fogarty spent an hour inspecting the main panel in the torpedo room.

Alone in the sonar room, Sorensen popped open his console and gazed at the maze of circuitry. Over the years he had modified it extensively, sometimes without authorization.

On his trip to Japan he had acquired not one but two of the miniature tape recorders, one of which he now inserted into a disguised panel. A quick twist of a screwdriver, and Sorensen became a criminal.

4

COWBOYS AND COSSACKS

The Strait of Gibraltar forms one of the great bottlenecks in the world ocean. Historically, control of the Strait has meant control of the Mediterranean. Since the end of World War Two the US Navy has considered 'the sea in the middle of the earth' an American lake.

Seven days after leaving Norfolk, *Barracuda* approached the Strait at slow speed.

'All right,' said the captain. 'Send up the buoy.'

A jet of compressed air fired a capsule from the top of the sail toward the surface. A few seconds later a radio transmitter floated two hundred feet above the sub. Springfield beamed a position report to the naval station at Rota, Spain, and received an immediate reply.

US NAVAL STATION ROTA: BARRACUDA SSN 593: SOSUS DEEP SUBMERGENCE DETECTION TEST SUCCESSFUL. FOLLOWED YOU ALL THE WAY ACROSS. PERMISSION GRANTED TO CLEAR STRAIT. NETTS.

In the sonar room Sorensen listened to the sonic beacon fixed to the bottom of the Strait, which guided submerged ships through the deep channel. He locked on and the ship slowly passed into the Mediterranean.

Presently they heard engine noise from another sub nearby. Before Sorensen could ask, Fogarty said, 'British. HMS *Valiant*.'

'Very good, very good, indeed. Be glad we're not a Russian or he'd blow our ears out.'

'Full speed ahead,' said the captain. 'We're through.'

Two days later *Barracuda* was 250 miles from Naples.

Springfield and Pisaro studied the CRT in the navigation console, which displayed an electronic chart of the Tyrrhenian Sea between Sardinia and the Bay of Naples. A blip in the center of the screen represented the ship. A flickering digital readout reported the changing longitude and latitude. The quartermaster sat quietly at the console, eyes following the blip, the only visible evidence of *Barracuda*'s progress.

Springfield had ordered a burst of flank speed. Driving *Barracuda* at forty-seven knots was like flying blind underwater. The noise rendered her listening sonars useless, and there was danger of colliding with another submerged vessel. Every fifty miles Springfield slowed the sub to a crawl and quieted all machinery to allow the sonar operators to 'clear baffles'. While the ship slowly turned 360 degrees, the sonarmen listened through the hydrophones, the passive sonars.

Pisaro blew cigarette smoke away from the console. 'We're almost at the edge,' he said, waving smoke out of his eyes. 'Five minutes.'

Springfield nodded and spoke into his microphone. 'Control to engineering, prepare for slow speed. We're going to clear baffles.'

'Engineering to control. Prepare for slow speed, aye.'

Springfield glanced at the blank screen of the sonar repeater. Willie Joe had the repeater disassembled for Fogarty's edification.

'How long, Willie Joe?'

'Ten minutes, Captain.'

'All right,' Springfield said to Pisaro. 'There's supposed to be a storm up above. If we're going to hear anything, we'd better get Sorensen up here.'

'Aye aye, skipper.' Pisaro spoke into the intercom. 'Control to engineering. Listen, Chief. Send somebody aft to drag Sorensen's butt back into the real world. I want him in sonar in five minutes.'

'Engineering to control. Aye aye. The ace will be in place.'

In the sonar room Sonarman Second Class Emile Davic sat at his operator's console, apparently watching the CRT screen. He was alone.

Davic stared diligently at the screen, but there was little to see except the green fuzz of ambient noise – washed-out signals from the passive array.

Three hours into his watch, Davic sipped a sixth cup of coffee, devoured a second Hershey bar and daydreamed about food in Naples. Spaghetti putanesca, tortellini in broda. Davic hated Naples. It was dirty and reminded him of the worst parts of New York, but he relished the food.

As a boy of twelve Davic had emigrated from Budapest to Brooklyn, where he lived alone with his mother. Confused and frightened by New York, Davic tried to insulate himself from the city. Eventually he became naturalized, but he never became an American. He didn't know how to have fun, to relax, and devoted his life to the study of modern languages and the cultivation of a bitter hatred of the Russians. Anything else seemed frivolous.

He had joined the Submarine Service to get as close to the Soviets as possible. When World War Three started, Davic didn't want to miss it. To him, serving on the sub was a solemn obligation that he approached with deep seriousness. On a ship where most sailors barely spoke one language, Davic spoke five: Magyar, German, English, French and Russian. He considered himself a dedicated cold warrior and regarded anyone less fanatic than himself a fool. Naturally, he despised Sorensen, whose open irreverence Davic found intolerable. Sorensen acted as if *Barracuda* were his personal property, provided by the navy for his amusement. In spite of himself, Davic envied Sorensen his talent and was jealous of his privileges.

Davic was contemplating now the photo of Admiral Gorshkov, examining the stony face. He was the one who had taped the Russian's portrait to the bulkhead.

Gorshkov, architect of the modern Soviet Navy, was the officer who had dragged the Russian fleet out of the nineteenth century and transformed it into a blue-water force. And that frightened Davic, who as a young boy had witnessed Soviet tanks in Budapest. He kept the photograph of Sergei Gorshkov as a reminder.

Barracuda was following a standard NATO deep-water route off Sardinia, and her routiné position reports had been forwarded to all NATO navies. The last time they had cleared baffles, the long-range sonar had shown nothing. Any moment now the captain would slow again. Davic felt that a contact was unlikely.

'Attention all hands. Prepare for slow speed.'

He felt the ship begin to slow and listened to the turbulence as it washed over the hull and swirled around the hydrophones. He reached up and turned on a tape recorder.

Barnes banged on the door to Sorensen's Beach.

'Sorensen.'

'Yo.'

The door opened. Dripping sweat, Sorensen stuck his head out.

'What's up?'

'They want you in sonar.'

'Where are we?'

'Hey, man, I'm back here making chips all damn day,' Barnes said, flicking a shard of stainless steel off his chest. 'I don't know. Switzerland?'

'Listen, Barnes, did you make my little box yet?'

'Your little watertight box? It's next. It's on the sheet.'

'I gotta have it tomorrow in Naples. Skipper's orders.'

'Like I say, it's on the sheet. Not to worry. What's it for, anyway?'

'You got me, sport.' Sorensen took off his glasses and winked.

'Oh, yeah,' Barnes said, flapping his arms and returning to his lathe. 'Big time secrets. When the captain goes to the crapper, it's a secret. What's for lunch? It's a secret. A sonar beacon in a watertight stainless steel box. Big secret. Shit.'

Sorensen shut the door. True enough, nothing stayed secret for long. He began collecting his stuff. A tape was still running. La Verne Baker belted out *Jim Dandy on a submarine. Got a message from a mermaid queen. Jim Dancy didn't waste no time. Jim Dandy to the rescue. Go Jim Dandy. Go Jim Dandy.*

He turned off the lights on the way out.

The door to the sonar room jerked open and Sorensen suddenly filled the tiny space. He sat down at the supervisor's console, logged in and adjusted a headset over his ears.

'Just carry on,' he said to Davic. Sorensen didn't look at the screen. He closed his eyes and listened.

The deep waters of the Mediterranean constituted a notoriously fickle sonar environment. Sound waves were bounced up and down by thermal layers and distorted by seamounts and an uneven bottom. It was impossible to determine the range of a contact heard on a passive array unless it was moving.

'Control to sonar, prepare for three hundred sixty degree revolution.'

'Sonar to control. Understand three hundred sixty degree revolution. Aye aye,' Davic replied.

As the ship slowed, the machinery quieted and the screens gradually cleared. The ship banked slightly as it turned. Davic heard static. 'There's signal interference from the storm,' he said.

'The storm is dying,' Sorensen told him. 'Ignore it.'

A third of the way through the turn, they clearly heard a propeller cavitating on the surface. Sorensen estimated the range as five miles.

'Sonar to control. Contact on the surface, bearing one one seven. Speed two knots.'

'Control to helm, Make our course bearing one one seven.

'Course one one seven, aye.'

The ship turned back to the left and once again the sonar operators heard the propeller.

'All stop,' ordered the captain.

The sub drifted, listening. Sorensen heard a second propeller. Twin screws. A small ship was barely making way on the surface.

'It's your watch, Davic,' Sorensen said. 'What do you think it is?'

As Davic logged the contact into the computer he mumbled, 'It could be anything, a coastal freighter, a fisherman.'

Sorensen opened his eyes and began watching the screen, listening intently. NATO routes avoided commercial shipping lanes and fishing grounds. He had a hunch.

'Fee fie foe fum, I smell the blood of a Russian bum.' He winked at Davic who stared wide-eyed at the screen, wondering what Sorensen heard that he didn't.

'Davic,' Sorensen said, 'that's a Soviet surveillance ship up there, a trawler, and he's got us pegged for sure.'

'What makes you think so?'

'Tomorrow the Sixth Fleet is going to sail from Naples, right up this alley. Now, if I was your friend Admiral Gorshkov, I'd wait for *Kitty Hawk* right about here. Sonar to control. Is the repeater on line yet?'

Willie Joe's languid voice came back through the

intercom. 'Another minute, there, Ace. One more circuit.'

Before Sorensen could reply, a streak flickered across the extreme edge of the sonar screen, a faint electronic shadow. Sorensen snapped to attention and began punching buttons on his console. The trawler had company.

Deftly, Sorensen locked his sonars on bearing one one seven and immediately heard the throb of a saltwater pump, the type of pump that circulated seawater around a steam condenser, the unmistakable signature of a nuclear reactor. A nuclear submarine was hovering under the trawler, listening to *Barracuda*.

'Bingo,' he said. 'Sonar to control. We have another contact, bearing one one seven, range estimated ten thousand yards, speed zero zero. Contact is submerged. Repeat, contact is submerged.'

'Control to sonar,' said Pisaro's voice, 'the repeater is coming on line now. We show nothing, sonar, *nada*.' The XO paused for a moment. 'Wait a minute, wait a minute. That's impossible. No goddamn Russkie sub has been reported in this sector of the Med. How in hell did he get in here?'

The faint streak returned at the same bearing. The contact was directly below the trawler. Pisaro swore. 'The son of a bitch must have been listening to us for half an hour. Quartermaster, sound general quarters.'

Throughout the ship loudspeakers drove one hundred men into furious but disciplined activity.

'General quarters, general quarters. All hands man battle stations. This is not a drill. This is not a drill. Man battle stations.'

Davic stood up and took off his headset. His battle station was forward as part of a damage-control team. He opened a cabinet and pulled on a white asbestos suit. Inside the plexiglas faceplate he looked like a chubby astronaut. 'I would prefer to remain in the sonar room,' he said into the microphone inside his helmet.

'Look, Davic, I don't assign the stations. Lopez does that,' Sorensen told him.

'That's *my* Russian, Sorensen,' Davic shouted in his electronic voice.

'Sure, he's all yours. He's in your log. Don't worry, you'll get your chance to go toe to toe with him.

Davic muttered a Hungarian curse and went out.

Sorensen called after him, 'What's the matter? Don't you ever go to the movies?'

A moment later Fogarty rushed in, sat down and put on his earphones. He heard a deep throb, an unnatural predatory growl, and suddenly he was very alert.

In sonar school Fogarty had listened with detached interest to tapes of Soviet submarines, but the tapes had been disembodied noises in a void. The tapes that Sorensen had played for him had been frightening, but still remote. The immediacy of the real thing came as a shock. His first Russian.

'What's he doing?' he asked Sorensen.

'Our friend Ivan is just sitting there listening to us with a big fat smile on his face. The joke's on us.'

Fogarty settled into his seat and watched the resolution of the streak improve as the range closed.

Invisible to the rest of the world, the two subs drifted five miles apart, listening warily for the slightest hint of a wrong move.

'Well,' Sorensen said, 'the game is on. Let's see if we can come out a respectable second best.'

'What game?' Fogarty asked.

'*The* game. The only game in town. The game we play with the Russians. Cowboys and Cossacks.'

Fogarty stared at him.

'Call it practice for World War Three.'

Sorensen switched on the overhead speakers and took

off his earphones.

'Listen to that dirty racket,' he said with a smile. 'His weapons control system is locked right on your beating heart.'

'Control to sonar. Prepare to lock on weapons control.'

'Sonar to control. Prepare to lock on weapons control, aye. Now we're going to return the favor,' Sorensen said. He pushed a sequence of buttons on his console and the sonar signals were ready to be fed into the weapons-guidance systems.

When Fogarty had practiced this drill it always made him nervous. Now faced with an actual adversary, he was surprised to discover how calm he felt.

'Control to weapons. Lock on sonar.'

Hoek's voice came through the intercom. 'Weapons to control. Lock on sonar, aye.'

'Very well.'

Hoek looked up from his weapons console to face the captain in the conning station, wondering if Springfield was going to give the order to load a torpedo. Rachets in hand, the torpedo room crew was standing by.

'Load tube number one, Mark thirty-seven, conventional warhead, wire-guided.'

'Load tube number one, aye.'

Barracuda dipped slightly forward as the weight of a torpedo was shifted into a tube. A trim tank automatically compensated and the ship levelled.

Fogarty shook his head. 'This is like playing with a loaded gun.'

'Indeed it is. That's the spice that makes it so tasty.'

'What if someone screws up?'

Sorensen shrugged and lit a cigarette. 'Who? The skipper? No way. Ivan? He's the same as us. Nobody wants to start a war. Not today. So they say . . .'

'We could have a war down here and nobody would ever know it.'

'You're a bright boy, Fogarty. You noticed there aren't any TV cameras down here.'

Fogarty still felt strangely calm and clearheaded. A torpedo could not be fired until the tube was flooded, a provocative act that would be heard by the Russian sonar operators.

Looking at the pictures on the wall, he tried to imagine the Russian sub. He had seen film of Russian subs on the surface. They looked mean, warlike. As for the men inside, he had only the residue of a lifetime of propaganda that pictured them as an enemy . . . We will bury you, and so forth. He wasn't sure if he believed all of it, some of it, or none of it.

'Well,' Sorensen said, 'what class of sub do you think it is?'

'I don't know. Most of their attack subs are November class.'

'She's starting to move. Sonar to control, contact is moving. He's showing himself to us.'

'Control to sonar.' Springfield's voice replaced Leo Pisaro's. 'Try and get a signature.'

'Aye aye.'

'Okay, Leo,' Springfield said to the XO, 'let's take a look. All ahead slow.'

The ship shuddered as the propeller revolutions increased. The instant *Barracuda* moved the Russian took off, making a great deal of noise as his speed increased. The streak on the screen resolved into a blip. Sorensen heard the unmistakable sounds of Soviet machinery, noisy reduction gears and coolant pumps, the swish of a prop, but it was not the classic signature of a November. He switched on the signature program that compared the sounds of the contact sub with the recorded sounds of known Soviet submarines stored in the program.

'It's a Viktor,' he said, a good fifteen seconds before the computer verified his judgement.

Fogarty glanced at the chart. 'The new one,' he said.

'Yeah. We don't know much about these Viktors. They can go deep, but they make a lot of noise.'

Springfield and Pisaro were alarmed by the Russian's unexpected appearance in the Mediterranean. How did it get through the Strait of Gibraltar without being detected and tracked? They studied the repeater and sipped coffee. Pisaro chain-smoked.

The Russian was running parallel to *Barracuda*'s original course. The Russian commander was announcing that the Mediterranean was no longer an American lake.

'Leo,' Springfield said quietly, 'move in on her. Crowd her. All ahead half.'

'Aye aye, Skipper. All ahead half.'

'Go right three degrees, course one two zero.'

'Right three degrees, course one two zero, aye.'

As *Barracuda* began to accelerate, the Russian went into a steep dive, machinery roaring like breaking surf. The Russian accelerated, the blip leaped across Sorensen's screen at a fantastic rate. *Barracuda*, the fastest submarine in the US Navy, was being left behind.

Abruptly Sorensen snatched off his earphones and reached over to yank Fogarty's away from his ears. He was too late. The high pitch of a powerful Feniks target-seeking sonar erupted in the young sonarman's ears. He winced in pain and swore. It was his first sonar lashing.

'Welcome to the wonderful world of sub wars,' Sorensen said to him.

Fogarty poked at his ears, his face contorted with pain. 'God*damn*. Why did they do that?'

'Hey, Third Class, didn't they teach you anything in sonar school?'

'They didn't do that.'

'When Ivan stings your ears like that, it means he could have put a torpedo up your ass. Bang, bang, you're dead. Our friend heard us a long time before we heard him.'

The Russian descended to twenty-one hundred feet and the sound abruptly ceased. The sub disappeared.

Sorensen stared at his blank screen. 'Jeez, I don't believe it. She vanished below a deep thermal. Sonar to control. We lost her.'

'Control to sonar. Say again.'

'We lost her, Captain. She's gone.'

'Good God.'

There was shocked silence in the control room. A deep thermal layer deflected the down-searching sonars at twenty-one hundred feet, but no one wanted to admit that a Soviet sub could be beyond that depth. In 1963 *Thresher* had imploded at two thousand feet.

Springfield was shaken. The Viktor had revealed herself as a far more formidable opponent than American naval officers had been taught to expect.

For three hours they searched in a spiral pattern, totally mystified. Finally, Springfield gave up.

'Unload torpedo.'

'Unload torpedo, aye.'

'Send up a buoy, Leo. Report the contact, then resume course for Naples.'

'Aye aye, Skipper.'

Sorensen was intrigued. In the grand game of Cowboys and Cossacks the Viktor was a new challenge. He put his hands behind his head and leaned back. 'Score one for Ivan,' he said. 'We lost this round.'

Fogarty was still poking at his ears. 'That was a slap in the face. I didn't like it.'

'Well, Fogarty, nobody likes it, so you can brood about it for a while. In the control room of that sub there's a guy sitting right now at his Feniks console, watching an obsolete oscilloscope, and he's probably feeling right pleased with himself, but don't take it personally. Sooner of later you'll get to do it to him, or to one of his pals. The only thing that bothers me is that he got away. That son of a bitch went pretty deep. And fast. A regular Maserati.'

'You really like this, don't you?' Fogarty said.

'Sure I do. There's nothing else like it in the world. This is what it's all about. We chase the Russians around the ocean, then they chase us, then we chase them some more. Shit, one hot sub doesn't mean anything. They get one, then we get one, the guys at Electric Boat keep busy and all the admirals are happy. After all, kid, it's just a game, isn't it?'

'It may be just a game, Sorensen, but the stakes seem pretty high.'

'So who wants to play penny-ante? That's no fun.' Sorensen's voice remained lighthearted, but his eyes were dead serious. 'Listen, Fogarty, down here we jam it to the max. We take it right to the edge. There's no other way.'

'It seems dangerous to me, Sorensen. If it gets out of hand we could have a war.'

'You afraid of a war, Fogarty?'

'Shit, yes.'

'Well, try to remember the other guys have just as much to lose as we do. If we get nuked we'll never know what hit us. What's with you, Fogarty? Are you some kind of peacenik? Ban the bomb, is that it? Or are you just chickenshit?'

Fogarty shrugged and looked away.

'Lighten up, kid,' Sorensen said. 'I'm not going to bug you about what you believe or don't. You do your job, you keep your ears sharp, you *play the fucking game* and you're going to be all right. I think maybe you've got a conscience, and that's okay.'

Fogarty looked into Sorensen's eyes and could almost feel a psychic probe rooting around in his mind. 'We can have a lot of fun in here,' Sorensen was saying, 'or it can be a real drag. You're a straight mid-western kid with smarts. All you really need is a sense of humor. We're the cowboys. They're the cossacks. So goddammit, start acting like a cowboy. Let me ask you something, Fogarty' – Sorensen's mouth twisted into a devilish smile – 'how did you feel when you first heard that Russian sub? Were you afraid?'

'No,' Fogarty admitted.

'Damned right. I was watching you. You were too excited to be scared. You got a big charge out of it. That's nothing to be ashamed of. When you see that Russian on the screen and listen to him growling like a goddamn nuclear shark, nothing else matters. It's you and him. That's where the action is. It's a big rush. Adrenaline maybe, or something even deeper. It's the ultimate drug. Underwater, what you believe doesn't count, only what you do, how you react. The rest of the world doesn't exist. Not your girlfriend, not your mother, not your god if you got one. Just you and Ivan.'

'Leave your mind behind.'

'You got it.'

A shy smile crossed Fogarty's face. 'I admit it was pretty exciting,' he said. 'Until my ears got blasted.'

'Think of what it did to the fish.' He jumped out of his seat and waved his arms around. 'Imagine a school of deaf tuna swimming upside down. Along comes a Great Barracuda. Zap, zap, he cuts 'em to ribbons, eats about twenty, and swims away upside down.'

Fogarty shook his head. 'Christ, Sorensen. That was terrible.'

They were both laughing when Lt Hoek opened the door. He was disappointed at having missed the original contact with the Russian sub and wanted to listen to the recording of the Viktor's signature. Sorensen surrendered the supervisor's console and started the tape.

They changed the watch. Sorensen and Fogarty were in the control room when they heard Lt Hoek howling in pain.

Springfield looked around and locked eyes with his senior sonarman. They both smiled. Hoek had a lot to learn.

The next morning Springfield prepared to take his ship into the Bay of Naples. Surfacing near a crowded harbor was always undertaken with great caution.

Fogarty was at the operator's console as the ship made a slow 360-degree turn, echo-ranging 360 degrees to make certain the surface was clear of shipping before raising the periscope. He picked up two freighters, a small tanker and a car ferry, all at a safe distance, but missed a flotilla of yachts in a restricted area.

'Up periscope.'

When Springfield put his eyes to the binocular lenses of the periscope he found himself staring into the startled face of a man in evening dress at the wheel of his boat fifty feet away. A naked woman lay on the deck. Several more people, drinks in hand, gawked at the periscope. Springfield could read the registration number painted on the hull. He swung the scope around and saw three more wooden and fibreglass sailboats within a hundred yards, impossible to detect on sonar.

'Control to sonar, you blew it. We've got sailboats.'

Sorensen clucked. 'Fogarty, you still can't navigate.'

'Leo,' Springfield said to the XO, 'take a look.'

Pisaro peered into the eyepiece and whistled.

When Springfield gave the order to surface, *Barracuda* surged out of the sea, a silent monster of the deep. The people on the sailboats lined the railings and watched the sub slip past. Her surface was mottled black, like the skin of a whale. The only sound was the hiss of water breaking over her bow.

Barracuda steamed into the Bay of Naples and tied up outside the breakwater next to the sub tender *Tallahatchie County*. Nearby, *Kitty Hawk*, flagship of the Sixth Fleet, was preparing for departure later that afternoon.

From high up on the superstructure of the massive aircraft carrier, a sailor looked down at the tiny submarine. Compared to the manifest might of *Kitty Hawk*, the sub appeared insignificant. With a dorsal fin and a tail protruding from the water, *Barracuda* looked like a fish to him, at worst a harmless little shark.

Jaded, polluted Naples spilled down the mountains to the bay, home port of the US Sixth Fleet. Over the millenia Neapolitans had seen many fleets come and go. When the giant *Kitty Hawk* and her escorts got up steam and sailed away, only a few young boys paid attention.

Barracuda was moored to the seaward side of *Tallahatchie County*. A canopy stretched from the tender over the top of the sail, veiling her profile from 'the eye in the sky', the Soviet satellites that frequently passed over Naples.

Springfield left the ship to carry the recordings of the Viktor to fleet headquarters, leaving Pisaro to pass the word. The crew waited expectantly for liberty call.

Pisaro called Chief Lopez into his cabin. The XO kept a box of Havanas exclusively for Lopez, one of his perks as chief of the boat. Flipping open his Zippo, Pisaro said, 'We're going to unload all your torpedoes, Chief, and replace them with dummies.'

Lopez puffed his cigar into life. 'All of them, Commander? I hate dummies. That pulls all the teeth out of *'Cuda*'.

'Nobody likes them, Chief. Anyway, that's the good news. The bad news is that there'll be no liberty call.'

Lopez looked forlorn but said nothing. Naples was his favorite liberty port. Pisaro knew how he felt. It was his favorite as well. He went on, 'We're going to be here less than twenty-four hours, and we'll be gone a week at the most. When we get back everyone gets three days ashore.'

'The crew won't like it, sir.'

'Your job is to listen to them bitch, Chief. Anyone who

wants can go onto *Tallahatchie* for thirty minutes.'

Lopez puffed hard on his cigar. 'Thirty whole minutes? I'll pass the word, sir. I'm sure it will make the men feel better about having no liberty and all—'

'Don't choke on the stogie, Lopez. Get outta here. And send Sorensen in with his beacon.'

In the sonar room Sorensen was assembling a waterproof, pressure-tight sonic beacon into the stainless steel box made by Barnes. As the other sonarmen crowded around, Sorensen tinkered with a soldering gun, a tiny screwdriver and a pile of highly classified miniature parts. He carefully torqued down the pressure seals and threw the switch. The box began to beep, and the sonarmen cheered.

Davic said, 'The Russians would kill for what's in that box.'

Sorensen turned it off. 'What makes you think so, Davic? Do you really think anyone would slaughter your fat ass for a bunch of transistors? In five years you'll probably be able to buy one of these things in a dimestore. A battery, a speaker, big fucking deal.'

Lopez looked in from the control. 'Sorensen, the XO wants to see you and your gizmo.'

Sorensen turned off the box. On the way out he handed the circuit diagram to Davic. 'Here, Davic, I want you to make one of these. You don't need a watertight case. I'm gonna hang it around your neck.'

Sorensen knocked on Pisaro's door.

'C'mon in, Ace.'

Spread out on the table was a chart of the Bay of Naples and the adjacent Gulf of Pozzuoli, a large inlet to the north, separated from the bay by the point of La Gaiola.

'At ease, Sorensen. Sit down. Light up if you like.'

'Thank you, sir.'

'You been topside yet?'

'No, sir. Too busy.'

'I wonder if it's a nice day. Naples can be a nice place. My grandfather came from Naples.'

Sorensen sniffed the air. 'I smell cigar smoke, sir. Does that mean there's no liberty?'

Pisaro laughed and ran his hands over his scalp. 'There's just no bullshitting you, is there? Well, you're right. No liberty. Next time.'

'Yes, sir.'

'All right, let's see your handiwork.' He reached for the beacon and switched it on, listened to it for a moment and turned it off. 'Is it going to work?'

'I can't say, sir. I haven't had it in the water.'

'What about a magnet?'

'I got one.'

'Well, then.' Pisaro looked over his chart and jabbed his finger at a spot in the middle of the Gulf of Pozzuoli. 'It's one hundred twenty feet down. Can you handle it?'

Sorensen peered at the chart and nodded. 'No problem.'

'Okay, you need to take someone with you. Who's it going to be?'

'Fogarty.'

'The kid? Is he qualified for scuba?' Pisaro opened his personnel files and pulled Fogarty's records. 'So he is. Is he any good at sonar?'

'He's a sharp cookie, Commander. He's got good ears.'

Pisaro studied the file. 'There's something about him I can't put my finger on. He's kind of sullen. I don't think he really likes the military—'

'For cryin' out loud, Commander, I don't like the military. I don't think you like it very much. If you'll pardon my saying so.'

Pisaro pretended not to hear this. He was reading Fogarty's file. 'He went to the University of Minnesota for a year. Hmm. Electronic engineering. Another wizard, I suppose. Why can't I get more guys like Willie Joe? Just

73

a good old boy who loves his submarine. Instead, I get the likes of you and this Fogarty. Get outta here. Go swimming.'

In wetsuits Sorensen and Fogarty popped out of the after hatch and carefully made their way along the deck. From the portside forward diving plane Hoek was supervising the loading of the dummy torpedoes. All of the torpedoes for the exercise, six Mark 37s and two Mark 45s, were wire-guided. Each torpedo was equipped with a reel of fine wire, miles long, that remained attached to the submarine when the weapon was fired. By means of an electronic pulse transmitted along the wire, the weapons officer could guide the torpedo to its target. The gleaming weapons were painted brilliant orange to indicate they were unarmed.

The two sailors dropped into a waiting rubber boat. Sorensen cranked up the outboard motor and a moment later they were skimming across the bay, heading for the Gulf of Pozzuoli.

Sheltered from the swell of the Mediterranean by the shoals of La Gaiola, the bay was calm. Shadows crept down the slopes of Vesuvius. The air was heavy with diesel oil and thyme.

Fogarty was awestruck by the crumbling magnificence of Naples. After ten days underwater he seemed to have surfaced in paradise. Waving his arms, he shouted into the wind, 'It's like a dream, it's beautiful.'

'You know what they say, kid. See Naples and die.'

Sorensen had visited Naples many times but had never looked at it as anything more than a backdrop for a debauch. He wasn't looking now. His face was turned into the sun.

As they rounded the point and entered the gulf, Sorensen slowed to get his bearings. Fogarty chattered excitedly about the villas along the beach, the ice-cream town of Pozzuoli visible four miles away, the range of mountains that loomed over the gulf.

'C'mon, Sorensen. Which one is Vesuvius?'

'How do I know? The one blowing smoke rings.'

'Where's Pompeii? It's supposed to be around here.'

Sorensen became annoyed. 'Look, Fogarty, I know this is all new to you, but try to restrain yourself. I'm not a tour guide and we've got a little job to do.' He started putting on his scuba gear. 'You check your tanks, kid?'

'Yeah.'

'Look, I don't mean to be hard on you. You'll have plenty of chances to play tourist. Hey, you know what you get when you nuke Naples?'

'What?'

'Plutonium pizza.'

'Jesus, Sorensen, you're a sick man.'

'You think it's a joke?'

'I hope it is.'

'Well, it's not. Listen, I live in a submarine. I'm a bubblehead, and that gives me a certain point of view.' He paused to gesture widely, taking in the entire region around Naples, 'This is a target. As long as Naples is the home port of the Sixth Fleet it will be destroyed in the first salvo. A million people are going to die here, blasted by the Russians. As far as I'm concerned they're already dead. They don't exist. I don't want to know who they are or how they live.'

'Do you really think we're going to have a war?'

Sorensen looked around. 'We're already at war. It's just that we don't shoot each other, but we do everything else. We're fighting for control of the sea. Whoever controls the oceans rules the roost. When the Russians put that sub in the Med, the one we stumbled across yesterday, they took a big step in that direction. They're not supposed to get through Gibraltar undetected, you know. That's bad news. If they can go on with this shit, sooner or later they'll be able to track our missile subs in the Med. That threatens our strategic deterrence – you know, the one they make all those speeches about – and that's not allowed.'

'But we track theirs too. We know the location of every one of their subs in the Atlantic and the Caribbean—'

'Except we're not them. We've had superior forces all along. We can waste them any time we want, only we don't. We aren't so sure that that would happen if the situation were reversed.'

'And we don't want to find out . . .'

'Maybe I don't give a shit. I don't know . . . we're all bugs crawling over a ball of dirt on the edge of some nowhere galaxy. You think we're all there is? If we go down like the dinosaurs maybe the whales will get their chance. They'd probably do a better job . . . Hey, ain't I profound . . . you'd think I knew something.' He looked at his compass and checked his bearings, then with a flourish zipped up his wetsuit. 'C'mon, sailor, drop anchor. We're here.'

Murky green light filtered down into the gulf. Sorensen and Fogarty followed the anchor rope to the bottom, where Sorensen consulted his compass. He carried the beacon and Fogarty the magnet.

Fogarty expected to find a bouillabaisse in the gulf, rascasse and eels, scampi and sole. Instead he found a garbage dump, long since fished out. The debris of centuries littered the bottom. Mixed with the silt were layers of slime, condoms, volcanic ash, broken statuary and Pepsi bottles.

It didn't take long to find their objective – a dark shape looming up from the deep, the mangled hulk of a World War Two German submarine. The stern was half-buried in the silt, and the rest of the wreck was covered with algae and rust. On the conning tower they read: *U-62*.

Sorensen took the magnet from Fogarty, swam to the

sub and attached the beacon to the hull. He switched it on, and they listened to the beep.

They swam slowly around the wreck. Half the bow was torn away, and around the edges of the gaping hole the metal was twisted outward. In one awful moment a torpedo had exploded inside the boat, sinking it instantly. Since the hatches were closed and the radars and periscopes retracted, it was clear that the accident had occurred while the boat was submerged.

Sorensen lingered, looking for a souvenir, but the old sub had been stripped by divers long ago, and besides, it was too dangerous to go inside without lights. Sorensen jerked his thumbs toward the surface, and together they began the slow ascent.

On the surface the wind died, the light faded and the bay turned smooth as a sheet of Formica. As they approached the breakwater the sub was a black silhouette looming against the gray washes of the tender.

Sorensen imagined he could see radiation seeping from the hull aft of the sail. To him, *Barracuda* glowed in the dark, her atomic fire burning with an intensity that could not be contained.

Back in the crew quarters Sorensen whistled cheerfully as he rummaged around in his tiny locker for a cigarette. He found books, tapes, electronics manuals and uniforms, but no smokes.

'Say, Fogarty, can I bum a cigarette?'

They were alone. Fogarty lay on his bunk in jockey shorts and glowered at the bulkhead. He had not said a word during the ride back to the ship.

'What's the matter with you?' You quit smokin' or what?'

Fogarty tossed a pack of Luckys across the passageway. Sorensen took one. 'Some folks would pay a fortune to go scuba diving in the Med.'

'Christ almighty, Sorensen. There were dead men on that boat—'

'Maybe, maybe not. The ocean is full of dead men and sunken ships. Their wars are over. Those guys on that U-boat died a long time ago. Fish ate them before you were born. It's ancient history.'

'They were sailors just like you and me—'

'They were not like you and me. They were Nazis. They were the enemy. It was lucky for our side that they blew themselves up.'

'Ah, come on, Sorensen, that's just it. A fish blew up inside their boat. I can't even imagine what it was like in there when that torpedo exploded. They never had a chance.'

Sorensen nodded. 'I wouldn't think too much of it. When we come back here next week we can borrow some tanks and dive down to old *U-62* again. We'll go in there with lights, and you can find out what it was like. It'll be an object lesson in what can happen if somebody makes a mistake underwater.'

'*U-62* didn't have nuclear torpedoes. If we blew up in the Bay of Naples, plutonium pizza.'

'C'mon, Fogarty, lighten up.' He punched the young sailor playfully on the shoulder. 'Listen, kid, you've got a bad habit. You think too much. It isn't going to make your life any easier, I guarantee you. Sooner or later everybody on this ship has to come to terms with the fact that we're a fucking bomb waiting to go off. You've got a head start. You're green, but you think about these things. You have to grow up fast, we need guys like you down here.' Sorensen grinned. 'At least on this ship we might get a chance to waste a Russian missile sub before she blows up New York City.'

'And until then?'

'Hey, man, we all live in our little yellow submarine.

78

Relax, try thinking of yourself as a pioneer exploring life underwater. The price for the privilege is that you have to work for the navy. So you put up with a lot of chickenshit. But at least you get a nice clean comfortable air-conditioned submarine to drive you around, all meals provided. You get the best toys and the best talent to operate them. And for excitement you get to play Cowboys and Cossacks with the Russians. Some deal, right?'

'Except a forty-million-dollar submarine designed to kill people isn't a toy.'

'Well, we haven't killed anybody yet, and as far as I know we aren't planning on doing it today. Listen, Fogarty,' Sorensen said, his voice slowing down and lowering in tone, 'as long as you are on this ship I'm your supervisor. For some stupid reason I like you. I think you will turn into a fine sonar operator, so I'm giving you a choice. Just keep your mouth shut, do your job, or get the fuck off this ship today. You hear me, sailor?'

Fogarty kept his mouth shut. Sorensen looked at him, then broke into a smile and slapped him on the back.

'Hey, okay, lighten up now and get your ass in gear. We have to report to the XO.'

6

NETTS

The ship buzzed with excitement. The word had been passed that an admiral was coming aboard to give *Barracuda* a special assignment, and the crew was busily preparing for an inspection. Sailors in freshly laundered jumpsuits executed routine tasks with an extra touch of crispness. Internal communications technicians checked every circuit. Settings on the inertial navigation gyros were adjusted. Radar monitored the traffic in the harbor. Only in the galley was there a note of discontent. The admiral would not dine, and Stanley felt dejected.

Sorensen and Fogarty were passing through the control room when Pisaro called out, 'Attention!'

Instantly the control room was transformed into a parade ground.

The quartermaster blew his pipes, and two men passed through the hatch.

'At ease,' said Pisaro.

Fogarty saw a short pudgy man of sixty in a flowered Hawaiian shirt, flat black sunglasses and a salt-and-pepper beard that wrapped around his jowls like a mask.

'Who is *that*?' he whispered to Sorensen.

'Netts,' said Sorensen. 'Vice-Admiral Edward P. Netts.'

'Never heard of him,' Fogarty said.

'The Russians have.'

The second man was impeccably dressed in custom-tailored tans.

'Who's that?' Fogarty asked.

'His aide, Commander Billings. I expect he'll be with us for a few days.'

Netts looked around the control room and spotted

Sorensen. Quietly, to avoid being overheard by the other men in the compartment, Netts asked Sorensen about the Viktor they had encountered. 'I understand it went below two thousand feet. Is that true?'

'Yes, sir. It did, indeed.'

Netts mulled over the unhappy implications. 'Is the beacon planted on *U-62*?' he asked.

'Yes, sir.'

'Did you go over the plan with the skipper?'

'Yes, sir. It's going to be a piece of cake, Admiral.'

'All right' – Netts turned to Pisaro – 'let's get on with it.'

The admiral was in no mood to see his special assignment torpedoed – he winced at the unintended pun – by a faulty stern plane, a leaky pipe or a crazed computer. He intended to inspect the ship.

At the navigation console the quartermaster was taking a satellite feed of up-to-date information on tide, current, wind and sea conditions. On the display screen an electronic chart of the Naples roadstead was ready and waiting with *Barracuda*'s course already plotted.

At the attack console Hoek took another satellite feed, which showed *Kitty Hawk* and her escorts on a radar screen. The fleet was three hundred miles from Naples, fifty miles off the southern tip of Sardinia. Netts stared at the screen. 'Do they have company?'

'Yes, sir, they sure do,' said Hoek, punching buttons. Two more blips appeared, trailing the rearmost destroyer by two miles.

'*Boris Badinoff* and *Natasha*,' said the lieutenant.

'What about subs? Any sign of the Viktor you met?'

'So far, *nada*.'

'Well, let's hope it stays that way, but don't bet on it. Can you show me Naples?' asked Netts.

'Certainly, Admiral.' Hoek punched more buttons and the screen showed the navigation chart. Netts studied the screen. Scattered among the freighters and ferries that appeared as blips on the screen were the buoys that marked the channel.

'Lieutenant, there's a sub waiting for you out there, probably ten or twelve miles out. There might even be two. I wouldn't be surprised if she's under one of those buoys. I suggest that you plot an attack course for each buoy more than ten miles out, just in case one of them moves.'

'Aye aye,' replied Hoek as he energetically began to push buttons. Hoek was ready for a fight. His breath was short, his chest felt constricted. He was due for a physical when *Barracuda* returned to Norfolk, and he knew he would never pass. This was his last patrol, and he wanted some memories to take ashore.

Netts led his party forward through officers' country. In the narrow passageways he paid particular attention to the control cables and pipes that ran through the ship, all open and exposed for instant maintenance and repair. The cosmetic paneling that at one time had covered them was ripped out after the *Thresher* disaster.

Sorensen and Fogarty made their way to the mess. The moment they arrived, Sorensen was cornered by Cakes, who asked, 'Who's the brass?'

'Big shot from Washington. Netts.'

The steward did a double take. 'Cap'n Netts? Ed Netts?'

'Vice-Admiral Netts.'

'No shit!'

'Why, Cakes? You know him?'

The steward's eyes seemed to shrink back into his head as if he were trying to hold back a memory that had forced its way into his skull. One hand jerked up to the side of his face and began tugging at his right ear.

A commotion forward signaled the approach of officers.

'Attention!' shouted Sorensen, and everyone snapped to.

'At ease, men,' said Pisaro.

Netts immediately walked over to the steward, stuck out his hand and warmly pumped his arm.

'Hello, Cakes.'

'Howdy, Cap'n.'

'How's the ear?'

'Mighty fine. Ninety-five percent.'

'Glad to hear it.'

What Netts and Cakes shared happened on August 23, 1944, when Admiral Chester Nimitz pinned the Navy Cross on Cakes Colby for heroism aboard *Sargo*, Netts commanding. During a depth charge attack in the Sea of Japan, Cakes had sealed himself into a flooding compartment and saved his ship.

With a friendly salute to his old shipmate, Netts descended a ladder and entered the torpedo room. He swept the room with a scowl, taking in the two dummy Mark 45 and twelve dummy Mark 37 torpedoes stacked neatly in racks.

The eight members of the torpedo gang stood at stiff attention, sweating in the intimidating presence of the admiral.

Netts said to Lopez, 'Chief, did you run checks on these fish yourself?'

'Yes, sir!'

'You happy?'

Lopez hesitated before answering.

'Out with it, man!'

'Sir! I don't like to go on patrol without no live torpedoes, sir!'

Nett's mood changed. 'At ease, men,' he said. 'I understand your point, Chief, but this is not a patrol, it's an exercise, and it's only for a few days.'

'Sir!'

'Yes, Chief.'

'What if a war starts during the exercise?'

Netts swiftly crossed over to the attack console and tapped Zapata's cage. 'In that case, Chief, you'll go up to the surface and sic this nasty little devil on the Russians.'

The admiral then turned abruptly, disappeared up the ladder and headed aft. The Chief had a point, but he couldn't stand there and debate it.

The reactor compartment was divided into two decks. On the lower deck were the reactor vessel and heat exchangers, heavily shielded in a room no one entered while the reactor was operating. The upper deck housed the control rods and a narrow passageway, the tunnel, that led to the reactor control room and engineering spaces. In the reactor control room Netts noted that the reactor was critical and nodded with satisfaction. In the maneuvering room he stood for a moment watching the technicians watch their displays.

Without a word he continued into the engine room, where Chief Wong was running a computer check on the injectors that fed steam into the turbogenerators to provide for the ship's electrical systems.

'Chief,' said the admiral, taking from his pocket a set of electrical diagrams and handing them to Wong, 'are you familiar with this setup?'

The engineer bent over the diagrams and clicked his tongue. 'Yes, sir. We tested it in transit from Norfolk.'

'I know,' said Netts. 'Well, you had better get busy.'

'Aye aye, Admiral.'

Netts examined the engineering log, noting that nothing extraordinary had happened to the propulsion plant since Norfolk. He paused a moment to stare at the turbines. 'Pretty nice steamboat you have here, Chief,' he said, and headed forward for his briefing with Springfield. Damn, he loved these steamboats.

Sorensen and Fogarty were sitting in the mess with forty

84

other sailors when the loudspeaker piped attention. Sorensen stared unseeing into his coffeecup and gritted his teeth, wishing he were on watch so he wouldn't have to listen to a speech.

'Attention all hands, attention all hands. The captain is going to address the crew.'

Springfield's voice resounded throughout the ship. 'As I am sure all of you are aware, we have a distinguished visitor aboard. Admiral Netts has come from the Office of the Chief of Naval Operations to give *Barracuda* a special assignment, and he is going to tell you about it now.'

'Gentlemen,' said Netts, 'today on all the oceans of the world we face a more powerful and dangerous adversary than even the Fascist powers of Germany, Italy and Japan that we defeated in the Second World War.

'In the last decade, under the leadership of Admiral Gorshkov, the Soviet Navy has been built up from a coastal defense force into the second most powerful navy in the world. If the Russians were to attack us today I'm here to tell you we would have a hell of a time stopping them.

'If I were Admiral Gorshkov and I were planning an attack on the US Navy, the first thing I would do would be to sink as many American missile submarines as I could find. In all likelihood, I wouldn't find many, if any at all. Therefore, I would attack what I could find. And that, gentlemen, means aircraft carriers. You just can't hide one of those damned things. An aircraft carrier may be a dandy platform for launching airstrikes against peasants in Viet Nam, but Viet Nam does not have attack submarines like *Barracuda* capable of shooting back.

'I'm letting my hair down with you people because I think of us as a family. So please indulge me.

'Our navy has spent and spent building aircraft carriers and carrier groups, and intends to spend more. In my opinion, an opinion which I do not share with many people in Washington, this is wrong. Terribly wrong. If war comes with the Russians, those carriers will be sitting ducks. They will be blown out of the water in the first fifteen minutes of the war, and then it will be up to the submarine forces to carry on the fight.

'The Russians will attack with strength and cunning. Their submarines have their problems, no question, but in those first fifteen minutes they will be able to inflict damage. No question about that either. They will destroy the fixed arrays that enable us to track their subs through the oceans. They will render our communications system useless. They will attack our ports, our naval stations, our fuel and supply depots. All that is to be expected. What my superiors do not wish to believe is that at the end of the first phase of the war at sea our carrier groups will be clouds of radioactive dust.

'Why am I telling you all this? Because in the next five days your mission will be to prove the truth of it.'

'Now, I'm sure Admiral Gorshkov would be proud to have a ship like *Barracuda* in his fleet. I know I am, but for the next five days you will be playing the role of a Soviet crew, and *Barracuda* will act as though it were part of the Black Sea Fleet.

'This ship is going to demonstrate that one attack submarine can penetrate the defenses of an entire carrier group and sink the queen bee. You can't put a live charge into *Kitty Hawk*, but you can sure as hell smash a pair of dummies into her hull and give everybody on her flight deck a good soaking.

'In my opinion the future of the Navy is at stake here. For the first time ever there will be no restrictions on the operations of the attacking submarine in an exercise of this sort. Captain Springfield will have absolute discretion to go where he wants, as deep as he wants and as fast as he wants. You men will do whatever it takes to sink the *Hawk*.

'That's is all. God bless you.'

When the speech ended a cheer erupted in the control room and swept like a wave through the ship. By the time it reached the mess, the crew was chanting, 'Nuke the *Hawk*, nuke the *Hawk* . . .'

Fogarty felt that Netts had confirmed his private feelings about a nuclear war at sea. He raised his voice with the others. It felt good to have something to cheer about.

Only Sorensen kept silent, the muscles in his jaw tightening. He slammed his coffeecup onto the table and stood up. The mess instantly quieted.

'You people are crazy,' he said. 'This isn't going to be a joyride. The fleet will have six subs looking for us.' He looked over the young faces in the mess. 'And while half the fucking US Navy is chasing us around in circles, there's *still* a Russian sub loose out there. Keep it in mind.'

He sat down and shook his head. The mess started to clear out.

'What gets me,' Sorensen said to Willie Joe, 'is that this bullshit could get us killed just so the admiral can boost his career—'

'Cool off, Ace,' said Willie Joe. 'This is gonna be fun. The fleet doesn't stand a chance.'

'I've known about this for two weeks, but I couldn't say anything. It's going to get crowded down there. Seven subs in one tiny piece of ocean, six of them and us.' Sorensen sighed. 'Okay, Willie Joe, you and Fogarty go up to sonar and start running signature programs for the fleet's subs. Give Davic the word.'

'Aye aye. You take it easy there, Ace.'

Sorensen rustled up a sandwich from Stanley. By now the mess was deserted. He took a bite of BLT, chewed without tasting, gave up and lit a cigarette.

'That was real cute, Sorensen.'

He turned around and saw Pisaro leaning against the bulkhead, arms folded across his chest.

'Evening, Commander.'

'You trying to put the fear of God into those boys, or what?'

'We're supposed to be pros down here, sir, not a bunch of jerkoffs.'

'What about esprit de corps? Isn't that worth something?'

Sorensen smiled. 'Tell it to the Marines, sir. No disrespect intended. My only concern is the safety of this ship.'

'I know that. And we both know that on this exercise the safety of the ship will be in your hands. If you're a little edgy, I need to know.'

'I'm all right.'

'You lay off the amphetamines.'

Sorensen raised his eyebrows and stared at the XO.

In the sonar room Fogarty said, 'Willie Joe, what's with Sorensen?'

'He figures anything but chasing Russians is a waste of time.'

'Do you?'

'I just put in my time, man. It don't make any difference to me.'

Hoek stuck his face into the room. 'Willie Joe, run a signature program for *Swordfish*, *Shark*, *Seawolf*, *Mako*, *Dragonfish* and *Stingray*.'

'Aye aye, sir.'

'What's in the log?'

'Just local traffic, Lieutenant. A small ship is approaching the channel.'

'Okay, sign it and that's it.'

'Aye aye.'

Sorensen came in, muttering something unintelligible.

'All right,' he said. 'If we're going to do this, we're going to do it right. Willie Joe, beat it. Take your white suit. Fogarty, check your bottom scanners. We ain't gonna nuke the *Hawk* if we can't make it out of the bay.'

All over the ship, division heads were logging in the first watch. In the control room the captain went through the departure checklist.

'Maneuvering room, report.'

'Steam, twenty percent. Turbogenerators on line.'

'Very well. Engine room, report.'

'Engine room standing by on number one turbine.'

'Very well. Sonar, report.'

'Sonar reports screws on the surface bearing one niner zero, range two two five zero zero yards.'

'Very well. Radar, report.'

'Radar reports a ship entering the channel, bearing one niner zero, range two two five zero zero yards.'

'Very well. Navigation, report.'

'Navigation reports gyros set, course plotted, standing by.'

'Very well. Helm, report.'

'Helm standing by.'

'Very well. Stern planes, report.'

'Stern planes standing by.'

Springfield turned to Pisaro. 'This is it, Leo. I'm going up to the bridge. Quartermaster, sound General Quarters.'

Throughout the ship loudspeakers heralded the quartermaster's voice. 'General Quarters! General Quarters. Prepare for maneuvering. All hands man battle stations.'

Two sailors were standing by on the deck near each hatch, their eyes on the bridge. Springfield ordered them, 'Deck party, stand by to cast off lines.'

He spoke through the intercom to the control room. 'Bridge to navigation, how is the tide?'

'Navigation to bridge, going out at one-quarter knot.'

'Very well. Cast off the bow line.'

The crew of the *Tallahatchie County* appeared over the gunwhales, smiling and waving.

'Bow line away.'

'Cast off the stern line.'

'Stern line away.'

'Steer left three degrees.'

'Left three degrees.'

'All ahead slow.'

Fogarty began feeding the signature programs of the six subs into his computer. The captain and lookout came down from the sail.

'Prepare to dive,' said the captain. 'Take her down, Mr Pisaro.'

Pisaro gave orders to retract radars, and the diving officer went through his panel.

'Mark three degrees down bubble.'

'Mark three degrees down bubble, aye.'

'Flood forward and main ballast tanks.'

'Flood forward and main ballast tanks, aye.'

'Flood forward trim tanks.'

'Flood forward trim tanks, aye.'

'Maintain slow speed.'

'All ahead slow, aye.'

The bow sank quickly under the surface of the bay.

'Stern planes down ten degrees.'

'Ten degrees down, aye.'

The game began.

7

TURBO-ELECTRIC

One the stroke of midnight an inbound tanker passed a large red navigation buoy eleven miles outside the Naples breakwater. The sailors on the tanker's bridge scarcely glanced at the revolving light buoy, and no one noticed a much smaller float that had attached itself magnetically to the buoy. Eight inches in diameter, the float had a two-foot-long antenna extending into the air and a thin wire descending into the depths. At the far end of the wire, 150 feet down, USS *Mako* hovered in ambush.

She had been on-station for six hours, waiting for the message from the Sixth Fleet shore command that would announce *Barracuda*'s departure. Having spent a dozen patrols lying off Soviet ports waiting for Russian submarines to exit, the crew was accustomed to picket duty.

The tide had turned and *Barracuda* was about to exit the bay under the tanker's sound screen. Captain Flowers joked that Netts himself was on the tanker, intentionally fouling the water with noise pollution. Like everyone else on *Mako*, Flowers wished for *Barracuda*'s ultimate success, but regretted that if it came it would be at his expense. His orders were to stop *Barracuda* the moment she emerged from the channel and put a quick end to 'Netts's Folly'.

'Radio to control. Target under way.'

Flowers wasted no time. 'Cut loose that buoy,' he ordered. 'Control to weapons, he's moving. Load dummies in tubes one and two.'

The weapons officer, Lt North, stared at the blip on his screen that was *Barracuda*, just as he had stared a month before at the blip that was *Leninsky Komsomol* when she sailed from Leningrad into the Gulf of Finland. Should *Barracuda* elude the picket and reach blue water, she could outrun *Mako* and reach the fleet in thirty hours.

The rules of the war game established a combat-free zone within a radius of ten miles around Naples. Outside the ten-mile limit, a submarine 'kill' would be registered by the firing of a dummy torpedo and a sonar blast, to be judged as a hit or a miss by umpires aboard each ship. Torpedoes fired at other submarines would contain no propellant. Immediately after being ejected from the tubes, they would sink. Only the torpedoes *Barracuda* fired at *Kitty Hawk* would make a run to the target. With no warhead the fish would bounce off the huge hull of the carrier, causing no significant damage.

'Control to sonar, listen up. He's moving.'

Mako's sonar room was larger, quieter and more comfortable than the cramped sonar room on *Barracuda*. With her more sophisticated sonars, computers and fire control system, plus the element of surprise, *Mako* seemed to have every advantage. The sonarmen expected *Barracuda* to proceed seven or eight miles into the bay and submerge under their noses.

'Sonar to control. We have her, bearing three four six. Course one two three. Speed four knots. Range nineteen thousand yards. She's turning. Bearing three four seven, three four eight, three four nine. Captain' – the operator's voice suddenly rose with astonishment – 'she's *submerging.*'

The sonar operators listened to *Barracuda*'s machinery as she submerged, prop cavitating noisily in the shallow water of the bay. The sounds were muddled by the tanker that was now between the two subs.

Suddenly the machinery noises stopped. They heard the tanker, the ping of the fixed beacon that guided ships in and out of the harbor, but no submarine.

'Sonar to control. We lost her on the passive array. She disappeared.'

'Springfield's guessed that we're here,' said the XO, Commander Poland.

'Control to sonar. Echo-range,' ordered Flowers. 'Find her.'

'Sonar to control. Echo-ranging.'

The bottom of the bay was studded with rocks, sunken ships, mounds of garbage and waste from the deeply dredged channels, all of which deflected and distorted the sonar pulses from *Mako's* echo rangers, transforming her sonar screen into an undecipherable maze.

In the control room Flowers scratched his jaw, took off his headset and rubbed his ears.

Poland said, 'She's gone turbo-electric. She's trying to sneak out on the quiet.'

The captain nodded, knowing that ballistic missile submarines occasionally left port under turbo-electric power in order to evade a waiting attack sub. All SSN officers were, of course, familiar with the tactic.

'The question is,' said Flowers, 'does Springfield come after us or try to escape?'

'I think he'll run,' the XO said. 'He's faster than we are and he'll try to get around us. He'll use the islands.'

Pointing at the electronic chart that displayed the Bay of Naples and the islands of Procia, Ischia and Capri just offshore, the XO said, 'If Springfield can get behind one of the islands and block our sonar he can escape. The channel between Capri and the mainland is the deepest and the safest for passage. I reckon he'll go south, here, around Capri. He's already moving in that direction.'

'All right,' said Flowers. 'We have to go somewhere and Capri is as good a place as any. We sure as hell can't stay here now that he knows where we are. Sonar, belay the echo ranger. All ahead half. Course one three one. Let's try not to run into the son of a bitch.'

Originally Springfield had proposed to Netts that *Barracuda* make a run for Capri, counting on *Barracuda*'s speed to get her past any picket. Netts rejected that as too obvious. He suggested that Springfield hide the ship in the Gulf of Pozzuoli until the picket either was sunk or gave up and returned to the fleet. After eluding the picket, *Barracuda* would run north, pass through the Strait of Bonifacio between Sardinia and Corsica, sail down the west coast of Sardinia and surprise the fleet with an attack from the north.

The plan was dangerous. First, *Barracuda* had to maneuver in the bay and then in the shallow gulf without colliding with a submerged obstacle. To do this it was necessary to echo-range and thereby announce her location to *Mako*. Both Springfield and Netts found this unacceptable.

Sorensen provided the solution. The Bay of Naples was seeded with fixed sonars that transmitted sonic beacons on regular frequencies to guide ships in and out of port at times of low visibility. Sorensen demonstrated how it was possible to echo-range on the same frequency as one of the beacons. 'All we have to do,' Sorensen told the captain, 'is time the pulse to coincide with the moment *Barracuda* is directly in line between the fixed array and the picket. If it doesn't work, we'll still be inside the ten-mile limit and he can't shoot us.'

'If it doesn't work, Sorensen,' Springfield said, 'this exercise will be over in five minutes, not five days.'

When Springfield submerged less than a mile out into the bay, he did the one thing no one on *Mako* expected. It was a most precarious gambit. The channel was barely deep enough to act as a sonar buffer, but the tanker coming through should provide enough cover to disguise his maneuvers.

Once underwater, Sorensen immediately picked up the tanker and the garbled but distinct sound of coolant pumps throbbing ten miles away. He logged it and told Hoek he heard only pumps and no gears or prop. He knew the sub was hovering, but the sound was too distorted by other noises in the channel for an absolute fix. Hoek, watching the sonar display on his attack console, guessed that the sub was under buoy number five, and busily plotted an attack.

Springfield took *Barracuda* on a wide sweeping turn to the left at very slow speed. When the ship was lined up between the beacon and buoy number five, he ordered sonar to echo-range once on the beacon's frequency. Sorensen sent one narrow-beamed pulse of sound out into the channel. A single blip appeared on the screen, a sub lying quietly at radio depth.

'Lieutenant, we've got him.'

'Bearing?'

'Bearing one five one.'

'Speed?'

. 'Zero zero, repeat zero zero.'

'Range?'

'One eight five zero yards. He's under buoy number five.' Sorensen recognized her signature.

'It's *Mako*,' he said a split second before the computer.

Springfield ordered, 'All stop.'

In the engine room turbine number one whirred to a halt. In the maneuvering room an engineer throttled back the steam. The main feed pumps, with less work to do, became as quiet as possible. In the heat exchangers just enough steam was produced to power the turbogenerators. Although with a loss in overall efficiency, the power from the generators could be used to run an electric motor coupled directly to the propeller shaft. The system had been devised to provide emergency propulsion if both main turbines failed. *Barracuda* would be slower than before, but she also would be almost totally silent.

When the propeller stopped turning, *Barracuda*'s momentum carried her forward several hundred yards. By the time she came to a complete stop, her turbogenerators and electric motor were engaged.

With a clear picture of the bottom and the traffic in the harbor, *Barracuda* made a tight 180-degree turn inside the bay, carefully picked her way through the wrecks and silt mounds and crept north around the point of La Gaiola and into the Gulf of Pozzuoli. Sorensen informed Springfield that *Mako* held her southerly course. Making a great deal of noise with her own machinery, *Mako* apparently did not notice *Barracuda*'s maneuver.

As soon as *Barracuda* cleared the point, Sorensen picked up the signal from the beacon attached to the hull of *U-62*. Most of the gulf was too shallow for submerged operation, but Springfield had studied the charts carefully and had determined that he could hide *Barracuda* behind the wreck. Using the beacon as a guide, Springfield cautiously maneuvered into a position that allowed the rusting hulk of the dead German sub to shield *Barracuda* from probing sonars. The ship hovered just above the bottom. Right on time the battery in the beacon went dead.

Sorensen kicked his chair away and stood at his console, listening to *Mako* conduct her search. After a few minutes she disappeared behind Capri.

'Control to weapons. Load a dummy in tube number one.'

'Weapons, aye. Loading dummy.'

In the torpedo room the torpedomen loaded a dummy Mark 37 wire-guided torpedo into tube number one.

'Flood tube.'

'Flooding tube, aye.'

Sorensen and Fogarty heard seawater rush into the torpedo tube. The ship tilted forward.

'Correct the trim, if you please, Mr Pisaro.'

The ship came back to dead level.

'Control to sonar. This is the captain.'

'Sonar to control, aye.'

'Well done, Sorensen.'

'Thank you, sir.'

'Now be quiet,' Sorensen said to Fogarty. 'This is a special treat. It's not often we get to lie quietly in shallow water like this. You never know what you might hear. Maybe we fooled that other ship and maybe we didn't. For all I know the Italians are going to drop sonar buoys right on top of us any minute. They go *splish*, just like that, sounds like a big fish jumping, and then they drop a Lulu and it's time to say adios.'

Suddenly he sat up with a jerk. 'Sonar to control,' he said into his intercom. 'Lieutenant, *Mako* is coming back this way, bearing one four three, course two five two, speed eight knots, range thirty thousand yards.'

In the control room every officer experienced a rush of adrenaline. *Mako* was going to pass right across *Barracuda's* bow and give her a clean shot. Hoek was tracking the target on his weapons console, waiting for *Mako's* tangent to carry her beyond the ten-mile limit.

Navigating on a course that would intercept *Barracuda* coming out from behind the island of Ischia, *Mako* crossed the mouth of the Gulf of Pozzuoli at an oblique angle. Her side-to-side sweeping sonar would pick up *Barracuda's* coolant pumps once the angle cleared *U-62*, but it would be too late.

'Sorensen,' said Hoek, 'get ready. When I give the order to fire, you give them a blast with the target-seeking frequency.'

'Yes sir, Mr Hoek.' Sorensen nodded to Fogarty. 'You do it, kid. You blast 'em.'

Fogarty watched the screen. 'He's around the point,' he said.

Sorensen held up his thumb. 'Go.'

'Sonar to weapons,' Fogarty said. 'Lock on weapons guidance.'

'Weapons guidance locked on sonar,' said Hoek over the intercom. 'Tracking target.'

'Five, four, three, two, one. Fire.'

The ship bucked as it spat out a torpedo, and the bow angled up for a moment until the trim computer automatically pumped water forward to compensate for the loss in weight. Sorensen listened to confirm the torpedo was a dummy. The motor never kicked in and it sank into the mud of the gulf.

Hoek was yelling through the intercom, 'Sorensen, what's the matter with you? Hit them with the target sonar.'

Fogarty stared at his console. The narrow-beam echo ranger was locked onto *Mako* and tracking her course, but Fogarty, remembering his own recent sonar lashing, couldn't help thinking of the sonar operators whose eardrums were about to take a pounding. Another moment's delay and those same operators would hear the sound of the dummy whooshing out of the tube, and they would return the favor. Reluctantly, he pushed the button on his console.

Glaring at Fogarty, Sorensen said, 'The next time you hesitate on a direct order will be your last.'

Sound, Fogarty had learned, traveled through warm shallow seawater at 4921.25 feet per second. 12.33 seconds later two men were screaming in *Mako*'s sonar room, and three more in her control room.

On *Barracuda* there were cheers. Hoek even did a little war dance in his seat.

Mako was now *hors de combat*, and five of her crew had ringing ears. The umpire aboard *Mako* immediately noted the 'kill', as did Billings, the umpire aboard *Barracuda*. Both ships sent up radio buoys.

'Well done,' said Flowers. 'Congratulations.'

'Sorry about your men,' answered Springfield. 'Buy you a drink in Norfolk.'

'Sink the *Hawk* and I'll buy you one.'

Springfield retracted his buoy, and *Barracuda* continued north for three hours on electric power, making sure there was no second picket. Finally the main turbine was cut in.

'All ahead full,' ordered Springfield, and *Barracuda* lunged forward like a dolphin.

8

BONIFACIO

Six hours after leaving Naples, *Barracuda* raced through the Tyrrhenian Sea, heading for the Strait of Bonifacio.

'Attention all hands, attention all hands. Secure from general quarters. The movie this morning will be *Bonnie and Clyde* at zero nine hundred in the mess. That is all.'

After eliminating *Mako* from the wargame, the crew was jubilant. In the galley Stanley was preparing cioppino from fresh fish taken on at Naples.

'What is it?' asked Cakes.

'Shark soup,' Stanley replied with a grin.

In the torpedo room Lopez was feeding Zapata and smoking a huge stogie. Aft, even the nucs got cute and painted the profile of a sub on the casing of turbogenerator number one.

Coming off watch, Fogarty went to the movie, and Sorensen went looking for Eddie Luther, the corpsman. With a peek at the watch sheet in the control room he learned that Luther was taking his turn on Sorensen's Beach.

Luther, a dapper little man with a taste for jazz and no scruples whatsoever, sold amphetamines.

No one was on duty in the steering machinery room when Sorensen banged on the door to the Beach. When it opened, Sorensen heard Cal Tjader playing on his machine. Silently, Luther passed Sorensen a packet of ten Dexamyl tablets in exchange for a ten dollar bill, and Sorensen headed for the sonar room to test all the circuits in his console.

Two hours later, on his way to the mess, Sorensen felt the ship reduce speed. As he was munching a hamburger, it came to a complete stop.

'Attention all hands, this is the captain. We have entered French territorial waters approximately thirty miles off the coast of Corsica. We are attempting to contact a French submarine operating in this area. All hands to maneuvering stations. That is all.'

Sorensen took up a cup of coffee and walked back to the sonar room.

The Strait of Bonifacio between the islands of Corsica and Sardinia was slightly over six miles wide at its narrowest point. Small islets guarded both sides of the eastern entrance, and dangerously shallow shoals surrounded the western exit into the Mediterranean.

There were three channels deep enough for submerged passage, two on the Italian side and one on the French. Each was a sonar trap. The bottom was seeded with fixed arrays of active and passive sonars impossible to elude. The echo ranges also served as submarine beacons to guide submerged ships through the Strait, which was frequently transited by submarines from all NATO navies, plus the French, but always with prior notice.

The Italians had extremely quiet diesel-electric subs and competent sonar operators. As part of NATO, the Italians would report *Barracuda*'s presence to the fleet, and so the element of surprise would be lost. The French were less predictable, though generally inhospitable toward incursions into their territorial waters.

Springfield decided to gamble on the French. So soon after withdrawing from NATO, the French Navy was not inclined to cooperate with their former allies in small matters. The worst they would do was deny *Barracuda* passage through the Strait and send her back the way she came.

When it arrived, contact was with *Sirène*, a diesel-electric of the Daphné class. Davic, on duty in the sonar

101

room, was not surprised to discover the French sub already on an interception course with *Barracuda*. Springfield ordered all stop, and they waited.

As soon as Sorensen arrived in the sonar room he could see the French sub moving slowly across his screen. The chop of her propellers came through the speakers.

'Get lost, Davic.'

'The French are pigs,' Davic, the linguist, muttered on his way out. 'De Gaulle thinks he's Napoleon.'

Fogarty came in and sat down.

'Practice your sonic codes,' Sorensen said. 'You're going to need them.'

Maneuvering in close proximity to another submerged ship was a tricky business. Sorensen never enjoyed it. A collision underwater could rupture the pressure hulls of both ships and send their crews to the bottom.

Threequarters of an hour after the first contact, *Sirène* came to a full stop five hundred yards away, her echo-ranging sonar pinging every three seconds off *Barracuda*'s hull with monotonous regularity. Sorensen didn't know how adept the French were at identification. They might mistake *Barracuda* for a Soviet sub, in which case there was no telling what her captain might do. While he was considering this possibility the pings ceased, were replaced by a standard NATO sonic code. The French sonar operator was tapping out an enciphered message in Morse over a gertrude, the underwater telephone. Sorensen transcribed the message onto a notepad, and the captain took it into the locked code room to decode it.

AMERICAN SUBMARINE: YOU ARE IN FRENCH WATERS. IDENTIFY YOURSELF. SIRENE S 647, DELONGUE COMMANDING.

Captain Springfield composed his reply as a plea from one submariner to another.

BARRACUDA SSN 593: SIRENE S 647: WARGAME TARGET KITTYHAWK PLEASE ESCORT THROUGH STRAIT ON PARALLEL

While the French captain decoded Springfield's message, *Sirène* did not communicate with the surface. Her captain alone was deciding what to do.

> SIRENE S 647: BARRACUDA SSN 593: FOLLOW SUB BEACON 18
> MINUTES N LONG 9 DEGREES 30 MINUTES W AT 8 KNOTS DEPTH
> 35 M RUN PARALLEL AT 100 M TO STARBOARD. DITES BON
> CHANCE A L'AMIRAL NETTS. GOOD HUNTING. DELONGUE.

'Well I'll be goddamned,' said Pisaro. 'Looks like Netts had it rigged all the time.'

Springfield said nothing, studied a chart.

Two nerve-racking hours were required to align both subs astride the beacon. *Barracuda*, on the right, was longer and broader of beam than *Sirène*, and the Italian operators of the fixed arrays would surely notice something peculiar about the passage. In order to resolve the anomaly they would go through channels, would inform their superiors, who would then query the French commander on Corsica. The French also would have both subs on their screens and yet be unsure of what was happening. By the time it was sorted out, *Barracuda* should be clear of the Strait, Captain Delongue would have explained the situation to his superiors and would receive either a pat on the back or a court-martial. The latter was a real possibility, and Springfield felt a certain distaste about requesting Delongue, a man he did not know, to take that risk.

Slowly the two subs moved into the Strait. The course marked by the beacons included three turns, the last of which curved around dangerous shoals off the Iles Lavezzi, a cluster of islets a mile off the tip of Corsica. Sorensen locked his side-to-side sweeping array to the left in order to report instantly any maneuvering by *Sirène*, and fed the data to the navigator in the control room. Fogarty monitored the bottom scanner to make sure the depth under the keel corresponded with the chart. The captain stood at the sonar repeater in the control room and kept his eyes on both screens while giving orders to the helm.

The first turn headed the ship on a southwesterly course that paralleled the Italian passage through the Strait. In the belly of the ship the inertial navigation gyros spun on their axes, sending the digital readouts of the longitude and latitude on the navigator's console spinning dizzily until the turn ended.

They were at periscope depth, but no periscope from *Barracuda* broke the surface. Springfield navigated on gyros and sonar alone.

Sirène also ran without benefit of periscope, radar or communication gear. In his log Delongue cited sea conditions and the presence of merchant ships in the Strait. No submarine captain would ever risk damage to his precious surface gear, but Delongue's real reason was that he didn't want to answer any questions until he cleared the Strait.

The second turn, to the right, brought them within half a mile of the main Italian fixed-arrays. Pings echoed back and forth between the two subs, and off the bottom and the surface, sending a weird and confusing signal back to the Italian operators on Sardinia. Sorensen imagined them listening to this strange mix, scratching themselves and trying to puzzle it out. He was sure they could hear coolant pumps and they probably were asking themselves if the French had secretly developed a nuclear attack submarine.

As the ships eased into the final turn, the depth gauge on Fogarty's bottom scanner suddenly began to rise.

'Sorensen, look at this . . . ?'

Sorensen twisted around to look at Fogarty's screen and recognized the rising pattern of bottom sand. He immediately unlocked the side-to-side sweepers from the

French sub and started looking for obstructions. If there was anything big resting on the bottom, they were going to hit it, but the screen showed nothing but the rising shoal a half mile away.

Sorensen spoke into the intercom. 'Sonar to control. Shoals bearing two nine seven, depth one two zero feet and rising. One one five feet.'

'Control to sonar,' said the captain, 'we have it on the screen. Mr Pisaro, take her up to sixty-five feet.'

'Depth sixty-five feet, aye. Rig for steep angles.'

The command rippled throughout the ship. Sailors in every compartment grabbed whatever was close and held on.

'Stern planes up twenty degrees.'

'Up twenty degrees, aye.'

'Pump forward trim tank number one to aft trim tank number two.'

The bow rose sharply and the prop drove the sleek hydrodynamic hull toward the surface. *Sirène* began to rise alongside, but not nearly so quickly. The diesel-electric sub did not have the power to drive herself rapidly up or down in a state of neutral buoyancy.

The shoals continued to rise. Springfield realized he would have to surface or reduce speed, steer to the left and fall in behind the French sub in order to avoid grounding on the shoals.

'All stop,' he said. 'I'll be damned if I'm going to surface in the Strait.'

From his diving console Pisaro said, 'That French captain is covering his ass, protecting himself from a court-martial sure as hell.'

'Sonar to control. *Sirène* is moving deeper into the channel. Range one one zero yards, one two zero yards, one three zero yards.'

'He's giving us room to maneuver,' said the XO. 'He can tell them he tried to make us surface and then he had to move to avoid a collision.'

'All right,' said the captain. 'By now, the Italians know something funny is going on, but they'll want to talk to the French before they do anything else. Let's just get the hell out of here. All ahead slow. Left full rudder.'

'All ahead slow, aye.'

'Left full rudder, aye.'

The ship banked left and quickly corrected her trim. Fogarty watched the fathometer as the shoals fell behind. *Barracuda* moved out of the Strait and into the open sea.

Sorensen spoke into his intercom. 'Sonar to control. Receiving message from *Sirène*.' He scribbled on his notepad and handed the message to the captain as he came through the door.

Five minutes later Springfield had the position and order of battle for the fleet.

9

KITTY HAWK

For three days and nights Admiral Horning, commodore of the carrier group, had directed the search for the elusive *Barracuda*. *Mako* had vanished, obviously 'sunk'. From the operations center on *Kitty Hawk* Horning had plumbed the depths with sonars and magnometers, crossed and crisscrossed the surface with frigates and destroyers, and sortied into the air hundreds of times with helicopters and antisubmarine airplanes. Five of his own submarines prowled under and around his armada, hydrophones open to every gurgle, yet *Barracuda* remained underwater and undetected.

Springfield had eluded the trap set by *Mako* and had disappeared. Admiral Horning's remaining submarines were having trouble operating in close proximity to one another, and his aircraft kept finding them instead of *Barracuda*. Alarms would scream, sonar officers would shout, 'Contact! Contact!' All for nothing.

And if that weren't enough, Horning had Netts gloating in the wardroom.

On the morning of the fourth day, after a sleepless night during which he had demanded a report every fifteen minutes from the operations center, Horning shaved, showered and dressed in fresh tans.

It had been twenty-five years since he had felt so rotten. During World War Two, as commander of a destroyer, he had escorted convoys of merchant ships across the North Atlantic through deadly wolfpacks of German U-boats. In that war an enemy submarine presented a terrible menace, but one he could deal with. Diesel-electric subs spent most of their time on the surface, wallowing in heavy seas, full of seasick sailors, submerging only to hide, attack or escape intolerable weather. Underwater, they were slow and at the mercy of short supplies of air, water and battery power.

A nuclear-propelled attack submarine was another matter entirely. A true submarine ship, rather than a submersible boat, a nuke remained underwater virtually all the time, sending a periscope above the surface only to communicate or to take a satellite fix for navigation. It made fresh water by desalinating seawater, and oxygen by electrolysis of the fresh water. As for power, sheer power, it was incomparable. The reactor core in *Barracuda* was good for one hundred thousand miles, and she could outrun any ship in the fleet.

Staring in the mirror at his fifty-six-year-old face, with its deep creases and silver brush, Admiral Horning accepted the simple, humbling truth: if this were a shooting war, *Kitty Hawk*, and probably the entire fleet, would already have been vaporized in a nuclear blast.

On entering the operations center he stood quietly to one side, observing the anxious, strained faces of his officers. In the eerie glow of electronic instruments they looked haunted. For an instant he looked directly at Captain Lewis, commander of the carrier. The haggard, unshaven man shook his head. No luck, no change, no *Barracuda*.

Netts was there, out of uniform, a bug on the wall, silently watching.

'Good morning,' Horning said to him.

'Good morning, Admiral. Sleep well?' Netts made no effort to keep sarcasm out of his voice.

'Well, where's your pet submarine, Mr Netts? I haven't seen any torpedo wakes streaking through these waters.'

'Perhaps we should contact the manufacturer. Faulty torpedoes are a terrible thing.'

Horning bit his lip. 'Perhaps we should wait until we see Commander Billing's report.'

'Fine,' said Netts, who turned his attention to the dawn breaking in pink streaks off the flight deck.

In rapid succession four antisubmarine airplanes were catapulted off the flight deck. They would drop sonar buoys into the water and listen to them via radio as they circled overhead. Only half the buoys would work. Some would sink. In others the transducers would fail and in many the radio gear would not transmit.

From another part of the flight deck a trio of ASW helicopters took off, dangling sonar arrays beneath them like weird parasites. More reliable than radio buoys, the helicopter-borne sonars could detect a local contact, but the operators could barely hear over the clamor of the rotors. If a sub were lying quietly, they would never hear it. Should it be moving rapidly and making enough noise for them to hear, they could not get an accurate fix without a second chopper. Even then it was dicey.

No other ship was visible. *Barracuda*'s mission was to simulate a nuclear attack. To avoid having a ship damaged or sunk by a blast that destroyed another, Horning had spread his perimeters to the maximum, with no ship within five miles of another. The dispersal also allowed him to search the widest possible area.

A communications officer handed Captain Lewis a message. 'It's from *Badger*,' Lewis said to Admiral Horning. 'She's tracking *Swordfish*, which is entering the perimeter between *Badger* and *Bainesworth*.'

'All right, if they can hear *Swordfish*, so can *Barracuda*. Concentrate the search in the other three quadrants. When are we scheduled to signal *Swordfish*?'

'Not for another two hours,' said the communications officer.

'Damn.' Horning looked at Netts, who shrugged and looked back.

On the bulkhead a large screen displayed the order of battle for the fleet. Each ship was an electronic silhouette. The screen was kept up-to-date by a constant flow of data from radar, sonar, satellite sensors, aircraft and even, occasionally, the word of a sailor on deck with a pair of binoculars. Netts thought it was a pretty picture and imagined that the picture on *Barracuda*'s sonar screen was much the same.

While the location of each surface ship was shown with precision, the whereabouts of each submarine could only be estimated. A technician punched buttons on the control panel, and *Swordfish* appeared on the screen between the destroyers *Badger* and *Bainesworth*.

The fleet had received messages from neither the French nor the Italians, and Horning had not guessed that *Barracuda* had run the Strait of Bonifacio and was preparing an attack from the north. Two of the fleet's subs were on station fifty miles south, hoping to intercept *Barracuda*'s approach from that direction. *Swordfish*, *Stingray* and *Dragonfish* were roving under and around the armada.

Netts knew that Springfield's plan was to position *Barracuda* in front of the fleet, lie quietly at depth and wait for the advance ships to pass directly over her. If the advance ships made contact, she would try to outrun them and attack the carrier before they got a fix.

Netts stared impatiently out to sea hoping that at any minute now a pair of torpedoes would streak out of the north, slam into the hulking *Kitty Hawk*, and Netts's Folly would be history.

10

BATTLE STATIONS, NUCLEAR

There was a stillness in the ship.

The captain had slipped under a thermal layer of warm water that deflected sonar pulses searching from above, and for twelve hours *Barracuda* had hovered a thousand feet down.

She was rigged for quiet. The noisy air-conditioning system was reduced to the minimum and the temperature had risen to eighty-three degrees. The fresh water still, which made a terrible racket, was shut down, so no one could shower. The ship was rank.

In the sonar room Willie Joe was on watch. Every few minutes he heard propellers and engine noises as one of the ships of the fleet passed over a convergence zone. Fifteen miles away *Kitty Hawk* was steaming north, directly toward *Barracuda*.

In the forward crew quarters Fogarty was reading a battered copy of *Catch-22*. In the bunks beneath him two sailors played a silent game of chess.

In the tier opposite, Sorensen cradled his tape recorder on his chest, listening to whale talk. Through the haze of cetacean whistles he heard someone softly call his name. He opened his curtain and saw Davic standing in the passageway.

'Sorensen—'

'Be quiet.'

'I want to apologize to you, please.'

'What are you talking about? Apologize for what?'

'For demanding that the Russian submarine be credited to me. I am ashamed.'

'That's all right, Davic. I don't keep score.'

Looking remorseful, Davic paced and muttered to himself in the small confined space. From somewhere in the darkness a rubber shoe flew out of a bunk and struck him in the back. A voice grumbled, 'Shut up, Davic. Let a man beat off in peace.'

Davic stopped pacing and whispered, 'Sorensen, I want to be on the first watch.'

'I have to qualify Fogarty. You know that.'

'Well, when is he going to qualify?'

Across the passageway Fogarty drew open his curtain and stared in the dim light at the back of Davic's head.

'It took you three months to qualify, Davic,' Sorensen said evenly. 'Fogarty hasn't been on the ship three weeks.'

'Hey,' a voice pleaded in the darkness, 'let us get some *sleep*.'

Angry faces appeared up and down the tiers of bunks. Davic opened his mouth to speak again, but thinking better of it, padded off in the direction of the mess.

'What's the trouble with him?' Fogarty whispered to Sorensen

'He wants your job.'

'He's a strange bird.'

'Fogarty, after you've been down here a while you'll find that everybody is strange. You never know the *real* reason a guy wants to live cooped up in a steel tube with a hundred other guys. Like you. I can't really figure out what you're doing here, no matter what you say.' Without waiting for a reply, Sorensen replaced his headphones and returned to the whales.

In the sonar room Willie Joe watched two ragged blips move slowly onto his screen, a pair of destroyers on the outer perimeter of the fleet. Five miles apart, the closest a mile from *Barracuda*, they were steaming at an oblique angle across the bow.

In the control room Captain Springfield, Pisaro,

Billings, and Hoek watched the repeater and listened through headphones to the muffled sound of the nearest destroyer, distorted by the thermal.

Then there was another, more ominous sound, much closer.

'Sorensen!'

The high, brittle voice belonged to Lt Hoek, who was standing in the hatch.

'Yes, sir.'

'You and Fogarty in the sonar room, on the double.'

'Aye aye, sir.'

Hoek lowered his voice to conspiratorial. 'We have a sub,' he said, eyes gleaming. Hoek was hot to win the war game and earn a unit citation.

'No kidding,' said Sorensen, deadpan.

'It's *Swordfish*. We're going to get right on her tail and follow her in.'

'Well, what do you know, Lieutenant. Sounds like fun.' He winked at Fogarty as they followed Hoek through the hatch and up a ladder.

Throughout the ship loudspeakers whispered, 'General Quarters. General Quarters. All hands man battle stations, nuclear.'

POTEMKIN

In the control room of *Potemkin* nine men were crowded into a space designed for six. After seventy-three days at sea, every minute of which had been spent submerged, *Potemkin*'s moment of truth was at hand.

Standing behind the sonar operator, his arm draped over the young officer's shoulders, Captain Nikolai Federov calmly gave the orders to maneuver *Potemkin* under the perimeter of ships that surrounded *Kitty Hawk*.

All eyes were on the sonar screen, where a splendid array of blips represented the US Sixth Fleet.

'Quite a sight, eh, Popov?'

'Yes, sir,' Popov whispered, his face gone white.

'Steady as he goes,' said the captain quietly.

'Steady as he goes,' repeated the helmsman.

Potemkin was an Alpha-class experimental submarine. Her sleek, orca-shaped hull was constructed of an alloy of titanium, a rare, strong, lightweight metal. The use of titanium in place of steel enabled *Potemkin* to cruise at fifty knots, a speed that had been thought impossible, and at a depth below four thousand feet. No other sub in the world could go that deep.

Potemkin was the most secret ship in the Soviet Navy. Only those in the highest echelons of command were aware of her presence in the Mediterranean. She was not officially attached to the Black Sea Fleet, whose bailiwick included the 'Med'. *Potemkin* was a fleet unto herself.

Potemkin had sailed submerged through the Norwegian Sea, the Iceland Gap and the Strait of Gibraltar without being detected. Federov had run the Strait by going deeper than the NATO sonar operators expected, positioning himself under a giant tanker and drifting through with the current and short bursts of electric power. Once in the Med, Federov concealed *Potemkin*'s identity even from other Soviet ships. The officers of the surveillance ships with whom he communicated, and who reported to him the movements of the American fleet, thought *Potemkin* was a Viktor.

During the cruise, the longest submerged patrol in Soviet history, *Potemkin* had exceeded her design specifications. Federov had tested her depth and speed, her weapons, sonars, and electronics, all with glorious results. As he approached the American fleet, at a depth of only four hundred feet, his orders were to test the ultimate effectiveness of one more system. Acoustical Reproduction Device Number Seven.

A Sony tape recorder was mounted above the sonar console. Transfixed, the men in the control room listened as the reels spun out the song of the *Swordfish*. The taped signature of the American sub was the heart of a complex apparatus designed to make American sonar operators think *Potemkin* was one of their own. An earlier test had demonstrated that the device could make the Americans believe Potemkin was a Viktor.

Seven American submarines and fourteen surface ships were involved in the exercise. In a locked vault in the captain's cabin *Potemkin* carried tapes of every American nuclear sub. Of the seven subs in the war game, Federov had elected to simulate *Swordfish* because she was the oldest and noisiest.

Federov was not fond of Acoustical Reproduction Device Number Seven. For ten weeks he had eluded detection without it. With the aid of the thermal beneath him, he believed he could station *Potemkin* directly under *Kitty Hawk* without the Americans suspecting he was there.

But orders were orders, the tape was rolling, the special

sound-absorbent silicon packing that quieted *Potemkin*'s turbine was in place, and she was running shallow and slow, just as *Swordfish* would do as part of the American defense.

Since testing the Viktor tape on *Barracuda*, *Potemkin* had encountered no American sub. Should the genuine *Swordfish* happen to be in radio contact with the surface fleet at that moment, *Potemkin* was going to attract a lot more attention than the designers of Acoustical Reproduction Device Number Seven had planned for.

On the sonar screen the nearest blip, a destroyer, turned toward *Potemkin*. A moment later everyone on board heard the ping of the American's echo ranger.

Federov looked around the control room at the tense bearded and sweating faces. He switched on the intercom. 'Engine room, how's the packing on the turbine?'

'Running hot, sir, but holding.'

'Destroyer range?'

'Five thousand meters,' said Popov. 'He's . . . he's turning back, Captain.'

On the screen the blip revolved back to its original course. A muffled cheer chorused through the control room.

'Silence!' ordered the captain.

'It's working,' gloated First Officer Kurnachov, who was officially responsible for Acoustical Reproduction Device Number Seven. Kurnachov was also the Political Officer, the representative of the Party, and he had great faith in the prowess of Soviet technology.

'Don't be so sure, Comrade First Officer. All this means is that, for the moment, the Americans are more screwed up than we are.'

Kurnachov turned back to his diving panel, making a mental note to write a memo about the captain's tasteless remark. 'The only thing I regret, Captain First Rank

Federov, is that we cannot surface and reveal the Alpha to the Americans, to throw it in their faces. Their metallurgists can't build a submarine of titanium. They would give anything to photograph our pretty ship.'

Federov, tuning him out, had the uneasy feeling that he was being sucked into a trap. In ten minutes he would be inside the American perimeter, steaming directly at *Kitty Hawk*. He wanted a drink. In his hip pocket was a silver flask filled with vodka, the cheap, flavorless table vodka the Ministry of Trade sold to the Americans under the label Stolichnaya. He was tempted to pull it out and down a stiff belt, but resisted. Later, after the test was completed, he would lock himself in his cabin with Alexis, the chief engineer, and empty the flask.

He was weary of playing war with the Americans. He either wanted to make war or make peace, put an end to the purgatory of waiting. If this were war, *Kitty Hawk* would be sunk by now, and perhaps *Potemkin* as well, but at least that would be a clean and honorable finish to this dirty business of game-playing and its gamesmanship.

Federov had spent fifteen years in subs, fifteen years in – what did the Americans call it in their journals? – inner space: the lightless, heartless, impersonal ocean that had swallowed him, his ship and his crew. Inner space – the hostile, menacing sea, relentlessly seeking every microscopic flaw in every tiny weld; ruthlessly testing every square millimeter of the pressure hull, looking for the weak spot, the casual error of every drunken shipyard worker, every lazy quality control inspector – *nyet*, his mind was wandering . . .

'Range to *Kitty Hawk*?'

'Twenty thousand meters.'

Suddenly Popov was out of his seat, his eyes fixed on the screen.

'*Captain*, there's another sub . . . he's right *under* us.'

12

SORENSEN'S RUSSIAN

'General quarters. General quarters. All hands man battle stations, nuclear.'

The announcement came over *Barracuda*'s loudspeakers in a whisper. Quietly, feet encased in rubber shoes, the crew rushed through the ship. They were about to 'nuke' the *Hawk* – their main target.

Willie Joe was positive the sub was *Swordfish*. Even though the thermal layer distorted the sounds made by the other sub, the computer had verified his judgement.

Sorensen and Fogarty relieved Willie Joe, who hurried forward in his asbetos suit to his damage-control station.

Springfield's tactic was quite simple and dated back to the Second World War. As *Swordfish* passed overhead, he would rise into the blind spot of her sonar, her 'baffles', and follow directly behind her prop. Sonars of surface ships would read the two submarines as one. When he reached optimum range he would launch a pair of fish at *Kitty Hawk*, then attempt to 'sink' *Swordfish*.

Optimum range for Mark Forty-five nuclear torpedoes was sixteen thousand yards, about nine miles. At that range the sonars could track a target and program the fire control computers, which in turn set the guidance systems aboard the weapons. Nine miles was sufficiently distant from the target to avoid *Barracuda*'s destruction by shock waves from nuclear blasts.

'Range to *Kitty Hawk*.'

'Eighteen thousand yards,' replied Hoek, reading from the screen in his attack console.

'Range to *Swordfish*.'

'Two hundred yards.'

'Fire control, set for sixteen thousand yards.'

'Fire control, set and locked for sixteen thousand yards.'

'Set for impact detonation.'

'Set and locked for impact detonation.'

'Torpedo room, load torpedoes in tubes one and four.'

In the torpedo room Lopez and his crew carefully slid Mark Forty-fives into the two uppermost torpedo tubes.

Lopez spoke into his microphone, 'Torpedo room to control. Torpedoes loaded in tubes one and four.'

'Flood tubes one and four.'

'Flood tubes, eye.'

The nose of the sub dipped slightly as the torpedo tubes were opened to the sea.

From the moment Sorensen sat down to listen to the approaching sub, he sensed that something was peculiar. He checked Willie Joe's log and punched up the signature program for *Swordfish*.

Apparently oblivious to *Barracuda*'s presence, the sub was almost on top of them. He discerned the sounds of coolant pumps, reduction gears, secondary pumps and the odd cadence of a faulty bearing on one saltwater pump that had been a chronic problem on *Swordfish* for years.

He bumped Fogarty with his elbow to get his attention. On a notepad he scribbled SWORDFISH. Fogarty nodded. Sorensen smiled his most wicked smile, drew a line through the word SWORDFISH and sketched a hammer and sickle.

Fogarty paled. 'You sure?'

Sorensen nodded. Soviet submarines frequently appeared during NATO exercises, making deep fast runs under NATO formations. This was a new twist, trying to sneak in with an acoustic cover.

'This is a real cute one,' said Sorensen, shaking his head.

Fogarty felt a deep twinge. 'What's happening?'

'Listen up,' said Sorensen. 'This is a Russian submarine.'

Fogarty listened. It sounded like *Swordfish* to him. Sorensen played the *Swordfish* signature program, and then Fogarty heard the difference too.

With every revolution of the Russian prop, *Kitty Hawk* and the war game faded into insignificance.

'Oh, boy.' Sorensen spoke into the intercom. 'Lieutenant Hoek.'

'Yes, sonar.'

'Can you step in here a moment, sir?'

Hoek entered the sonar room.

'Sir,' said Sorensen, his face innocent of any expression.

'Yes, Sorensen.'

'I know the *Swordfish*, sir. I know every sound she makes. She's a noisy boat, if you don't mind my saying so, Lieutenant, but not as noisy as she was before her last refit. They fixed the bearings in her saltwater pumps. What we are listening to here is the way *Swordfish* used to sound, not the way she sounds now.'

'What are you trying to say, Sorensen. What does all that mean?'

'I don't know, sir, except I think the submarine we are listening to is not *Swordfish*.'

Hoek chewed his lip. 'Well, who is it, then?'

Sorensen lifted his eyebrows. 'The Israelis?'

'Don't be smart, Sorensen. The Israelis don't have nuke boats.'

'Are you sure, Lieutenant? They have everything else.'

Fogarty fought to keep a straight face.

'Maybe it's the French, sir?' Sorensen suggested.

'Why would the French want to make us think they were one of our subs?'

'I haven't the foggiest, sir, but somebody is trying to pull a fast one. Someone wants us to think that is one of our subs out there, but it isn't. It's a dirty trick.'

Hoek's eyes lit up as the dawn broke. In the core of his finely honed, Annapolis-trained mind he at last came to the correct conclusion. 'It's the goddamned Russians.'

'You really think so, sir?'

Hoek could hardly contain himself. He rushed back to the control room to inform the captain of his discovery. Seconds later the captain made a rare appearance in the sonar room. 'What do you think, Sorensen?'

'It's gotta be a Russkie, sir, probably that same Viktor we ran into on the way out here. It sure as hell isn't the old *Swordfish*. They fixed that pump for sure. I spotted it right off the bat and we checked it against the tape. That boat has some kind of gadget rigged to make it sound like *Swordfish*. She fooled those destroyers.'

'Play the tape.'

Springfield listened. The distinction was obvious.

'All right, carry on. Good work, Sorensen.'

As the Russian sub passed directly overhead, the sound was an exact imitation of *Swordfish* before her pumps were repaired. Everyone aboard *Barracuda* heard the Doppler effect.

'Attention, all hands. This is the captain. Prepare for steep angles. Take us up, Leo. We have to assume she knows we're here, and that she's testing her cover on us. For the moment we will let her think it works. Put us in her blind spot. In any case, she may hear us blow our tanks.'

Pisaro pushed a sequence of buttons on his diving panel. Compressed air expelled the seawater from two trim tanks, and *Barracuda* rose six hundred feet directly behind *Potemkin*. She matched the Russian's speed and began to follow a scant two hundred yards behind.

In the sonar room Fogarty tracked the carrier while Sorensen monitored the sub, which suddenly began to turn.

'Sonar to control,' Sorensen said. 'Contact is turning

left twelve degrees.'

'Helm, left twelve degrees. Keep right on her.'

The helmsman pushed his joystick over to the left and *Barracuda* banked like an airplane.

As far as Springfield was concerned the war game was suspended. They would stay on the tail of the Russian sub until they either obtained a positive identification or lost it.

Billings, the war game observer aboard *Barracuda*, was not convinced of anything. In his opinion a Russian sub that intruded on the war game would run under the fleet at high speed, then disappear. It wouldn't linger. The repair on the faulty pump on *Swordfish* was probably shoddy, and the pump had reverted to its noisy state. The sub was indeed *Swordfish*. The war game was not over, it was reaching its climax. Seething, feeling the full weight of his vested interest in a successful conclusion of the exercise, he interrupted, 'Captain, we're only seventeen thousand yards from *Kitty Hawk*. You can fire your torpedoes now and then chase the sub.'

'Commander Billings, I'm following that sub now.'

'What if she's not a Russian? What if your man is wrong?'

'If Sorensen is wrong, I'll keelhaul him. Will that make you happy, Mr Billings? I'll serve him to Netts for breakfast.'

'You can still fire your torpedoes.'

'I don't think I want to do that this close to a Soviet submarine. She might get the wrong idea. She will also get a dandy tape recording of our system. I'm sorry, Commander, but you know my standing orders as well as I do. Your boss, Admiral Netts, wrote them.'

'Speed of target increasing to twenty-one knots.'

'Make our speed twenty-one knots, Mr Pisaro. Stay with her. Torpedo room, unload torpedoes.'

'Torpedo room, say again.'

'Unload torpedoes, Chief. Get those fish out of the tubes.'

'Aye aye, sir. Understand unload tubes one and four.'

'Mr Billings, you had better find something to hold on to. We're not playing games any more. Engineering, prepare for high power. Give me seventy percent.'

'Engineering, understand seventy percent steam.'

'Keep right after her, Mr Pisaro, keep right on her butt.'

13

DISASTER

'Sit down, Popov, and get hold of yourself.'

Federov's voice was harsh. Every man aboard *Potemkin* was an officer, but some, he decided, didn't know how to act the part.

'Identify him, if you please, Mr Popov.'

'It's a Skipjack class, Captain. It must be *Barracuda*.'

With seven American subs taking part in the war game, Federov had expected an encounter before this. When the American rose up and began to follow, he deduced that he had come upon the sub that was playing the role of attacker. One of the defenders would either try to contact him or simulate a torpedo attack. It was quite a situation – he was pretending to be an American and he was being followed by an American pretending to be a Soviet, but there was no one in the control room with whom he could share the irony of it.

He had to determine if the American commander was going to continue his attack on the carrier or follow *Potemkin*. He ordered the helmsman to turn left twelve degrees and the engine room to increase speed to twenty-one knots. The American followed him through the turn and increased his speed to match.

'First officer Kurnachov, I think we have successfully completed our test of Acoustical Reproduction Device Number Seven. I am not certain the American submarine following us has been fooled by our tricks. We have proved we can penetrate their defenses with the device. Now I think we shall use all our resources to withdraw.'

'I disagree, Comrade Captain,' Kurnachov said. 'I believe we have fooled the American submarine. He follows because he believes we are *Swordfish*. In any case your course is taking him toward the carrier that is his target.'

'Then we shall have to take him somewhere else, Comrade First Officer Captain Second Rank Kurnachov.' Federov loved to give him his full ridiculous due. 'Right full rudder. Increase speed to thirty knots. Bearing one seven seven. Depth three hundred meters. Ten degrees down.'

Kurnachov was shocked. 'Captain, Acoustical Reproduction Device Number Seven has never been tested at over twenty-four knots.'

'Then consider this a test.'

Potemkin abruptly tilted downward and accelerated into the depths. In the engine room the chief engineer watched awestruck as the silicon packing on the turbine slowly turned into a pool of glassy liquid. The quiet hum of the whirring blades transformed into a deep roar.

'Captain,' the engineer said into his microphone, 'we have to stop the turbine. The packing melted!'

One hundred fifty feet away the noise burst into the quiet of the control room.

The captain glared across the control room at the first officer. 'All stop. Quiet in the boat.'

The noise ceased. *Potemkin* continued to plunge on momentum silently downward at a steep angle, banking steeply on her diving planes. Throughout the ship, black-uniformed sailors struggled for equilibrium. Air conditioners were switched to low power and all nonessential systems shut down. In the engine room the turbine came to a halt; reactor operation was reduced to a minimum. Gradually, the ship leveled off.

Kurnachov jumped up from his seat and went across the control room toward the engine room.

'First Officer Kurnachov, return to your diving panel. Where do you think you are? Right full rudder. Zero angle

125

on the diving planes.'

With her prop no longer turning, *Potemkin*'s momentum still carried her more than two kilometers. The ship glided to the right on her diving planes and slowly came to a stop.

'Engine room, damage report.'

'The packing melted, Captain, but the turbine is all right.'

'Popov, do you hear the American sub?'

'No, sir. I hear the aircraft carrier. Range eight thousand two hundred meters and closing.'

Federov turned on Kurnachov. 'Remove every American tape from Acoustical Reproduction Device Number Seven and put in the Viktor tape, Mr Kurnachov, and do it now. That's an order. And if you ever move from your station again, I'll have you before a court-martial and you'll spend the rest of your life in an old sailors' home. *If* you're lucky.'

The captain hurried back to the engine room to ascertain for himself the status of the turbine. Unlike American submarines in which every component of the drive train was duplicated, *Potemkin* had only one turbine. What she sacrificed in safety, she gained in speed by reducing weight.

'Comrade Chief Engineer, how bad is it?'

Federov and the engineer had sailed together for many years. For one to address the other with the formal party salutation was a secret code between them that meant yes, once again, they miraculously had survived an attempt by the masters of Moscow to sink them.

'Comrade Captain First Rank, Acoustical Reproduction Device Number Seven is now a useless piece of shit, but *Potemkin* is still an Alpha.'

'You mean, Chief Engineer, we should get up a full head of steam and show the Americans a thing or two, such as how fast our marvelous *Potemkin* can go?'

'Nikolai Petrovich, you read my mind. I am astounded at your insight.'

'Alexis, my old shipmate, we may try to do just that.'

In the control room the first officer sullenly removed the *Swordfish* tape from the Sony. When Federov returned, he ordered the first officer to accompany him to his cabin.

Federov locked the door. Kurnachov smiled, malevolence in his heart. 'Comrade Captain First Rank, I believe you deliberately increased the speed of this ship to sabotage Acoustical Reproduction Device Number Seven.'

'You can believe whatever you want to believe, or whatever the Party wants for that matter. That's your privilege.'

'Your orders were to test the device.'

'My *orders* were to test this ship. The device be damned. I am growing impatient with you, Kurnachov. You seem to forget that we are at sea. My responsibility is to carry out my mission and return my ship and crew safely home. This is a new class of ship, and all these wonderful technological devices are equally new. One of them has been put to the test, and it has failed. So be it. My duty is very clear. The Americans know nothing about the Alpha. At worst they think we are a Viktor. They have never experienced a submarine with a titanium hull. We must disappear before they collect too much information.'

'This does not alter the fact that we have been detected.'

'The Americans have detected something but they don't know what. Have you forgotten that our orders were to allow ourselves to be detected? That was the whole point of the damned device. Be detected and deceive. Well, we didn't fool them. But they still don't know what we are. If you want to accuse me of sabotage, do it now. If you do, you shall have to relieve me and take command of *Potemkin*. You have the entire American Sixth Fleet above you and an American submarine on your tail. You have a jittery crew that has been at sea far too long, and half of them know more about the Party line than about operating this ship. First Officer Kurnachov, this would be an excellent moment to demonstrate your seamanship.'

The captain unlocked the door and returned to the control room. Kurnachov began formulating his report on the captain's remarks about the Party and Soviet technology. Then he reconsidered. He would act.

On the sonar screen the American fleet could be seen coverging on their position. Popov could hear the screws of *Kitty Hawk* only three miles away. The short burst of speed by both subs had produced a great deal of noise.

The captain plugged in a headphone and listened.

'Where is the American submarine?' he asked Popov.

The terrified operator just shook his head. *Barracuda* was not on the screen.

Sorensen was astounded at the Russian sub's rate of acceleration. *Barracuda* was the fastest submarine in the US Navy, but the Russian ship took off like a corvette.

'Contact increasing speed and descending,' he said over the intercom. 'Range increasing to four zero zero yards, four five zero yards.'

The Russian plunged into the depths. 'We got us a real Cossack sub driver,' Sorensen muttered, then spoke into his mike. 'Captain, she's running much faster than anything we've ever seen before. Speed, estimated thirty-five knots.'

'Stay on him, sonar. We're going right down with him.'

Springfield ordered a steep dive and increased speed *Barracuda* angled over and rocketed down.

Thirty seconds into the dive the Russian sub erupted with a sudden burst of noise that caused Sorensen to jump out of his seat. It was, at last, the sub of his dreams – the mystery sub.

Then, abruptly, there was no noise at all. The Russian's prop stopped turning and all machinery noises ceased. Soviet subs were notoriously unreliable. With no duplication of vital machinery, a breakdown of any component of the drive train frequently incapacitated the ship. If that were the case, the Russian captain would have to surface, a development most embarrassing for him.

Sorensen sat back down, ignoring Fogarty's questioning look, and took a deep breath.

Springfield ordered, 'All stop.' Drifting on momentum, *Barracuda* descended through a thermal layer and unwittingly passed under *Potemkin*. At thirteen hundred feet, very close to her test depth, she came to a halt.

The Russian was not on the screens. She was in a blind spot, above *Barracuda*, obscured by the thermal. Fear of collision swept through the control room.

Since Springfield did not know the Russian's location, he intended to let her know where *Barracuda* was.

'All ahead, dead slow,' Springfield ordered.

'All ahead, dead slow, aye.'

'Control to sonar. Echo-range.'

The broad beam swept all around, but there was no contact.

Sorensen hammered on his console. 'C'mon, you son of a bitch, make some noise.'

Springfield sent for Davic, the only one aboard who could speak Russian. He was going to try to talk to the Soviet ship on the gertrude.

'Captain First Rank Nikolai Petrovitch Federov, by the authority invested in me, I relieve you of command of

Potemkin. Return to your cabin at once.

Face flushed, sweating, black eyes too bright in the control room, Kurnachov held a pistol. Still standing over the sonar console, Federov's first impulse was to laugh. The laughter died in his larynx when Kurnachov cocked the hammer.

'Put the gun away, Kurnachov, before you blow a hole in the ship and kill us all.'

'Return to your cabin, *at once*.'

Popov started to stand up. 'Captain, *no*.'

Federov pushed him back into his seat. Everyone else in the control room remained at his station. With dignity Federov assumed his military bearing and left the control room without another word.

Still brandishing the pistol, Kurnachov paced around the control room, unsure what to do. After a minute of waffling, he called out, 'Stern planes, down twenty degrees. Reverse engines. Slow revolutions.'

No one moved. Alexis, the chief engineer, appeared in the control room hatch. 'What the hell is going on here?'

Kurnachov moved across the compartment and put the barrel of the pistol in his face. 'Chief Engineer, get back to the engineering room.'

The engineer stood his ground. 'Where is the captain?'

'I am now the captain. Do as you've been ordered.'

'Good God. An *apparatchik* in command of *Potemkin*.'

Shaking his head, the engineer left the control room. Still, nobody moved.

'Planesman, stern planes down twenty degrees or I will charge you with mutiny. I'll also shoot you, you son of a bitch.'

The planesman turned his wheel.

'Reverse engines. Slow revolution.'

The hull shuddered once as the turbine started to revolve. The ship began to angle down at the stern and descend backward into the unknown. Kurnachov's heart was beating so fast he thought he might have a seizure. He felt giddy with power. He was in command for the first time in his life. He had, he believed, saved *Potemkin*.

On *Barracuda* Davic stood in the control room, holding his asbestos helmet under his arm as he listened to the captain's instructions.

'Tell him to surface. Tell him we will make no attempt to interfere with him or to board his ship.'

'Aye aye, sir.'

Davic switched on the gertrude. '*Pogdorny Sovetski . . .*' he began.

Before he could continue, Sorensen's voice interrupted over the intercom. 'Sonar to control, sonar to control. I hear him. Captain, he's right on top of us. He's backing down out of the thermal. *Left full rudder.*'

The helmsman was cranking his joystick before Springfield could give the order. Barely making way, *Barracuda* slowly turned to the left.

For one terrible moment everyone froze as *Potemkin*'s portside stern plane brushed *Barracuda*'s bow. The impact reverberated through *Barracuda*'s hull like a giant gong.

Collision alarms began screaming, circuits popped, sirens went off. Every soul aboard expected the sea to pour into the ship.

In the torpedo room the solid steel bulkhead bulged into the compartment and snapped back into place with a thundering bang. The young torpedomen were terrified. One dropped to his knees and began to pray, holding a crucifix.

'Get on your feet, Baker,' Chief Lopez ordered. 'Seal the hatch.' He yanked the young sailor to his feet and pushed him toward the rear of the compartment. Johnson, the mate, already was spinning the wheel. If the torpedo room flooded, the ship theoretically would remain buoyant if water could be kept out of the other compartments.

Lopez braced himself for a sudden pitch forward, praying to the Virgin of his childhood for the pressure hull to hold. Making a grinding noise, the keel of the Russian sub slid down the starboard side of the hull, rolling *Barracuda* over to the right and sending men sprawling. There was a lurch, another metallic crunch . . . and the ships separated. Baker lay screaming on the deck, his leg fractured.

Barracuda swung back to the left and righted herself. On top of the fire-control panel Zapata's glass cage slid to the steel floor and shattered. Miraculously uninjured, the scorpion skittered away and hid in the shadows of the torpedo racks.

Lopez rushed to the fire-control panel and saw that one of the outer-tube-door indicators had changed from green to red. Tube number four was ruptured, having been the exact point of impact by the tip of the Russian sub's stern plane. Lopez was certain the inner door would burst open.

'Torpedo room to control. Tube number four open to sea.'

In the control room an indicator light on Pisaro's diving panel changed from green to red. He blanched.

'Torpedo tube number four open to sea,' he said, making the greatest effort to sound calm.

'Blow all ballast tanks, surface,' ordered the captain.

As water was expelled from the ballast tanks, the sub slowly began to rise.

'Fire yellow distress rocket.'

'Rocket away.'

'Control to torpedo room, damage report.'

'Torpedo room to control. Tube number four open to sea. Inner door is holding. We've got a small electrical fire here.'

'Casualty report.'

'We got a man with a busted leg.'

132

'Attention all hands. Damage control team to torpedo room, on the double. Corpsman to torpedo room.'

'Sonar, where's the Russian?'

Sorensen switched on the active sonar, afraid of what he might hear. Instantly an erratically pulsating sphere of sound expanded around *Barracuda*.

He stared at his screen. It took him a moment to realize that the sonars on the starboard side of the hull were damaged. He played with his console to compensate.

'Fogarty, switch to bottom scanners. Sonar to control. I hear no reactor noises. He's lost power.'

Fogarty activated the down-searching bottom scanners and made contact. 'Oh no,' he said, and closed his eyes.

Sorensen looked at Fogarty's screen and slowly removed his headphones. He switched on the overhead speakers. Shaking his head he said, very quietly, 'Sonar to control, he's sinking. He's already down to two thousand feet. He's going down without power. He can't blow his tanks.'

Sorensen began to fidget. The sub was going to sink until the pressure of the sea became too great. Then she would implode. What they had feared would happen to them a moment before was about to happen to the Russians. The Soviet sub was too heavy. Somehow the collision had left her without power, and she had no pumps and negative buoyancy. In a few seconds her hull would rupture, the sea would come crashing in and instantly raise the atmospheric pressure in the boat to the point of incandescence. In a blinding flash the Russians would fry before they were crushed. None would live long enough to drown.

Springfield entered the sonar room and stopped in midstep. Sorensen was pale. Fogarty looked like he was watching an execution.

Sorensen said, 'Three thousand feet.'

The captain stared at the screen in disbelief. 'Three

thousand feet.' The sub already was far deeper than any other submarine had ever dived.

Springfield didn't need this, the Navy didn't need this, the Russians certainly didn't need this. There would be a Court of Inquiry. The Russians would make their own investigation and it was going to be one hell of a mess.

'Thirty-one hundred feet,' said Sorensen. He imagined the scene aboard the Russian sub . . . the men in there knowing they had only moments to live, some praying, others weeping or gone mad with panic and fear. But most, he was sure, were trying their best to make their machinery do the impossible. They were trying to get power to the pumps to blow her tanks and make her rise—

'Good God,' said Sorensen, '*they fired a torpedo*.'

He stood up and backed away from the console. On the screen the slowly sinking blip divided in two. They heard the whine of an electric motor. A guide wire between the blips was clearly visible. Someone aboard the doomed sub was attempting to steer the torpedo.

With her tanks blown *Barracuda* was rising swiftly. They were going to die on the surface.

Springfield shouted, 'Evasive maneuvers. All ahead full. Right full rudder.' But before the helm could respond, the torpedo went awry and plunged straight down to four thousand feet.

While all eyes were on the torpedo, the Russian sub imploded – painfully loud cracks separated by a fraction of a second as each of the ship's compartments ruptured in close sequence. At tremendous velocity the sea poured through the fractured pressure hull, pushing the air inside into a smaller and smaller bubble until the air itself exploded, blowing out the bulkheads between the individually pressurized compartments. The explosions and fires lasted only the briefest instant until the full weight of the sea smashed the hull and everything in it into tiny, scarcely recognizable fragments.

Debris filled *Barracuda*'s sonar screens. A cloud of tiny blips drifted to the bottom and scattered over a vast area.

'My God, my God . . .' Springfield said over and over. 'Did you get it all on tape, Sorensen?'

'Yes, sir . . .'

'Seal that tape and bring it to my cabin.'

'Aye aye, sir.'

'You people in here are not to say a word about this to anyone. Understand?'

'Aye aye, sir.'

Springfield returned to the control room. 'Take her up to the surface, Leo. We'll have to send off a message to ComSubLant. You have the conn. I'm going to inspect the torpedo room.'

14

STALEMATE

In the operations center on *Kitty Hawk* the sonar contact alarm had sounded with a waspish buzz. On the screen the blip representing *Swordfish* had divided like an amoeba and had resolved into two separate contacts, both of which were heading directly toward *Kitty Hawk*. A moment later the echo-ranging sonars of the surface ships had begun to interfere with one another, and the blips had dissolved into electronic chaff.

Admiral Horning had realized that he was caught in a terrible dilemma. Neither sub had been positively identified as *Barracuda*, although he was certain that one was his nemesis.

With a sudden roar of propulsion machinery, both subs had descended below the thermal layer, and the sonar data became increasingly erratic until the sounds had stopped altogether. Helicopters had dropped sonar buoys around the carrier, but the noises generated by the huge ship garbled everything. This was the penultimate moment. *Barracuda* had to slow to fire her torpedoes, and a thousand pairs of eyes had scanned the horizon, expecting the deadly white streaks at any moment.

Netts felt vindicated. One submarine had neutralized the entire fleet. *Kitty Hawk* wallowed helplessly before the onslaught of *Barracuda*. He was reminded of the final chapters of *Moby Dick*. Horning had found his whale, and the sea beast was about to eat him alive—

Without warning the loudspeakers had roared out the sound of a collision, metal grinding on metal, the shrieking horror that said death in the sea. After fifteen interminable seconds the screeching had stopped and was followed by a long silence. Finally, the sound of a submarine blowing its ballast tanks had meant one of the subs was attempting to rise. After another long pause . . . a series of violent eruptions and then the groans and crunches of a ship breaking up.

Everyone on the bridge of *Kitty Hawk* saw the distress rocket break the surface a mile away, streak into the sky and explode into a yellow cloud.

A moment later, in the midst of a boiling white sea, *Barracuda* bobbed to the surface. A hatch in the sail opened, and two men in scuba gear scrambled out, climbed down to the diving plane and jumped into the sea. Netts held his breath, waiting for the hatches in the hull to open. If the sub were about to sink, the crew would scramble out. Instead the hatches stayed closed and a blinking light on the bridge began flashing a message.

COLLISION WITH SUBMARINE. IDENTITY UNKNOWN. CREWMAN WITH BROKEN LEG. SEND MEDICAL ASSISTANCE. SPRINGFIELD.

Captain Lewis, commander of *Kitty Hawk*, immediately dispatched a helicopter to lower a surgeon to the sub. Springfield continued to signal with lights rather than radio so as to keep his transmission out of the hands of the Soviet trawlers trailing the fleet. If *Barracuda* were in imminent danger of sinking, he would not hesitate to say so. Nevertheless, Captain Lewis ordered rescue teams to stand by, ready to take off the crew in a hurry.

Admiral Horning was furious. The destroyers had let Springfield slip through the perimeter. No ship had fired at *Barracuda*, and she had not launched her weapons, so the war game was technically a stalemate, but Horning knew he had lost. All hell had broken loose down below, then *Barracuda* had reared up out of the sea like a nuclear sea monster only two thousand yards from his flag. He glared at the sub with deep loathing.

As dozens of reports came in from the fleet, the communications officers were trying desperately to make sense out of the confusion. One message was a routine communication from *Swordfish*. She was seventy-four miles from where the destroyers had reported her earlier. Several ships reported the sounds of bulkheads bursting as a ship sank.

Two subs were unaccounted for. *Dragonfish* and *Stingray* were scheduled to make routine position reports within the hour. With growing horror, Horning realized that if the sub that sank was not *Swordfish*, it had to be one of them. Who would take the blame? This was shaping up as a real disaster for the navy, the kind of foul-up that destroyed careers and raised hell with congressional committees. It was Netts's Folly. Now let his head roll.

Staring at the screen, Netts was trying to digest the fact that he had lost a submarine. Having arrived at the same conclusion as Horning, that the sunken sub was either *Dragonfish* or *Stingray*, he was thinking of neither the war game nor his career. His thoughts were with the men who had just died. *Dragonfish* carried 116 men, *Stingray* 112.

A communications officer announced, 'Receiving message from *Dragonfish*.'

Both admirals acknowledged the report of *Dragonfish* with stone faces. That left *Stingray*, Oakland commanding . . . Brian Oakland smashed to bits at the bottom of the sea, three daughters left in Charleston and a mistress in Holy Loch. Fred Basana, the XO, was a fourth generation naval officer, father killed at Midway. Fried to a crisp. George Milliard, Chief of the Boat, crushed, mangled, destroyed—

'Receiving message from *Stingray*.'

Netts was stunned. 'What the hell is going on here?'

he said to Horning.

'I think your Captain Springfield is going to have some explaining to do.'

Fifteen minutes after *Barracuda* surfaced, Baker, the injured torpedoman, was in the carrier's sick bay. The divers made their report on the damage to the outer hull, and Springfield was satisfied with his inspection of the torpedo room. He signaled to the carrier that his ship was seaworthy, the damage minor and that he and Commander Billings wished to board *Kitty Hawk*.

Before he left the sub Springfield spoke to the crew.

'Attention all hands, this is the captain. We are going to remain on the surface for approximately two hours. All hands who wish to go up to the bridge for a few minutes will have the opportunity to do so.

'We have not suffered major damage. The pressure hull is not ruptured. I want to take this opportunity to congratulate each of you for an outstanding performance during this action. I am going to recommend the ship's company for a unit citation, and there will be individual citations as well. In particular I want to mention Chief Lopez and the entire torpedo gang who put their lives at risk to save ours, and Sonarman Sorensen, whose quick reaction saved the ship from certain destruction. There will be special rations in the mess. That is all.'

The sonar room was a shambles. Technical manuals were scattered over the deck. The cabinet had fallen over and spilled thousands of tiny electronic parts. The ashtrays overflowed with butts. A cup of coffee was splashed over Fogarty's console.

Sorensen felt himself coming unstuck. He collapsed, gasping for breath. The tension streamed out of his eyes. The sound of the Soviet submarine – the mystery sub – plunging straight toward him reverberated in his ears, a sound he would never forget. It had seemed as though the suction of the Russian propeller was pulling him in. 'Left full rudder.' He remembered shouting that. The ship had taken forever to respond.

And then the hit.

Gradually he brought himself under control. He looked at Fogarty, who was pale and drenched in sweat. His jumpsuit was ripped down one leg.

'Holy shit, Fogarty. You look like you've just been in a train wreck.'

Fogarty's hands were trembling as he lit a cigarette. 'What did he do? Ram us on purpose?'

'I don't think so. Sub drivers generally aren't suicidal. This was just bad seamanship.'

'How many . . .' Fogarty stammered, 'how many men do you think were on that ship?'

'Hard to say. Eighty, ninety, maybe.'

'Christ.'

'It was quick, real quick. When it imploded, it was all over.'

'But the waiting. Sinking, knowing they were going to die . . .'

Sorensen understood what Fogarty was feeling. Inside himself he felt the same thing, but he shut it down. Not allowed. He said, 'As far as I'm concerned, the fool backed into a blind spot and sank himself and his crew. That was one stupid Russian sub jockey. Goddamn Ivan the Idiot . . .'

'It could've been us.'

'But it wasn't. Maybe next time.'

'Do you think the Russians know?'

'I don't know, I don't think so. Not yet. But the fleet is up there, and right now all their radio people are jabbering like crazy at one another. The Russians are picking it up, and they know something happened. That sub has to make routine reports, and after it misses a few

140

they'll start to wonder why. Sooner or later they'll find out.'

'Then what?'

'Then maybe we have sub wars. Who knows?'

Hoek came in, took one look at the mess and left without a word. Sorensen began to run checks on all the equipment. Several of the hydrophones arrayed along the starboard side of the hull were not functioning, and he had to log a damage report. Fogarty got down on hands and knees and began sorting through the spilled diodes and transistors.

The ship rolled on the surface but nobody minded. Being a little seasick was better than being dead.

Ten minutes later Davic and Willie Joe came in to relieve Sorensen and Fogarty. Davic's dream had come true. *Barracuda* had sunk a Russian sub.

'My God, Sorensen, what happened?'

'If you were thinking about reading the log, Davic, forget it. It's sealed. Captain's orders. It's coded red into the computer. Even I can't get it out.'

'I don't need to know the details. Just tell me, it is true? It was the Viktor? Did it sink?'

'You know how it is. The silent service.'

Davic could see in Sorensen's eyes that it was true, and that was good enough. On the profile sheet of Soviet subs he scrawled an X over the drawing of the Viktor. He beamed at Fogarty, who looked away in disgust.

Willie Joe shook Sorensen's hand. 'Congratulations.'

'For what?'

'Didn't you listen to the skipper? They're going to give you a medal. You're a hero.'

'Well, ain't that just dandy. You hear that, Fogarty? I'm a hero.'

'Yeah,' Fogarty said, 'the first hero of World War Three.'

'Go on,' said Willie Joe. 'You're outta here.'

Sorensen had heard the ultimate sound effect. The collision and the implosion of the Russian sub were engraved in his brain, a far more accurate recording device than anything made by Sony. Just to make sure, however, he had recorded the entire sequence of events on his own machine, even though he knew possession of that tape was a felony.

In the seclusion of Sorensen's Beach he played the tape over and over, backward and forward, fast and slow. Several questions about the sinking began to nag at him. Why did the Russians fire a torpedo? Were they trying to sink *Barracuda* or *Kitty Hawk*? The sub imploded below three thousand feet, an incredible depth. The *Thresher* had imploded at a depth of just over two thousand feet. How could the Russians go so deep? Was the collision an accident, or did the Russians ram them intentionally? No sane captain would do that, but no sane captain would fire a torpedo either.

It was a puzzle that was missing an undetermined number of pieces. The torpedo bothered him the most. Had the Russian torpedomen actually fired a shot without orders? Could they do that? Why would they? The torpedo had been wire-guided; he had seen the wire on his screen. When the sub imploded, the wire was severed and the torpedo's motor apparently had stopped. It did not explode. During the massive acoustical barrage of the implosions it had disappeared. Presumably it sank. What kind of warhead did it carry? Just the notion that it might have been a nuke was terrible to contemplate.

He tried to imagine the wreck of the Russian sub. Eight thousand feet down, he knew, there was no light, no perceptible movement in the water, nothing but pressure beyond imagination. In the cold black desert of the ocean bottom pieces of the shattered sub had by now settled over a debris field many miles square. The reactor and heat exchangers, weapons, electronics, enciphering machines and ninety men, smashed to bits, reduced to junk. It chilled his heart.

Davic and Willie Joe had to clean up the sonar room. As members of the damage-control team they had been too busy immediately after the collision to be scared. In asbestos suits, breathing bottled air, they had charged into the torpedo room, fire extinguishers at the ready. Now that it was over and they had a moment to reflect on what had happened, and what almost had happened, they began to react.

Davic, who rarely spoke to Willie Joe, began to babble about his future in the CIA. Willie Joe wasn't paying attention. As he sorted through a pile of diodes, those bits of plastic with tiny wires sticking out of them, he developed a case of the jitters. His hands shook. Ignoring Davic, he said, 'My wife, she sure loves that Navy Exchange they got there in Norfolk . . . She's been looking at this color TV they got there and I figure if I make first class at the end of this cruise, well, hells bells, I'll watch the World Series in color, oh shit . . .'

He had dropped a handful of tiny electronic parts onto the cork floor. They bounced. The collision alarm was still screaming in his head. 'Maybe I should just retire. I'm just glad it didn't happen on my watch.' He got down on his hands and knees and began picking up the parts.

'Nothing ever happens on my watch,' Davic said. He pounded his fist into his palm. 'I can't stand this not knowing what happened. Do you think Fogarty will tell us?'

'No.'

'We can ask.'

'I'm not that curious, Davic. Why don't you come down here and help me pick up these things?'

Davic sat down on the deck and picked up a transistor.

'It's not fair that Fogarty knows and I don't. It's just not fair.'

Fogarty lay in his bunk staring into space, listening to the elevator music that filtered into the forward crew quarters. His tattered copy of *Catch-22* lay across his chest.

'Yo, Fogarty.'

He opened the curtain. Davic and Willie Joe stood in the passageway next to his bunk.

'Yes?'

Davic said, 'Tell us what happened down there. Please.'

'I can't do that, Davic. Tell him, Willie Joe.'

'I did.'

Davic grabbed Fogarty's arm. 'We sank those bastards, didn't we. Sent them cocksuckers to visit to David Jones.'

Fogarty had to smile at Davic's convoluted English, and Davic read the smile as confirmation.

'We are the first ship in the US Navy to put in the bag a Russian. That'll teach them bastards to fuck with us.'

'Davic, whatever happened, it was an accident.' He brushed Davic's hands away from his arm.

'Whatever they got, they asked for it,' Davic said.

'That's crazy.'

A dozen sailors leaned out of their bunks. Frustrated and angry, Davic was on his toes, thrusting his face into Fogarty's bunk.

'What's the matter with you, Fogarty? Do you feel *sorry* for the Russians?'

Fogarty refused to be provoked. 'Sure. They were men and this was an accident. We're not at war with them—'

'Well, shit, Fogarty, what are we here for? Why don't we just get rid of the fuckers once and for all? Just nuke them all at once.'

'Just like that?' Fogarty snapped his fingers.

'Just like *that*. If we don't do it to them they'll do it to us.'

Fogarty propped himself up on one elbow and faced Davic directly. 'When the Russians learn they've lost a sub they aren't going to like it. They're going to blame us, even if it wasn't our fault—'

'So what? What can they do to us?'

'Didn't Admiral Netts just use *Barracuda* to prove what they can do to us? Where've you been the last four days? Get out of here, Davic. You're a vampire. Go fly around in the dark with the other bats.'

Davic flushed. Fists clenched, his urge to punch Fogarty struggled with his training and discipline. He knew a fight could land him in the brig.

'Fogarty, you have no guts. You don't belong on this ship—'

'Fuck off.'

Davic lunged. Off-balance, Fogarty barely had time to twist around and catch Davic's leading hand in mid-air and snap back the wrist. Davic screamed and sank to the floor. Fogarty let go.

'Touch me again and I'll break your arm.'

Fogarty's tone left no doubt that he could do it. He looked down the passageway. The entire compartment was staring at him.

Davic climbed to his feet, rubbing his wrist, not quite sure what had happened except that his wrist was beginning to swell and that it hurt like hell.

The sailors in the compartment were leaning out of their bunks, heads going from Davic to Fogarty and back again.

'Did you see that?'

'No, man, it was too fast.'

'Right on, Fogarty.'

'Try it again, Davic.'

At which point Sorensen stepped through the hatch

and froze. From his angle he couldn't see Fogarty, but he could see Davic.

Willie Joe spoke up. 'Hey, Sorensen. We got us a karate expert here.'

'And who might that be?'

'Me,' Fogarty said.

Sorensen looked from Fogarty to Davic. Fogarty turned his head.

'A fight?' Sorensen asked.

Willie Joe replied quickly, 'No, nothing like that. A little demonstration.'

'Karate?' Sorensen said to Fogarty. 'You?'

Fogarty nodded. 'It's not karate. It's *tae kwan do*. It's Korean.'

The sailors stared at Fogarty with new respect. 'I don't smash bricks, if that's what you're wondering,' he said to Sorensen.

Sorensen looked at Davic's swollen wrist. 'You'd better go see Dr Luther, tough guy. Looks to me like you slipped and fell into a bulkhead during the collision.'

With a drop-dead look at Fogarty, Davic went out.

'What was that all about?' Sorensen asked.

'You got me.' Fogarty shrugged. 'Davic is nuts.'

Willie Joe put his arm around Sorensen's shoulders. 'You're a hero of the people, boy. Ain't that so, Fogarty?'

Fogarty looked at the sailors hanging out of their bunks. 'You said it, Willie Joe. Sorensen saved our ass.'

Willie Joe made a show of digging around in his locker until he came up with a Coca-Cola bottle that he presented to Sorensen.

'Looky here,' he said. 'I been savin' this for a long time, Ace. It's for you.'

It was dark rum. Sorensen held it up. Looking at Fogarty, he said, 'Here's to all the dead comrades. Cheers.' He chugged two swallows and passed the bottle to Willie Joe. The rum went around the compartment and came back to Sorensen, who finished it and rinsed out the bottle. Willie Joe passed out Sen Sens to everyone who had had a drink.

Sorensen then put on a tape of Jerry Lee Lewis, and a moment later the compartment was full of sailors singing along with the music.

'Attention all hands, this is the captain. We have been ordered to put into the naval station at Rota for repairs. Transit time will be forty-eight hours. Our depth will be restricted to two hundred feet. Prepare for maneuvering. That is all.'

In the torpedo room Chief Lopez discovered that Zapata was missing. He cleaned up the broken glass from the cage and searched the compartment thoroughly, but the scorpion was nowhere to be found. Lopez felt queasy. A sub had thousands of nooks and crannies where a bug could hide. It was only a matter of time before someone got stung. Lopez was sure it would be him.

Several hours after they were underway, Lopez reported Zapata to the XO as 'missing in action'.

Pisaro blinked, not sure whether to laugh or show concern. The scorpion was not all that dangerous. It's sting was hardly worse than a bee's.

'How long can that thing live with nothing to eat, Chief?'

'Months, Commander. Maybe a year.'

'You're shitting me.'

'No, sir.'

'All right. Organize a search. Give the crew something to take their minds off the collision.'

Lopez drew a crude picture of a scorpion adorned with a Mexican sombrero and crossed cartridge belts and printed a wanted poster on the ship's mimeograph machine. He offered a reward of twenty-five dollars for the return of Zapata, dead or alive, and organized search-and-destroy patrols. For twenty-fours hours sailors armed with flashlights and hastily constructed nets systematically ripped out every panel, emptied every locker, tossed every bunk. By the time they reached Gibraltar every cubic inch had been searched twice, but Zapata remained AWOL.

Lopez now reported Zapata's continued absence to Pisaro, who shrugged it off. 'Leave him to the guys on the drydock at Rota,' he said. 'It'll keep them on their toes.'

'I think he's still in the torpedo room, sir. I don't see how he could get out. The hatch has been closed since the collision except when someone goes in or out.'

'Don't worry about it, Chief. Zapata is a survivor, I'd bet on it.'

The ship locked onto a NATO submarine beacon and passed submerged through the Strait of Gibraltar into the Atlantic. As *Barracuda* turned north toward the Bay of Cádiz and the huge Spanish naval base at Rota, the word was passed that most of the crew would get three days' liberty.

At dawn the sub reduced speed and began to rise from cruising depth.

Springfield went aloft to pilot the ship into the harbor. As they followed a radar beacon into the inner harbor a cool mist rose off the bay, shrouding the giant navy base. Just outside Cádiz the crew of a Russian trawler, *Deflektor*, on permanent station in the bay, trained glasses and electronics on the passing sub. Inside the breakwater at Rota, opposite Cádiz, the Spanish aircraft carrier *Dédalo*, her deck covered with antisubmarine helicopters, loomed over the smaller ships and tugs that lined the piers.

A tug pushed *Barracuda* against a massive floating

drydock, and lines were secured fore and aft. Two days had passed since the collision, and the Russians had not muttered a word about their missing sub.

15

CARBON DIOXIDE

The collision had sent men and machinery flying about like poltergeists inside *Potemkin*. Kurnachov had cracked his head against a periscope housing and fallen unconscious to the deck.

Potemkin had revolved 360 degrees around her keel, turning completely upside down. The reactor had scrammed, plunging the ship into total darkness for several seconds before the emergency electrical power kicked in. The prop no longer was turning, but the stern planes were angled down and the ship was in a state of negative buoyance. *Potemkin* was sinking. Dazed men struggled for footing. Much of the instrumentation had gone blank, and acrid smoke from an electrical fire billowed through the after-hatch into the control room.

Federov had groped his way out of his cabin, through the darkened passageway and into the control room. There, after stumbling over the prostrate Kurnachov, he discovered the lights on the diving panel were still green – the pressure hull was intact.

'Stern planes up to zero degrees,' Federov ordered. 'Seal the hatches. Get those fires out. I want damage reports.'

Federov's return to the control room inspired the crew to shake off their daze and follow orders.

The intercom still operated. 'This is the steering machinery room. Portside stern plane fails to respond. Attempting to operate manually.'

'This is electrical engineering. All systems functioning on emergency power.'

'This is reactor control. We have steam. Injection pressure normal, but we have a scram.'

'Blow after ballast tank. Not too fast. Don't make any noise. We've got time.'

The instruments popped back to life. With a glance, Federov realized that the most serious danger came from the atmosphere machinery. The carbon dioxide scrubber and carbon monoxide burners were not functioning.

'All hands put on gas masks and oxygen tanks.'

Slowly air was bled into the ballast tank, and the bubble in the buoyance gauge rose to the center. The rate of descent slackened.

At three thousand feet the engineers were able to crank the stern plane up to zero degrees. The fires were out and the carbon monoxide burners were reignited. Only the carbon dioxide scrubber remained out of action.

'Torpedo room, load decoy number five. Flood tanks. Sonar, where is the American sub?'

'Rising, Captain, almost on the surface.'

'Fire decoy, maximum speed, down angle twenty degrees. All hands prepare for decoy concussion.'

When Kurnachov woke up in his cabin, his head was bandaged and his left arm in plaster. He gazed without comprehension at the displays in the console next to his bunk. Ordinarily the readouts gave the ship's position – speed, depth, reactor status and atmosphere condition. Now even the chronometers were blank. He had no idea how long he had been unconscious.

At first Kurnachov thought the display system had been damaged in the collision. The ship was moving ahead slowly, but at what depth and direction he had no way of knowing. He picked up the intercom telephone. It was dead.

When he tried to sit up he discovered the manacle on his ankle. The chain that secured him to his bunk was wrapped in rags to keep it quiet.

His cabin was stripped of papers, books and charts. All

insignia of rank had been removed from his uniform. Even his gold Komsomol pin was gone. Kurnachov sank back onto his bunk to consider his fate . . .

Several hours later Federov brought him a tray of sausage and kasha.

'Release me,' Kurnachov demanded. 'I am still master of this ship.'

Federov set down the tray and stood in silence over the former first officer.

'Where is my Komsomol pin? I demand that it be returned to me.'

Federov began to speak, but loathing choked his voice. Finally he got out, 'The crew voted. You've been expelled from Komsomol.'

'They can't do that, they have no right—'

'Former Captain Second Rank Kurnachov' – he spat the words – 'you have demonstrated an incredible lack of seamanship, killed one of my men, provoked the Americans, compromised the secrecy of *Potemkin* and abused your authority. All these will be included in the charges against you. But what galls me, you son of a bitch, is that all you can think of is your fucking status in the Party. Enjoy your breakfast. Choke on it.'

Federov emerged from Kurnachov's cabin to find the surgeon waiting in the corridor.

'Captain,' he said, his voice urgent, 'it's Polokov. He's bleeding internally. He needs blood.'

'Give it to him. Ask for volunteers.'

'Yes, sir.'

'And Bolinki?'

'Still in a coma.'

'How much IV solution do you have left?'

'Enough for five days.'

'Do what you can. Send the chief engineer to my cabin.'

'Yes, sir.'

Chief Engineer Alexis Rolonov, son of a Leningrad shipyard worker, had spent a large part of his life covered with grease. As he sat in Federov's cabin, a swatch of black streaked across his forehead, his hands were coated with a fine film of oil.

'How goes the portside stern plane?' the captain asked.

'The hydraulic system is ruined but it can be operated manually.'

'The reactor?'

'We can start it any time.'

'And the carbon dioxide scrubber?'

'That's going to get serious. It wasn't designed to be turned upside down. The lithium hydroxide filters were spilled and scattered. We have only partial function.'

'No spares?'

'Nikolai, how can I say this? Some son of a bitch in Murmansk stored a spare packet of what he thought was lithium hydroxide, and Kurnachov checked it off. This is it.' Alexis tossed a plastic bag full of white crystals onto the desk. It looked like rock salt. 'It isn't lithium hydroxide. It's lithium *chloride*. We use it to make—'

'Mineral water,' Federov said, closing his eyes. He took a series of deep breaths, shrugged. 'Lithium chloride . . . Are you thirsty, Comrade Chief Engineer?' Federov's eyes were open now and full of anger. 'How much time do we have?'

'Normal carbon dioxide concentration is two percent. We're now up to three percent. Without filters, four days, five at the most, then it's going to be carbon dioxide narcosis. They say it's rather pleasant.'

Federov tried to vent his fury with a joke. 'Perhaps we should stop at Gibraltar and borrow some lithium hydroxide. We can give the English Kurnachov in exchange. They can try him in their Admiralty Court for dereliction of duty and banging into one of their subs.'

The notion of Kurnachov standing in front of a wigged British judge made Alexis smile. 'Your honor . . . your honor . . . ' he stammered, 'I plead guilty as charged. I plead guilty to any charge. Convict me, hang me, just don't hand me over to the KGB.'

Alexis stopped joking and cleared his throat. Federov reached for a tin of cigars, then changed his mind. 'The air is thick enough.' He pulled out his flask of vodka, swallowed two mouthfuls and passed it to Alexis.

'How are Bolinki and Polokov?' the engineer asked.

'They're going to die if we don't get them off this ship, which we can't do in the immediate future. Gorshov wanted a one-hundred-day cruise and he's going to get it, but we may all be dead.'

'Well, we are making history—'

'Fuck history. *Potemkin* was rushed through production too quickly. Inadequate sea trials, insufficient training for the crew, too many gadgets, and no backup systems. In another three years these titanium subs will own the seas, but now, thanks to our comrade political officer, we've tipped our hand. I want to strangle him with my bare hands.'

'Relax, Captain. At least because of our difficulties the next series of ships will be better. After all, we have a titanium submarine, which the Americans have been unable to manufacture.'

'In spite of what you think, Alexis, the Americans are not stupid. They don't have political officers.'

'Perhaps because of Kurnachov, once and for all we will be rid of these fools.'

Federov shook his head. 'We stand a better chance of getting rid of the Americans than our own idiots.'

Alexis smiled. 'My friend, in time this too shall pass. The Americans tend to be arrogant. They've become diverted. They are preoccupied with Viet Nam, which drains their treasure, their blood and their will. With thirty *Potemkin*-class submarines we will put an end to their primacy on the seas. Their missile submarines are no match for this,' the engineer said, softly rapping the hull. 'But we need to buy time . . .'

'We should live so long, Comrade Chief Engineer.'

Alexis tried to phrase his next question delicately. 'What are we going to do about the carbon dioxide?'

'What are you going to suggest, Alexis? That I surface, pass through the Bosporus into the Black Sea and make for Odessa?'

'I feel the words must be said. It's my duty—'

Federov smiled. 'You have done your duty. Good. You will continue to do your duty but the answer is no. We are not going to surface and steam through Istanbul. Our orders are to avoid detection at all costs, even if we have to scuttle *Potemkin* ourselves. We are going through Gibraltar.'

'But the scrubber, Captain. We need the filters.'

'We can snorkel. We can escape detection by running very slow, very quiet and very deep.

'And if we're detected?'

Federov ignored the question and turned his attention to a chart.

Running *Potemkin* on minimal reactor power and maintaining a depth below three thousand feet, Federov had maneuvered his ship toward Gibraltar. He hugged the North African Coast, taking care to avoid major shipping lanes and NATO operations areas. No one was looking for him at that depth, and even if they were, he believed, their sonars would not find him . . . He'd heard only vague rumors of an advanced American sonar system being deployed and tended to discount them. He was always hearing how the Americans were getting ahead, followed by a spurt in his own country's military expenditures. He exercised extreme caution, though. Without the silicon packing on the turbine, *Potemkin* generated a great deal of noise at any velocity above eight knots, so Federov maintained a slow speed and a steady westerly course.

After five days the carbon dioxide concentration was four percent. The crew was breathing at an increased rate, pumping more and more carbon dioxide into the atmosphere. The men were weakening and their resistance to infection was crumbling. An outbreak of colds ravaged the engineers.

To vent the sub's noxious atmosphere Federov had to snorkel, had to rise near the surface, push a tube into the ocean air, pump out the carbon dioxide-rich atmosphere and suck in fresh air, just like an old-fashioned diesel-electric sub. However, by doing so Federov knew he also ran the risk of exposing the snorkel to hostile radar. He had to be certain that he was beyond detection before he raised the metal tube above the surface. Federov cursed his bad luck. The failure of one simple subsystem had reduced *Potemkin* to a primitive submersible craft. He needed air!

As the fifth day drew to a close, *Potemkin* was fifty miles off the Libyan coast. The submarine had to snorkel, though Federov was still leery of approaching the surface and exposing *Potemkin*. In no more than another four hours the CO_2 concentration would reach a point of extremely dangerous toxicity and the crew of *Potemkin* would be subjected to carbon dioxide narcosis. Federov studied his charts. It seemed as safe a place as he would find.

'Prepare to surface,' he ordered. 'Ready the snorkel. Alexis, take us up to one hundred fifty meters.'

Potemkin rose slowly from the depths, circling at five hundred feet to clear baffles.

Only halfway through the circle, Popov intoned, 'Contact, subsurface. Two screws, diesel-electric. Range five thousand metres, bearing one five two, course three three one, speed eight knots.' He hoped his tone masked his fear.

On the sonar screen the sub was a two-dimensional streak on one quadrant of the screen, above and ahead of *Potemkin*, going slowly.

Keep going, Federov silently urged the intruder . . . not even wanting to think on what it would mean if the other sub stopped.

'Identify, please, Popov.'

'French, Daphné class. Probably *Sirène*.'

'All ahead, dead slow. Down planes fifteen degrees. Make our depth eight hundred meters.'

In the engineering room, four coughing, sneezing men cranked down the stern planes, and *Potemkin* descended.

Federov spoke quietly into the command intercom. 'Torpedo room, load tubes one and two—'

'Nikolai, you can't shoot him, you can't know if—'

'If he's looking for us, Alexis, if the Americans have announced that reports of our death were premature, what choice do I have? If this French captain reports our position, more will come looking, the British will blockade the Strait of Gibraltar. We will have no escape. And we will all die here if we do not snorkel . . .'

'Range to target, five thousand seven hundred meters.'

'Flood tubes.'

For a moment aboard *Sirène*, just a fleeting moment, the sonarman though he saw a blip on his screen, but it was too slight, too faint, and he well remembered how once before he had been severely reprimanded for sounding a false alarm . . . and now whatever it was, if it was ever anything, had disappeared. In his experience only whales dove so deep, and in his log he recorded *baleine*.

Now at eight hundred meters, having gone quickly down

157

from five hundred feet, *Potemkin* was too deep for discovery by the Frenchman's sonars. But it was not safe, not unless the French ship cleared the area.

'Popov,' Federov asked, 'what is the depth under our keel?'

'Four thousand six hundred meters. We're over the Tunisian Trench.'

'Range to contact.'

'Range five thousand nine hundred meters, captain. I've lost an active sonar. I don't think he's stopping . . . no, he seems to be moving . . .'

Keep moving, *please*, Federov silently intoned to himself.

And as he did, a tired and disgruntled Frenchman some eight hundred meters above him and five thousand nine hundred meters distant leaned back from his console, sighing mightily, and made the easy decision not to report what he probably had not seen, thereby allowing the *Sirène* to proceed.

'Captain, still no active sonar. Range now six thousand meters. I'm losing him.' And he allowed a bright smile as he said it.

Federov smiled back at him. 'All ahead slow, right full rudder,' and then to Alexis, 'he seems to have missed us, but we can't snorkel with him in the area . . . Attention all hands, put on oxygen masks' – he knew this was mostly an empty gesture, the masks having long since become all but useless – 'there will be a delay before resurfacing.' Greeted by mumbling and curses. 'Torpedo room, unload torpedoes.' Greeted by relief.

Federov and Alexis exchanged glances, each knowing that this was a reprieve only. They could take in some good air now, vent the carbon dioxide, but it would build up, and they could not snorkel all the way back to

Murmansk. They were not a ship on display . . .

An hour later *Potemkin* rose to a depth of sixty feet. The snorkel and a radar antenna broke the surface for half an hour and then disappeared. A lonely old Tunisian fisherman saw what he thought was a strange blue light in the sea and called his mate, who was asleep. By the time he woke up and arrived on deck, the strange light was gone, and the fisherman, who of late had been accused of seeing things because of failing eyesight, never mentioned it to anyone.

16

DRY DOCK

Seventy crewmen were transferred to barracks ashore, leaving a skeleton crew of twenty-nine men on *Barracuda* to supervise the repairs to the bow.

Pisaro called Sorensen and Lopez into his office. 'At ease,' he said, offering his tin of cigars. 'Sit down and light up if you like.'

Lopez selected a Havana, and Sorensen stuck a Lucky in his mouth.

Pisaro leaned back in his chair. 'We're going to do the work of ten weeks in ten days. So, the word for everybody is "no slack." That goes for crew and civilians alike. They've flown in a "tiger team" from the naval shipyard at Portsmouth, New Hampshire. These guys are the best, they know their jobs, but they don't have to live with their work. We do. Lopez, I want you all over the welders. They're going to take off your roof, Chief. You make sure they put it back right.'

'Check, Commander.'

'Sorensen, you stand over the electricians every minute while they replace the sonars. Anything they touch, you test.'

'Aye aye, sir.'

'Very well. You'll want some help, Ace.'

'Yes, sir. I sent Davic ashore, but I need Willie Joe. I might as well keep Fogarty, too. He'll have a chance to see the system torn apart.'

'Very well. Any questions?'

'Yes, sir,' said Sorensen. 'Will there be a court of inquiry?'

'You bet, but not until we return to Norfolk. Our orders

are to get *Barracuda* back to sea as quickly as possible.'

Lopez asked, 'What about liberty for the men who are staying on the ship?'

'We'll see how it goes with the repairs, Chief. The men ashore are already going in rotation. Anything else? No? Then that's all. Dismissed.'

A Navy tug nudged *Barracuda* into the well of the floating dry dock. A canopy was stretched over the sail, the gates locked, and the water pumped out. Gently, the sub settled onto the steel braces of the huge repair ship. Naked, with the entire 252 feet of teardrop hull exposed, *Barracuda* was a beached Leviathan of massive proportions.

The tiger team from Portsmouth, a polished and professional assortment of specialists in the art of submarine repair, turned on portable floodlights and began to erect scaffolding over the bow and eighty feet down the starboard side where the Russian sub had scraped along the hull.

While the scaffolding was under construction, Sorensen went up on deck to see what the Russians had done to his ship. He had to lie on his belly and skitter crablike over the hull to get a look at the damaged sonars. For half an hour he lay spreadeagled, trying to match what he saw with what he had heard during the collision. It looked as though Godzilla had walked across the bow, gouging out steel with every step.

The point of impact was directly in the center of a torpedo tube door. The Soviet sub had sideswiped two torpedo doors and six sonar transducers. The outer hull, the thin shell of steel that contained the ballast tanks, had sustained a small puncture, but none of the tanks was ruptured. No vital piping was damaged.

He tried to imagine what had happened to the Russian sub. How had she sustained enough damage to sink and implode? Did her reactor scram? Did she suffer stern plane failure? Was her hull ruptured? Did she lose her prop? He climbed back through the hatch and into the ship, his mind racing through the possibilities. He stood in the control room, watching the electricians, pondering what to do. Finally he knocked on Pisaro's door.

'Come in. What is it, Ace?'

'Sir, I request permission to listen to the tape of the collision. I would like you to listen with me, Mr Pisaro. I want to edit the tape.'

'What do you mean, Sorensen?'

'If we could just listen to the tape, sir, you'll hear what I mean.'

'All right.'

A minute later Sorensen and Pisaro were alone in the sonar room. Pisaro broke the seal on a reel of tape, and Sorensen threaded it into one of the big recorders.

They listened to the voices on the command intercom, the machinery noises, and then the clash of the collision reverberated around the room, followed by the torpedo motor and the implosions. When it ended, Sorensen reversed the tape to the point where the Russian fired the torpedo, and again they listened to the high whine of the torpedo's gas turbine motor.

'What does it sound like to you, sir?'

'It sounds like a Russian torpedo, Sorensen. I think hearing that sound and living to tell about it is a fucking miracle.'

'It appears that way, sir. I heard the motor, and I saw a guide-wire on the screen, but I won't swear that is a torpedo.'

'What else could it have been?'

'I don't know, but everything that sub did was strange. It was trying to make us think it was *Swordfish* when it wasn't. I don't trust any of the sounds I heard from that sub. Just because it sounded like a torpedo doesn't mean it was a torpedo.'

'Please explain.'

'Maybe they jettisoned some secret equipment. I don't know. I don't think they were trying to sink us. It doesn't make sense, unless there was an electrical circuit failure that fired a torpedo accidentally. But in that case the torpedo already would have been armed and loaded in a tube. Look, Commander, everything that boat did was an acoustic trick. Suppose they thought they weren't going to implode. They thought they could blow their tanks and surface, which would have put them right in the middle of the fleet. In that case they might jettison all their secret equipment, acoustic gadgetry, code books, ciphers, everything. Only, for some reason, they couldn't blow their tanks. They had no power. All the machinery noises had stopped. Maybe in the collision they ruptured their ballast tanks. Who knows? On the other hand if they were sure they were heading for the deep six they might have jettisoned all the equipment in order to prevent us from going down and salvaging it with the *Trieste*, like we did the *Thresher*.'

'All right. Now what do you want to do?'

Sorensen quickly made a copy of the tape and gave the original back to Pisaro. He ran the duplicate forward to where the Russian fired the torpedo, then played it at a slow speed up to the sound of the first implosion, where he stopped it. With the filters built into his console he laboriously removed each implosion and explosion from the tape, then took out the sounds of the ship breaking up, the wrenching of metal, the screaming of the sea. It was tedious work but after an hour he had a tape of the sounds that were left.

The torpedo motor was still there. It was faint, but it was clear, and the sound continued to the end of the tape.

'Son of a bitch,' Pisaro swore. 'I'll have to show this to the skipper right away.'

*

163

After Pisaro left the sonar room Sorensen popped open his console and removed the tape from his concealed recorder. He was about to take it back to Sorensen's Beach when Fogarty came in, slumped in his seat and stared, brooding, at the large X drawn through the Viktor on the profile sheet.

'What's buggin' you, kid?'

'What do you think, Sorensen? For example, is this going to get us into a war?'

Sorensen shrugged. 'Only a little one.'

'C'mon. The electricians were in here this morning. They said every sub in Portsmouth and Groton has put to sea. There's an alert. World War Three could start any minute. The whole world could blow up and no one will know why it started.'

'Fogarty, the Russians are not going to start World War Three over one lost sub. If it had been a missile sub, that would be different. Besides, it was an accident.'

'But it's crazy. Back home nobody is coming on the six o'clock news to say, "Well, folks, kiss your mama goodbye. We just sank a Russian sub and the Russians don't like it."'

'We didn't sink a Russian sub.'

'The Russians might not see it that way. If it were out in the open, if people knew the truth, that might defuse the situation.'

'What good does knowing about this do anybody? It will just get people excited. Look, kid, you can't be the conscience of the navy or even of this ship. You're a pain in the ass.'

'Doesn't it matter to you whether we have a war or not?'

'Sure . . . still, I figure at worst we'll have a little skirmish. If we're lucky we might get a chance to see if any of this shit works. The world isn't going to end, if that's what you're afraid of.'

'I don't know,' Fogarty said, 'the people at home have the right to know—'

'They do? Since when?'

'You think they don't?'

'I know they don't, not since the National Security Act. Reality is classified, kid.'

'But that's crazy.'

'Fogarty, the only thing worse than spying for the Russians is telling your own people the truth. Look, everybody who has ever been on this ship has thought the same thing. Me, too. Wow! What if people knew about all this stuff, you know? All this secret stuff and all the games with the Russians. But the truth is, they don't want to know.'

'That's what you say. I say they'd sure want to know about something like this—'

'Don't be so sure. Look, here's Joe Blow sitting at home watching his TV and he hears, 'Sub Sinks. War Threatens,' and he goes nuts. And when you tell him, you also tell the guy watching the news in Moscow. Did you give him two seconds' thought? He learns that ninety of his country's finest are lying dead on the bottom, and he starts screaming for war. Is he going to believe it was an accident? Is that what *Pravda* is going to say to him? Don't be a dummy. It works both ways. If it was us down there, would you want every maniac in America to know about it? Don't you know what they would do? Half the United States Senate would vote to nuke the Russians in a minute. So we don't tell people anything. It might be wrong, but the other way is worse.'

'So we just forget about it, like it never happened.'

'Something like that. Yeah. Learn to live with it like I have. I just ride around in my submarine, and when I go ashore I act like every other stupid drunken sailor you ever heard of. That way I don't have to think about all this shit. Wise up, Fogarty. Look at it this way, if the

Russians were going to start a war over this they already would've done it.'

'Maybe they don't know about it yet.'

'Don't bet on it. They know more than you think, and so do we.' Sorensen bit his tongue. 'Look, kid, I know you feel bad about the Russians. It was just their tough luck.'

'It could have been us, Sorensen.'

'I know.' He thought about telling Fogarty he now had evidence that maybe the Russian sub didn't sink. But he wasn't positive, not yet, and he wanted his point to sink in.

There was a knock on the door. 'Comin' through.' Willie Joe came in, followed by a pair of electricians carrying coils of cable over their shoulders. One was wearing a Boston Red Sox baseball cap. 'You the sonar guys?' he asked.

'No,' Sorensen replied. 'I'm Captain Nemo.'

'Right, chief. You ready to test about five hundred circuits?'

17

LIBERTY CALL

After a week in dry dock, the welding of the bow was completed and new sonars and torpedo doors installed. *Barracuda* was moved to a finger pier where electricians continued to work on the circuitry.

Sorensen and Fogarty were in the control room, pulling hundreds of feet of inch-thick cable up from the torpedo room and arranging it in coils. 'This is going to help you qualify in record time,' Sorensen said. 'You might even make second class.'

Panting with exertion, Fogarty said, 'Pulling cable? You're nuts. You're just trying to keep me busy, keep my mind off what's happened—'

'C'mon, quit yer bitchin'. Heave.'

They grunted and moved four hundred pounds of cable six inches. Fogarty wiped his brow.

'I sure could go for a cold beer.'

Sorensen dropped the cable. 'That's the most sensible thing I've heard you say since you've been aboard. I could go for a dozen myself.'

'You been in Rota before?'

'Once.'

'What's it like?'

'It's just another scumbag Navy town, kid. Don't you get your hopes up.' Sorensen raised his voice. 'Willie Joe.'

The redhead leaned out of the sonar room.

'Yo.'

'You finish the circuit test on the new down-searching array?'

'Not yet.'

'Forget it. Come give us a hand.'

Willie Joe picked up a coil of cable. For an hour they dragged the coils out of the ship and stacked them on the pier. When the last coil was placed on top of the pile they lounged on the pier and watched the civilians work.

A light warm rain started to fall. They could see running lights on the bay. The Russian trawler moved along its picket line from Cádiz to Rota, then turned around and went back.

'What are they so interested in?' Fogarty asked.

'The *Vallejo*,' Sorensen replied. 'What else?'

The USS *Mariano G. Vallejo*, a missile submarine, was berthed at the next pier. Her sixteen Polaris A-3 missiles and their warheads represented more firepower than all the bullets and bombs in all the wars in history.

One of the missile hatches was open, and a team of technicians was removing the nose cone from a missile. The yardbirds stared inside at the bundles of wires and warheads. One grinned and whooshed his hands in a gesture of explosion.

Willie Joe sat down next to Fogarty, who appeared concentrated on the big missile ship.

'Say, Fogarty,' he asked, 'where'd you learn that karate?'

'It's not karate, it's *tae kwan do*.'

'Tie what? What's that?'

'Korean martial art.'

'I never figured a guy like you would know that stuff.'

'Oh, yeah? What kind of guy are you supposed to be to know it.'

'I dunno. Mean.'

'Maybe you've seen too many movies, Willie Joe.'

'Did you go to a school and all like that?'

'Sure.'

'Will you teach me some of those moves?' Willie Joe tried to smile, but his teeth were bad and his attempt to hide them twisted his smile into more like a smirk.

'Why do you want to learn?'

'So I can whip your ass. What do you think?'

Before Fogarty could answer, they heard pipes followed by the quartermaster's voice blaring from the loudspeakers on the pier.

'Now hear this. Liberty call, Liberty call. Liberty for the first division will commence at twenty hundred hours. Cards will be good for twenty-four hours. Be advised that by order of the base CO, all personnel are restricted to the naval station and the town of Rota. The city of Cádiz is off limits. That is all.'

'That's us,' said Sorensen. 'I'll buy you sweethearts a beer.'

Pisaro came down the gangway hollering, 'Sorensen, what are you jawing about?'

'How much we love the navy, sir!'

'Is that a fact. Listen, Ace, I want you back here tomorrow night at twenty hundred hours. Make sure you're on time.'

'Aye aye, sir.'

'And sober.'

'Yes, sir.'

By the time they changed, members of the third division were straggling in. Among them was Corpsman Luther.

'I was hoping you'd show up,' Sorensen said. Luther nodded and they slipped quietly into the tiny dispensary where the medical stores were kept.

'What's happening in town, Eddie?'

'The usual. A new guy named Buzz took over the Farolito.'

'What's he like?'

'He's an old bubblehead with a red nose.'

'That figures.'

A moment later Sorensen emerged with enough Desoxyn to keep him going all night.

'Let's go, let's go,' he said, hustling up the ladder. He popped a pill into his mouth. 'Where's Willie Joe?'

'He caught the bus,' Fogarty said. 'We have to walk.'

He was getting to feel as mean as Willie Joe figured he was.

Nothing looks more like a sailor than a sailor on liberty in civilian clothes. Fogarty had the haircut, the brand-new plaid shirt from the Navy Exchange, the creased Levis, the clumsy black leather shoes, and the all-American smile. Even Sorensen, who took pains to look like anything but a GI, was doomed to failure. The wraparound sunglasses and custom-made cowboy boots helped, as did the faded jeans and Guatemalan shirt, but there was nothing he could do about his swagger or his natural tendency to walk in step with his buddy.

The main gate to the naval station was in the middle of the town. Sorensen and Fogarty flashed IDs at the American and Spanish Marine guards in the sentry box and passed through the barriers. They repeated the process at a second checkpoint manned by the Guardia Civil, policemen with three-cornered leather hats and snub-nosed machine pistols. They crossed railroad tracks and skirted around a traffic rotary that spun off cars and trucks in five directions. Directly opposite the gate, at the foot of the Avenida de Sevilla, an eight-foot painted plaster statue of the Virgin Mary looked down on them from atop a thirty-foot pedestal. A halo of blue light surrounded the head of the idol. Sorensen looked up at the Virgin's merciless eyes and said, '*That* tells you *every*thing you need to know about Spanish women. You leave them alone.'

They stood on the Avenida de Sevilla, rocking on their heels, surveying the scene. A string of seedy bars and cheap hotels tailed away from the gate, their faint lights barely illuminating the dank slum. The rain had stopped, and the cobbled streets glistened. Tiny trucks and motorscooters buzzed past, sending a fine spray into the night. A few sailors in white hats, and many more in civilian clothes, milled from bar to bar, sharing narrow sidewalks with whores, hustlers, priests and old women dressed in black.

'So this is Spain,' said Fogarty, staring into the darkness.

'They call this the Coast of Light,' Sorensen said. 'Light fingers, mostly.'

'So where do we go from here, Sorensen?'

'Same old drill. Get drunk, get laid, get stoned, in that order.'

'That's it?'

'So what are we, tourists? C'mon.'

They strolled through the Avenida de Sevilla, passing bars, cafés and bodegas. A hundred yards from the gate they stopped in front of El Farolito, 'the little lighthouse', and pushed through the door.

A blast of loud rock and roll greeted them inside. They stood for a moment on a small landing, looking down into the partially subterranean bar, while their eyes grew accustomed to the cherry glow of an old diesel sub 'geared for red'. A white hat flew through the air and landed on a table full of beer bottles. In the rear a pair of castanets danced above a ring of clapping sailors.

Machinist's Mate Barnes reclined on the steps that led down to the saloon, playing a drunken air-guitar in accompaniment to Jimi Hendrix. They stepped over him and picked their way through the crowd to the bar.

The bartender was a blotchy man of fifty.

'*Dos cervezas*,' said Sorensen.

'You can talk American here, Mac. A Bud okay?'

'Two cold ones.'

Two bottles appeared on the bar. 'You fellas off the *Barracuda*?'

They nodded.

'Hear you're in for repairs.'

More nods.

'Hear you sank a Russian boat.'

Sorensen did his best to look surprised. 'That so? Where'd you hear that?'

The barkeep looked around the room as if he were searching the horizon for a ship. 'The word gets around. Guys from your boat been comin' in here for a week. Seems like everybody knows what you don't.'

'Well,' said Sorensen, 'that's news to me.'

'Sure, the silent service. I served in subs for thirty years, Mac. I know the score.'

'So let me buy you a beer, Chief. To your happy retirement in sunny Spain.'

'I never made chief. If you want to get along in here, call me Buzz.'

'Okay, Buzz. Have a beer.'

Buzz's face cracked a cheerless smile. 'Never touch it.' He moved on down the bar.

Sorensen looked at Fogarty and laughed. 'You want to tell the world about the collision? Seems the world already know. So much for navy security. If an old alky lifer knows, then everybody knows. The Russians, everybody. Drink up, Fogarty. To freedom, truth, justice and the right to know.'

Sorensen threw back his head and poured down half a bottle of beer.

Fogarty looked around. It was a large L-shaped room with sawdust on the floor and a high ceiling obscured by smoke. Several of his shipmates were lying in the sawdust, some in puddles. Others were dancing to the thumping tempo of *Crosstown Traffic*. Here and there in booths and tables clusters of Spanish men and women aloofly watched the action. Gypsies meandered through the crowd selling switchblades and watches.

Halfway down the bar a crowd of sailors broke into a

cheer. Sorensen and Fogarty edged through the crowd. A spring-loaded rat trap rested on the bar. Buzz cocked it and set it in front of Willie Joe.

'Place your bets.'

'Double or nothin',' someone shouted.

'Ten he makes it.'

'Five he don't.'

'Place your bets, let's fade the main. Ten down and five to go.'

The game was simple. All Willie Joe had to do was reach in, trip the spring bar and get his fingers out of the way before they were mangled and broken.

With no hesitation Willie Joe stuck in his fingers, touched the metal bar and jerked his hand away.

Buzz cocked the trap and put down ten dollars. 'All right, who's next?'

Willie Joe looked around and spotted Fogarty. 'Hey, sailor, let's see if you have any guts.'

'You think it takes guts to do this, Willie Joe? All it takes is stupidity—'

'You chicken?'

In a flash Fogarty had reached into the trap with his hand turned palm up and tripped the lock, caught the guillotine bar in mid-air and crushed the trap to bits in his fist. He brushed the pieces of pine and steel onto the floor.

'Willie Joe,' Fogarty said, 'when you can do that, I'll teach you a few moves.'

Buzz wailed, 'Hey, hey, you can't do that. Where am I gonna get another trap like that? That was my big money maker.'

Fogarty smiled and pushed the ten-dollar bill across the bar. 'I'm sure you'll think of something.'

Sorensen laughed so hard he spilled his beer. 'Besides,' he said to Buzz, 'you should be ashamed of yourself. My people can't do their jobs with busted fingers.'

173

Fogarty went in search of the head. Sorensen popped another pill, ordered another beer and scrutinized the whores, most of whom were frumpy Englishwomen from Gibraltar. There were also a few Scandinavians, Germans and Gypsies.

'Hey there, Ace.'

From across the room Lopez waved his hat. A gaudy overstuffed Gypsy perched on his lap, and two torpedomen slumped over his table, passed out. Lopez lifted one off his chair and dropped him in the sawdust. Sorensen sat down.

'I wanna buy you a drink, hero,' Lopez said.

'Why aren't you in the CPO club, boozing it up with all the other old men?'

'Because that's what they are is a bunch of old men. Hey, baby . . .' He grabbed at a passing barmaid and ordered, 'Dos cervezas.'

'You gonna get a new bug, Chief?'

Lopez crossed himself and mournfully shook his head. In rapid Spanish he told the whore the tale of the lost scorpion. She made a face and stuck out her tongue.

'Chief, what do you know about Russian torpedoes?'

'They kill you dead.'

'If it's a wire-guided fish and the wire breaks, what happens?'

'I dunno. With ours, the fish dies. Motor stops and she sinks. Can't have a torpedo run wild, no no no.'

'You think theirs are the same?'

'The Russians aren't stupid.'

'I dunno, Chief. We're alive, they're—'

'Yeah, they're dead.'

The beers arrived. 'Here's to all the suckers,' Sorensen toasted, 'on both sides of the curtain.' He wouldn't correct Lopez about the Russian sub, not until he was one hundred percent certain. Why spoil his leave? . . .

'Oh, que guapo guerito,' said the whore, flirting with

Sorensen.

'You like?' Lopez said. 'Take her. I give her to you as a present. You saved the fucking ship. You deserve it.'

'Thanks, Chief. Maybe later.'

Lopez spotted Fogarty walking back through the bar, and asked, 'That the kid who did the number on Davic?'

'That's him.'

'You never reported it.'

'I didn't see it. There was nothing to report. Seems like you found out anyway.'

'I'm chief of the boat, Sorensen.'

'Did you tell Pisaro?'

'No.'

'All right.'

'But I will next time.'

Lopez buried his face in the whore's neck and spoke into her ear. Daintily, she climbed off his lap and Lopez stood up. 'Time for business,' he said.

Arm in arm, Lopez and the whore headed for the door.

Sorensen waved Fogarty over to the table and ordered another beer.

'Nice party, hey, kid?'

Fogarty nodded. 'It's all right.'

Sorensen laughed. 'Relax, Fogarty. Throw all that heavy shit out of your mind and have yourself a time. Grab one of these Brits and fuck her brains out.'

'I never did a whore before.'

'Bully for you. You're not queer, are you?'

'I wasn't the last time I checked.'

'You're not going to ease up, are you?'

Fogarty shrugged and drank some beer.

'Fogarty, you're a good boy, aren't you? All your life you've been a good boy. I'd bet anything that you've never been in trouble. I mean, real trouble. With the police, knock up a girl, burn down the house, like that.'

'No.'

175

'You've never done a mean thing in your life, right?'

'I wouldn't say that.'

'You know karate, or whatever it is, but I'd bet you never really beat anybody up.'

'You'd lose.'

'No kidding. Who'd you mess up?'

'My brother.'

'Okay. That's not too hard to figure out. Like he beat up on you for years, so you went out and learned how to fight, then one day he picked on you and pow! Right?'

'Something like that. Pretty close.'

'But you never went out on the street and kicked ass. You're not that kind of guy. You're a good boy. You believe in peace, love, all that shit.'

'I don't have to prove that I can break a few bones, if that's what you mean.'

'How about a few Russian bones, Fogarty? Would you break them if you had to?'

'I hope I don't have to.'

'So do I, kid, and don't forget it. But the question is, what are you going to do if and when the shit comes down? Maybe deep down you didn't really want to join the navy. Maybe you wanted to stay in school. Maybe you wanted to be an electrical engineer. Am I getting through to you?'

Fogarty nodded.

'What happened? You run out of money? You flunk out, what?'

'It was the money, partly.'

'Yeah, I thought so.'

'I joined the navy to see the world.'

'There's lots of ways to see the world, and the Submarine Service is at the bottom of the list.' Sorensen smiled, pleased at his turn of phrase.

Fogarty shrugged.

'Fogarty, I'd say you're all fucked up.'

'That's what I like about you, Sorensen, your delicate way of putting things . . . But I guess you're right. Sure, I'm all fucked up. Ditto the navy, and the world, for that matter . . .'

'Hey, belay that shit. You're not drunk enough yet. It'll look a lot better later. Whoa, what's this?'

Cakes Colby was headed for their table. Thumbs in his belt, hat tipped down low on his forehead, he planted himself in front of Sorensen. 'There's nucs and there's pukes, and then there's you, Jack. You want some reefer?'

'What would an old Tom like you know about reefer?'

'Son, how do you think I made it through twenty-five years of fixing coffee for snotnosed officers? Everybody has to get over one way or another.'

18

HOTEL PENNSYLVANIA

The decrepit Hotel Pennsylvania was built around a covered central patio with three floors stacked like doughnuts. The single sofa in the lobby was threadbare; the green tile on the floor was chipped. Dirty windows looked onto the narrow Calle de Pescaderos, a side street off the Avenida de Sevilla.

A boyish red-haired clerk stood behind the front desk, which was cluttered with dictionaries and notepads, the paraphernalia of self-taught English.

'Welcome, American sailors. Bery welcome to you and you and you.' The clerk nodded to Sorensen, Fogarty and Cakes in turn, exposing a set of gold teeth behind a fixed grin.

'You are wanting three rooms, jes? For the privation. We are very accommodate you here at El Hotel Pennsylbania. I am Rodrigo to help you in all things.'

'How much are the rooms?'

'Ten dollars Americans in advance and three nights the liberation. Is bery resonant, no?'

'This guy has got beri-beri,' Sorensen said.

'One night, Rodrigo,' Cakes told the clerk.

'Four dollares the singular night.'

He asked for their military IDs, copied the numbers and gave them keys to adjoining rooms on the third floor. As they were signing the registration forms he asked, 'You want girls? *Muchachas*? Nice girls. Clean. Speaking English girls from Hibraltar. Liquores? Booze, you say? This is the correct idiot? I got Him Beam.'

'You got him beer?'

'Sure. What kind you like? I got Herman, Dutch? It is

the next door a bar for all drinkings.'

'I don't care as long as it's cold. Two six packs.'

'*Para servirle, señor.*' Rodrigo went through a curtain into the bar and returned with a dozen bottles of San Miguel and stuffed them in a paper bag.

They went up to Sorensen's room. It was plain and clean with cheap prints of bullfighters on the walls. Sorensen opened beers, threw open the windows and stepped out on the balcony. Fogarty flopped on the bed, commenced guzzling beer. Cakes rolled a joint, twirling it under his nose, lit it and sucked mightily, then passed it to Sorensen, who took a hit.

'This is good shit, Cakes. You always have the best dope.' Sorensen passed the joint to Fogarty.

'Ain't you got no sounds, man?' asked Cakes.

Sorensen shoved a Miles Davis tape into his recorder and turned it on.

'This is your last cruise, Cakes?'

'Yep. This is it.'

'What're you gonna do?'

'I got me a lunch counter in Harlem. I've had it for years. My boys run it. I'm gonna sit in the backroom and watch the dough roll in.'

'Sounds like you're set up pretty good.'

'I make out.'

Cakes rolled another joint. Fogarty said, 'I can't get used to the idea I'm in Spain. It's like a foreign movie with no subtitles.'

'This isn't Spain,' Sorensen told him. 'This is Rota. This is just a pit stop for horny sailors. Spain is over there across the bay.'

Through the balcony doors they could see over the rooftops and across the water to Cádiz, shimmering like a fantasy five miles away.

'Why can't we go to Cádiz?' Fogarty asked.

'Ever hear of Palomares?'

'Palomares? No.'

Cakes said, 'It's where the Air Force lost an H-bomb.'

'That's right,' Sorensen said, 'it's about a hundred miles from here. One day a couple of years ago a B-52 loaded with hydrogen bombs collided with the tanker that was refueling it and dropped its load on this diddlysquat village named Palomares. One of the bombs fell in the ocean, and the Air Force couldn't find it—'

'Yeah,' Cakes put in, 'It took the Navy to save their ass. We found it with *Trieste*.'

'Right,' Sorensen said. 'Before Palomares nobody in Spain ever heard of a hydrogen bomb. When six of them fell on a village and scattered hot plutonium all over the school, the marketplace, the church, the cows and the chickens they got educated. Their country had been turned into a nuclear arsenal. There were bombs all over the place, including Rota, on the boomers. *Vallejo*, tied up to the dock down there on the waterfront, has sixteen Polaris missiles. Tick off the sixteen largest cities in the Soviet Union and that's what that one ship can do. The Spanish don't want any part of it. The Andalusians are not like the Neapolitans, who don't give a shit about anything. These people don't like being a target, and they don't like us. Over in Cádiz there've been demonstrations and a few scuffles. A white hat in Cádiz is an invitation to a fight. So it goes, so it goes. See, Fogarty, not everybody is like us, fearless nuclear warriors.'

'I think I'm getting high.'

'It's decent weed.'

'Nuclear warriors,' Fogarty repeated with a bland smile.

'*Fearless* nuclear warriors.'

'Bum ba bum bum. We hold these truths to be self-evident, that all nukes are created equal. Boom ba boom boom. Ain't that right, Cakes?'

Cakes stood up, swaying to the music, holding the joint

with all his fingers like a big stogie.

'I,' he said, drawing out the word in a deep baritone, 'I am the nigger of the apocalypse. I am death in the deep. I am the end. I am your worst nightmare. I am General . . . Electric!'

Fogarty looked amazed. Sorensen whooped and hollered and rolled on the floor. Cakes sat down with a big chuckle and sipped his beer. They listened to Miles wail into the night.

'How long you been on *Barracuda*, Cakes?' Fogarty asked.

'Same as Jack, here. Since before she was commissioned, nine years.'

'Oh, yeah, Fogarty, me and Cakes know each other's dirty little secrets. Cakes was there the day we invented Cowboys and Cossacks.'

'Oh, baby, them Ivans ain't never going to forget us.'

'What happened?'

'It was during the Cuban missile crisis. *Barracuda* was on station in the Caribbean when we got orders to patrol one sector during the blockade. The Russians were ninety miles from our shores, and the only thing between them and Miami Beach was us, *Barracuda*. Now, that kind of situation shoots a lot of adrenaline into your blood. We had this macho president who was just like us. You want to talk about belief? We *believed* in John Kennedy, every last man. He left no doubt as to what would happen if the Russians didn't back down. Man, we had our tubes flooded and guidance systems locked-on the whole time. We were ready to die.'

Cakes was nodding his head in agreement. Sorensen went on, 'We would have died for Kennedy without a second thought. As it was, nobody died. It was suddenly ridiculously easy to kick the Russians out of our ocean. We made these wild runs under the Russian ships. They had a couple of diesel-electric subs and we blew their ears out. They took one look at us and split. When we got back to Norfolk you'd have thought we'd just won the Battle of Midway. At that moment, Fogarty, I'm telling you, the world was perfect, as perfect as it will ever be. Hell, in March 1963, I reenlisted. Kennedy was in the White House, America was number one, *Barracuda* was number one. We were invincible . . . And then the world fell apart. First, the *Thresher* sank. It was like the *Titanic* all over again. The perfect invincible nuclear sub imploded during sea trials. That was a mind-fuck. Then Kennedy gets assassinated and the world turns upside down. On that day I learned about perfection. In the five years since Dallas the reality has been exploding in our faces. Race riots, Viet Nam, mass murderers, you name it, we got it. So next year my reenlistment comes up again and I'm thinking maybe I've had enough of this shit. But I ask you, Fogarty, how many civilian sonar operators do you know? The truth is, I don't know if I can live in the real world any more. I don't have a lunch counter in Harlem like Cakes. All I have is *Barracuda*, so I just do my job. I like my job. I'm very stoned.'

Sorensen walked out on the balcony and looked down into the dirty street. A pair of Guardia Civil policemen sauntered past the hotel, machine pistols slung over their backs. To his right he could see the sea wall and a slice of bay. A slice of an imperfect world. Dirty. Radioactive. He looked up at the sky, hoping to see stars. He saw clouds.

What do whales talk about? What is it like to live on dry land and have kids?

Inside, Fogarty was saying to Cakes, 'I guess you've seen a lot of changes in the navy in twenty-five years.'

Cakes blew smoke around the room. 'Some things are different, some ain't. Now we got white boys smokin' dope, that's different. We got crazy Stanley, that's a whole lot different. There ain't nobody shootin' at us no more. I like that part, but otherwise the navy hasn't changed in two hundred years. We got nuke boats and all that shit, but it don't mean nothin', nothin' at all. You go to sea and you come back to the same place you started. It's all one big circle. It's all right with me.'

'What do you think of the Russians?'

'Who gives a fuck? I don't never think about them. I like their vodka.'

'What about the sub that went down?'

'You mean them dudes that sank?'

Sorensen said nothing. The Russian sub was alive. She never sank, and he had the proof on tape. The torpedo wasn't a torpedo at all, it was the sub itself. The implosions were faked. Now wasn't the time to tell them . . .

'Yeah. What do you think about them?'

'Nothin'. There ain't nothin' to think about. It was their tough luck. I'm glad it was them and not us.'

'Were you scared?'

'Listen, I'm always scared. I'm scared right now, smoking this dope with you, but that don't stop me none. What are you talkin', man? Scared. You don't know what scared is until you been depth-charged.' Cakes stood up. 'I'm going back to the bar and screw one of them fat whores until she yells uncle. Uncle Sam, that is. How 'bout you boys?'

As Cakes was reaching for the door, there was a knock.

Sorensen opened the door an inch. Rodrigo stood outside. 'He is down the stair to see you, a sailor Americano.'

Stepping into the corridor, Sorensen saw Willie Joe drunkenly climbing the stairs, a ten-gallon Stetson propped on his head.

'It's okay, Rodrigo. He's a friend.' He slipped the clerk a dollar. Willie Joe flopped on the bed.

'Anybody got a drink?'

Fogarty passed him a bottle of beer.

Finally Cakes said, 'Well, I'm still going to party.'

'Let's do it,' said Sorensen.

They stood up to go back to the bar, all except Willie Joe, who mumbled, 'Battle stations, battle stations, pussy off the port bow . . .' closed his eyes and passed out on Sorensen's bed. They left him snoring in a dreamless sleep.

The party in the Farolito was still going full blast. Buzz was pouring cognac for a dollar a shot.

'Straight up, all around,' Sorensen ordered. Buzz wrinkled his nose at Fogarty and poured three shots of brandy. Sorensen counted a dozen sailors passed out in the sawdust and was tempted to join them.

Cakes walked down the bar to speak to one of the fat Gypsy whores. A few minutes later they left together.

In the rear a lone dancer went through the motions of flamenco in slow motion. Fair and blonde, the descendant of a rampaging Vandal, she kicked the floor and snapped castanets to music only she could hear.

'See you later,' Sorensen said. He carried his drink across the bar to the table nearest her, sat down and began to clap a rhythm to her dance.

At first she appeared not to notice him. Then she slowly danced around his table. She was young, nineteen or twenty.

'*Como te llamas?*' he asked.

'*Rosa. Y Tú?*'

'Jack.'

'Okay, Zhack,' she said, and sat down on his lap, leaned against his chest and put her arms around his neck. Taking a Lucky from his pack, she lit it and stuck it in his mouth.

'You got any money, Zhack? These saylors spend all their bugs on liquores and womans. You got any bugs left, Zhack?'

184

'I got enough.'

Her hand slipped down to his crotch. 'You want to spend with me? I eat you.'

'Let's go.'

He waved at Fogarty on the way out.

Fogarty drank alone for an hour, staring at the whores in the mirror behind the bar. He wasn't sure about how to approach the women. He wasn't interested in fat Gypsies and was ready to stumble back to the hotel when one of the women sat down on the bar stool next to his. Tight jeans clung to her hips, and a peasant's blouse hung over bare shoulders. On her feet were expensive handcrafted sandals. She wasn't especially pretty but she had attractively strong and intelligent features. She looked older by several years, he thought. Guessed.

'Hello, sailorboy. Buy me a drink?'

'Sure.'

Fogarty signaled to Buzz for more brandy.

'And I'd like a cigarette.'

He lit a Lucky and handed it to her. 'Are you English? You sound English.'

She smiled. 'Indeed I am. A bloody Brit, that's me. And you're a Yank.'

'A Yank? I never thought of myself as a Yank.'

'None of you ever does.'

Her smile completely transformed her face and made her very pretty.

'What's your name, Yank?'

'Fogarty.'

'That's it? Just Fogarty?'

'Mike Fogarty.'

'My God, an Irish Yank. A mick.'

'You don't like the Irish?'

'Of course not. They're bloody wogs, the whole grotty lot.'

'Wogs?'

She smiled, and in a precise Home Counties accent said, 'A wog, my dear boy, is a westernized oriental gentleman, to wit, a person of color or one who is not English. That includes the Welsh, the Scots, the Irish, the French and the inhabitants of any country that ever was part of the British Empire, or ever an enemy of England.'

'That's everybody!'

'Precisely. Some would extend the definition of wog to include members of the Labour Party. I'm afraid this is all too terribly English. Since we don't rule the world anymore, we have to make jokes about ourselves.'

'I think you're great. What's your name?'

'I'm called Liz.'

She knocked a few ashes onto her chest and brushed them away. Fogarty saw tiny freckles under her collarbone.

'Are you . . . what I mean is . . .'

'Am I one of the whores?'

'Yeah.'

'I am.' She smiled again. 'Ten dollars US and I'm yours. For twenty dollars you can have me all night.'

Fogarty was dazzled, but he was also so drunk he could hardly walk. She helped him up the stairs and out of the bar. A taxi carried them the short distance to the hotel.

19

THE ADMIRAL

Sorensen lay in bed listening to the sound of a maid slowly working up the marble stairs to the third floor. She lifted her pail of water one step at a time, set it down with a clang, dragged her heavy body after it, slowly mopped each slab of stone. She repeated the process two dozen times. When she reached the third floor she shuffled down the corridor, unlocked one of the rooms and banged the door behind her.

Somewhere in the hotel a radio came to life and a muffled female voice sang a slow ballad.

A pool of blonde hair lay across Sorensen's chest. Rosa stirred, sticky with sleep, and sat up with a groan.

'Oh, por Dios, la cabeza.' She got out of bed and went into the bathroom. Sorensen saw the marks of childbirth stretch across her belly. When she came out he gave her a fistful of pesetas and she left. He pulled on his clothes, went into the corridor and knocked on Fogarty's door. No answer. He put his ear to the door, smiled at the sound of huffing and puffing, went down to the Farolito for breakfast.

As the afternoon wore on, the Farolito was taken over by the crew of Vallejo. This was their last blowout before the big missile sub began a sixty-day cruise under the Med, and they pulled out all the stops. A radio was going full blast, filling the room with Armed Forces Radio Network rock and roll. Two sailors were teaching a whore the dirty chicken. A group of civilians from Portsmouth clustered at one end of the bar, playing with a new rat trap. One of the welders was reading aloud the box score of a Red

Sox–Yankees game from the *Stars and Stripes*.

Buzz poured Sorensen a beer.

Cakes sat in a corner, drinking alone. Sorensen carried his beer across the bar to the table.

'Want company?'

'Sure, Ace. Sit down. I'm ready. I'd just as soon get back on the ship and go home.'

'What's the matter, you broke?'

'I think I got the clap. Hell, I know I got it.'

'Luther will fix you up.'

'That faggot corpsman? He loves to stick a needle in my black ass.'

Sorensen drank beer for a while, then switched to brandy. About two o'clock he came out of the head and pushed up to the bar. Buzz pointed across the room and said, 'There's a fella lookin' for you.'

Sorensen looked around and noticed a tweed jacket sitting in a booth, away from the crowd.

It was *Netts*, sitting alone with a bottle of brandy and two glasses. He gestured for Sorensen to sit.

'Evening, Admiral.'

'Don't salute, Sorensen, I'm not in uniform.'

'Yes, sir.'

'I'm going to skip the bullshit. What happened down there?'

'You mean during the collision, sir?'

'Don't be a wiseass. Of course I mean during the collision.'

'What exactly do you want to know, sir?'

'What was he up to, that damned Russian?'

Sorensen hesitated. By now he was stoned and drunk. A din from the rowdy sailors swirled around him. He caught a flash of Rosa dancing in a crowd.

'Have a drink,' said Netts, pushing the bottle and a glass across the table. 'I know you're on liberty and it looks to me like you're having a good time. Just tell me what you know about this Russian sub.'

Sorensen poured some brandy.

'It's hard to say, sir. They seemed to be testing acoustical systems.'

'Submarine disinformation, deception, fakery, tricks?'

'Yes, sir. That's about the size of it. Dirty tricks.'

'We've got a few of our own.' Netts looked around the bar, then back at Sorensen. 'I listened to the tape you made for Commander Pisaro, but I don't quite know what to make of it. It's damned peculiar.'

'I'd like permission to ask a question, sir.'

'Go ahead.'

'Have the Russians said anything about their missing sub?'

'No. To admit it's missing would be to admit it was there in the first place, and they aren't about to do that. As a matter of fact they aren't searching for it at all. *Badger* has been on station directly over the site of the collision, and the Soviets haven't even buzzed her with an airplane. No reconnaissance ships, nothing.'

'Why not, sir?'

'That's what's under my skin. I don't know why not. You heard that sub implode. It's on the tape.'

Sorensen drank his glass of brandy and poured another. 'Admiral, I'm not convinced that boat sank. I mean, we all heard the implosions, but we heard a lot of things that turned out to be something else. Fact is, I think they faked it. I don't know how, I can't *prove* it—'

Netts cocked his eyebrows, questioning.

'Admiral, I believe what you hear at the end of that tape, what we thought at first was a torpedo, is the Russian sub bugging out on a tiny electric motor. She never sank.'

'Sorensen, do you know what you're saying?'

'I think so, sir.'

'That torpedo was four thousand feet deep.'

'Yes, sir. Four thousand one hundred thirty-five to be exact.'

A strange smile flickered across the admiral's face, a Cheshire-cat smile. Netts poured himself a drink. 'You're saying the Russians have built a submarine that can go that deep. If so, it's a revolution in hull technology.'

'Yes, sir, I know. It's bad news.'

'Not only that, if she's still loose in the Med, it won't be long before she's in the Ionian Sea, threatening our FBMs.'

'Yes, sir.'

'If that's the case we need to know more about this submarine. Hull sections involved in the collision with the Russian sub have been cut out of *Barracuda* and sent to Washington for analysis. They may turn up something on a spectroscope but it will take a few days. Meanwhile *Barracuda* is going back to sea. You and Springfield are going to find this son of a bitch, record every sound she makes and then do everything you can to force her to the surface and take her picture.'

Netts's face was flushed, he was speaking in a controlled shout. He poured and downed another shot of brandy.

'Do you know where she is, Admiral?'

'No. She got into the Med without our detecting her at Gibraltar, but she hasn't passed back into the Atlantic. The SOSUS net that *Barracuda* tested will pick her up right away. When she does go back into the Atlantic, we'll be all over her . . . If I had my way I'd come aboard *Barracuda* and shove a torpedo up her ass. But I can't do that. I have great faith in you, Sorensen. You're an asset to the navy.'

'Thank you, sir. I'm flattered you would say so.'

'Have you ever thought about accepting a commission?'

'No, sir. I like it fine where I am.'

'You think about it.'

Sorensen nodded, knowing he wouldn't think about it at all. Netts pushed the bottle across the table and stood up.

'Drink up, bucko. I'll see you in Norfolk.'

Not if I see you first, bucko, thought Sorensen as he watched the admiral's back move away and out the door of the Farolito.

20

NO BAND

Sorensen returned to his room in the hotel, opened a warm beer, picked up his tape recorder and knocked on Fogarty's door.

Fogarty was asleep, dreaming he was inside the sinking Russian sub. Blaming him for their fate, the Russians were stuffing him into a torpedo tube . . .

Sorensen pounded on the door and woke him up. 'Fogarty, you in there?'

'Yeah, just a minute . . .'

'You still got one of them ladies of the night in there with you?'

It was three o'clock in the afternoon. Fogarty unlocked the door. His eyes were red and puffy.

'No. She's gone.'

'You hung over, kid?'

Fogarty's head and chest felt like pincushions. He stumbled into the bathroom and surrendered to his stomach.

Sorensen walked into the room and flopped on a chair. Fogarty returned, looking pale.

'You all right?' Sorensen asked.

'I drank too much.'

'What's the matter, Fogarty? Didn't they teach you how to party in Minnesota?'

'Go to hell.'

Sorensen laughed. 'These Gypsy whores are all right. Not like the Italians. There's none of this Oh, Mister GI, take me to America bullshit.'

'Mine was English.'

'Your what?'

192

'My whore.'

'No foolin'? Good for you. You got your wallet?'

A look of panic on his face, Fogarty pulled on his pants and shoved his hands in his pockets. His wallet was there.

'Just kidding,' Sorensen said. 'These ladies couldn't stay in business five minutes if they were picking pockets.' He held out his beer. 'Want breakfast?'

'Pass.'

Fogarty sat down on the bed and wallowed in his hangover.

'We're due back on the ship in a couple of hours,' Sorensen said. 'Want to go back to the Farolito? There's a party on.'

Fogarty tried to shake his head, but the motion made him woozy. 'Twenty dollars,' he groaned.

Sorensen laughed. 'Kid, you been had. Mine cost ten.'

Fogarty tried to smile. 'It was worth it.'

'Oh? You feel like a real sailor now?'

This time Fogarty was able to shake his head. 'Not yet, Ace. Maybe I never will.'

'You still worried about the Russians?'

'Shit, yes.'

'Forget 'em, sailor.'

Fogarty looked disgusted. 'You can be one cold son of a bitch, Sorensen.'

Sorensen nodded. 'I'd say that was a pretty fair assessment.'

'The nuclear warrior.'

Sorensen shrugged, took a pull on his beer, shoved a tape into his machine. Bob Dylan sang the opening lines of 'Just Like Tom Thumb's Blues'. *When you're lost in the rain in Juarez, and it's Easter time too . . .*

While Fogarty closed his eyes and listened to the music Sorensen opened the windows and stepped onto the balcony. He watched a guided-missile frigate clear the harbor, pass *Deflektor* and head into the Atlantic, a gray ship in a gray sea.

Below, the street was nearly deserted. At the end of the block the *sereno*, the block watchman, contemplated the seawall. It was the hour of siesta. Sorensen went back into the room and pushed the rewind button on his recorder. He fished a roach out of his pocket, lit it, finished off his beer.

'Fogarty,' he said. 'I want you to get your head straight before we get back on the ship.'

'What's the matter with my head?'

'There's nothing in it but half-baked ideas. You're not dumb, you're just impatient, or maybe the word is naive. I know because I used to be the same way.'

'Thank you, doctor.'

'How old are you? Twenty-one?'

'Yeah.'

'You know, Fogarty, I think you're going to be a good sonarman. You've got good ears.'

'Thank you. Coming from you, that's a real compliment.' He meant it.

'Yeah, well, I want to give you a little test. I want to find out just how good you are. But to do that I have to let you in on a little secret.'

Fogarty sat up straight and squinted in the dim sunlight coming through the windows.

'What kind of secret?'

Sorensen grinned. 'Personal.'

'Personal?'

'Yeah, that means I personally will strangle you if you tell anyone.'

Sorensen retrieved his tape recorder, turned off Bob Dylan and put in a new tape.

'I wired this recorder into my console in the sonar room.'

'But that's illegal, Jesus.'

Sorensen grinned. 'Yeah, that's my secret, and now it's yours too. If I did everything the navy's way I couldn't do my job. This way I can listen to any tape any old time I want.'

'Why'd you bring it off the ship?'

'I wasn't about to leave it there for one of the yardbirds to find.'

'Does Willie Joe know? Davic?'

'No. They're a bit too straight. Me' – he smiled – 'I'm *bent*. Anyway, listen to this.'

And Sorensen proceeded to play the original, unedited tape of the collision. Fogarty recognized it immediately. He heard the voices on the command intercom, then the crunch of metal on metal. Coming through the miniature speaker in the recorder it didn't sound quite so terrifying.

'My God,' Fogarty said when the tape ended. 'That's incredible.'

'I kind of like it myself.'

'That's a dangerous piece of tape, Sorensen.'

'Only to me. Now, here comes the test.'

Sorensen flipped over the tape and punched the play button. Once more they heard the Russian sub sinking. The torpedo motor howled across the sea. But this time there were no explosions, no bursting bulkheads.

Fogarty jumped up and shouted at Sorensen, 'What did you do to the tape?'

'Shut up and *listen*.'

The torpedo motor continued on for several seconds, and then the tape ended.

'What did you do to the tape?'

'That's the test, Fogarty. You tell me.'

Fogarty lit a cigarette, laughed nervously. 'What kind of a game is this, Ace?'

'This is the home version of Cowboys and Cossacks. C'mon, Fogarty, tell me what you hear.'

'Play it again. Play it from where she shoots.'

Sorensen backed up the tape and they listened to it again.

Fogarty said, 'You took out the implosions.'

'Correct.'

'What's left is the torpedo. You're trying to find out what happened to the fish.'

'Could be. What do you think happened to it?'

'It was wire-guided. It sank when the wire broke.'

'You sure?'

'No . . . the motor keeps running.'

'Very good. What else?'

'Maybe it's not a torpedo.'

'Real good. So what is it?'

'A decoy?'

'Nope.'

Fogarty picked up the recorder, carried it to the bed, sat down and listened once more to the torpedo. The motor churned out a high-pitched whine that reminded him of the little electric motors he used to put in his model subs.

And suddenly, he understood. Or did he? 'You want me to believe that it's the sub? It never sank?' When Sorensen didn't reply, he sat perfectly still for a minute. Finally he said, 'I can't believe it.'

'You don't want to believe it, but it's true.'

'You're trying to con me.'

'Why would I do that?'

'I don't know. Something's not right.'

'You bet something's not right. That torpedo's not right.'

'But it went down to four thousand feet. No sub can go that deep.'

'This one did.'

'It's impossible.'

'God*damn*, Fogarty. Can't you shake your mind loose? It used to be impossible, but it isn't anymore.'

'It just doesn't make sense—'

'Then tell me why the Russians aren't looking for their missing sub.'

'How do you know that?'

'Netts told me,' Sorensen said cheerfully. 'He came all the way from Washington just to chat with the Ace. You like that?'

'You talked to Admiral Netts?'

'Sure. I'm a big hero, remember?'

'Why would the Russians fake a sinking of their own ship?'

'First, to make enough noise to cover their exit. And if we thought she was sunk, we wouldn't look for her. Come on, Fogarty, *think*, for chrissake.'

'Play the tape one more time.'

Sorensen did, and Fogarty felt the first twinges of anger.

'So it was a trick.'

'Looks like, kid.'

'I grieved for those people—'

'I know you did. An honorable thing to do. Hey, it's not *your* fault.'

'Damn . . . I'm still not sure I believe it.'

'Oh, you believe it, Fogarty. You know it's true.'

'How long have you known?'

'Since I played what you just heard. The skipper is going to tell the crew about the Russian sub tonight. And we're going after her, and we'll find her.'

'How can you be so sure?'

Sorensen sucked on his beer and looked at Fogarty. 'Because of the new system, the deep submergence sonars. The way they work is simple. They laid down cables, like ordinary undersea telephone cables, only as they laid it down, every twenty miles they spliced in a hydrophone. In four thousand miles of cable, there's two hundred sonars, but they're reliable because they send back their signals through the cable. We now have a grid of cables with a total of thirty-six hundred hydrophones in the

Atlantic. Some spots, like the Caribbean and the Iceland–Greenland–UK gap, are saturated with phones. Sooner or later the Russians will figure it out. When they do they'll pull their fleet back into the Norwegian Sea and expand their operations in the Pacific and the Mediterranean. For us right now, it means we ought to be able to track this sub, wherever she goes. The game is going to get very interesting. When we go back to sea tonight we have to be ready for anything. What I want to know, Mr Fogarty, is if you're going to do your job. That's all I ask. Just do your job and cut the crap.'

Fogarty picked up the miniature tape recorder and hefted it. He was scared, but he figured that was only natural. He remembered hearing what he thought was the torpedo charging through the water directly at him . . . but what if—

'I think I will have a beer,' he said, opening a bottle. 'Look, Ace, explain to me how you wired this into your console.'

'Sure, kid.'

'And stop calling me "kid".'

'The hell you say.'

Lopez was standing with the Marine guards at the foot of the submarine pier. 'All right, you're the last ones. Let's go.'

The pier was crowded with sailors and technicians preparing *Barracuda* and *Vallejo* for departure. As they walked along Lopez said, 'You ain't gonna bring no reefer on board, are you, Ace?'

'Why, Lopez? You want to get loaded?'

'Just checking.'

'What's happening in the real world, Chief? Any traffic out there?' Sorensen waved his arm in the direction of the Atlantic.

'Seems the whole fuckin' ocean is full of Russians. It's

gonna be hot. The skipper wants to see you right away. Go change.'

Sorensen showered, changed into a jumpsuit and knocked on Springfield's door.

'Come in.'

'Chief Lopez said you wanted to see me, sir.'

'Sit down, Sorensen.'

'Thank you, sir.'

'Coffee?'

'Thank you, sir. Black.'

Springfield poured two cups of coffee and handed one to Sorensen. 'I understand you spoke with Admiral Netts.'

'Yes, sir.'

'He wants to give you a commission.'

Sorensen rattled his coffeecup. 'We've been through this before, Captain.'

'I know. How many times?'

'Six.'

'And you've turned us down each time.'

'Yes, sir. I like it fine where I am.'

'I told Netts you would say that, but there's a catch. You can't stay where you are. None of us can. *Barracuda* is going back to Electric Boat for a major refit. She'll be up there in Groton for two years.'

'That's it? They're going to disband the crew?'

'Pretty much. We're sending you to Mare Island and assigning you to *Guitarro* as chief of the boat.'

Sorensen almost dropped his coffee. 'Chief of the boat? You're putting me on, Skipper? No sonarman in the navy is chief of the boat.'

Springfield smiled. 'Some navy traditions are flexible. Netts is willing to make an exception in your case. You'll have to take a couple special rating exams but you'll have plenty of time for that.'

'You said *Guitarro*? I never heard of her.'

'She's a new attack sub still on the ways. You'll have

the most advanced electronics and sonars. Space on the boat has already been designated as Sorensen's Beach.'

Sorensen hadn't expected this, and he wasn't sure how he felt about it . . . a new ship, a new crew, a new captain and chief of the boat all at once. Too much . . .

'I don't know what to say, Captain. Thank you. I'll have to think about it.'

'That's fine, Sorensen. You think about it as long as you like. Right now we have more immediate concerns. Netts and Pisaro tell me that in your opinion the Russian sub never sank, that it was an acoustic trick of some sort.'

'Skipper, what we thought was the torpedo was the sub itself. I think they fired some kind of decoy that sank and imploded.'

Springfield tapped a pencil on his desk. 'That means that sub went down to at least four thousand feet.'

'Yes, sir.'

'A Mark thirty-seven won't go that deep. We couldn't shoot her down there, except with a nuke, a Mark forty-five . . .' He shook his head at the prospect. 'But what if you're wrong, Sorensen? What if she did sink?'

'Then I'm wrong. If she's on the bottom, we'll find her.'

'Well, I'm betting you're right. It's the safest thing to do. Admiral Netts has had the tape of the sinking analyzed and the sound engineers don't agree. Still, we have to assume that sub is still loose. We don't know where it is or what shape it's in but we do know one thing. That sub got into the Mediterranean undetected, and as far as we know it hasn't come out.'

'If it got in sir, I won't be surprised if it can get out.'

'Well . . . we've increased the number of patrols through the Strait and beefed up the fixed arrays, but this sub isn't our only problem. Four days ago three more Soviet attack subs passed through the Iceland gap and headed south into the Atlantic. We're tracking them through the North Atlantic with SOSUS right now. One of them is riding a picket line about thirty miles out. Clearly the Russians believe they can penetrate the Med, and it seems as though they designed this new class of subs to do just that. You know, until now our missile subs have been able to operate without any trouble in the Ionian Sea. From there they can strike at targets as far away as Moscow. But if the Russians get attack submarines into the Med, they jeopardize our FBMs. This is a whole new ball game for the Soviet Navy. We think they're going after *Vallejo*, so the first thing we're going to do is help her shake her tail. We're going to have to deal with this picket first. When *Vallejo* is clear, we're going on station outside the Strait. If we're lucky, we'll catch the mystery boat coming out. Any questions?'

'Yes, sir. Is there a designation for the new sub?'

'Alpha.'

'It's one hell of a sub, sir.'

'It is. No question about that.'

'We'll keep sharp ears, Skipper.'

'Very well. Get ready to take her out."

Sipping Alka-Seltzer, Sorensen was running circuit checks on the new sonars when Fogarty came into the sonar room and sat down. Fogarty switched on his screen and punched up the bottom scanners.

'How's your hangover, kid?'

'Awful.'

Sorensen punched him lightly on the shoulder. 'Relax, Fogarty, we're home. What's the depth under our keel?'

'Thirty-four feet.'

'All right. Sharpen your spurs, cowboy. Here we go.'

They heard Pisaro's voice come through the intercom. 'Attention all hands, attention all hands. Maneuvering stations, maneuvering stations. Prepare for slow speed.'

The reactor was hot, the steam lines were charged, the course was plotted, captain and lookouts were on the bridge. Overhead the night sky was cloudy, obscuring the heavens. Always obscure, the sea was calm.

On the pier opposite, the captain of *Vallejo* prepared to follow *Barracuda* into the bay. Springfield waved and ordered the bow and stern lines away.

'All ahead slow.'

With a shudder the ship moved away from the pier, passed outside the breakwaters and slipped by the Russian trawler. Rolling in the swell, Springfield turned his ship into the moderate sea and headed for deep water.

'Strike the colors,' he said. 'Clear the bridge. Rig for dive.'

No band played. No admiral made a speech. No crowd waved goodbye. *Barracuda* steamed out of Rota in the dead of night and slipped furtively into the Atlantic.

21

ARKANGEL

Ten miles outside Rota, Springfield gave the order to dive.

'All hands prepare for steep angles and deep submergence. Flood forward ballast tanks.'

'Flood forward ballast tanks, aye.'

'Stern planes down six degrees.'

'Stern planes down six degrees, aye.'

'Radio to control. Intercepting Soviet transmission.'

'Belay the dive. Belay the dive. Stern planes zero degrees.'

'Stern planes zero degrees, aye.'

'Control to radio. Where is the point of origin?'

'Radio to control. It's in a priority code from Cádiz.'

'Control to radio. Did you get it all?'

'Radio to control. Message complete. Shall we decode?'

'Very well, radio, decode the message. A little practice never hurts. If it's anything more than a report of our position, let me know right away.'

'Aye aye, skipper.'

'Stern planes down six degrees.'

In the torpedo room Lopez checked the serial numbers of the live torpedoes against the log and cheerfully dusted off the warheads. Once again fully armed, *Barracuda* carried twenty Mark 37 torpedoes with conventional high-explosive warheads, in both wire-guided and acoustic-homing modes, four Mark 45 torpedoes with quarter-kiloton tactical nuclear warheads and two chaff decoys designed to confound and mislead an enemy torpedo. Lopez hummed a happy tune.

The young torpedomen gathered around a plaque

newly installed over the firing console.

ZAPATA M.I.A

Johnson, the mate, was scrutinizing the new plating in the curved snout of the compartment. Patches of fresh gray paint still glistened in the bright light, but the welds were invisible.

'I dunno, Chief,' Johnson said. 'This was a damned fast job on these torpedo doors.'

'Those tiger team boys know their stuff,' Lopez replied. 'Regular hotshots.'

A thin wiry man, Johnson seemed to grow even thinner as his eyes narrowed. When he spoke his voice was like two stones scraping together.

'Lopez, the scuttlebutt is that a Russian sub is riding a picket line thirty miles out.'

'That's right. They do it all the time.'

'Yeah, but this one's waiting for us.'

Lopez watched the torpedomen rivet their eyes on the mate.

'No shit, Johnson. Why would they do that?'

'They want revenge because we sank their boat.'

'Bullshit. They're waiting for the boomer, *Vallejo*.'

'How do you know, Lopez? They want to even the score. Wouldn't you?'

'Johnson, you've got a big mouth. If I hear this from anybody else, I'll know where it came from. All of you, listen. The Russians are not interested in us. There's a shitload going on here that you people know nothing about because you don't need to know. Don't sweat it. When we get back to Norfolk, all of you will get thirty days' leave. Think about that and forget the Russians. After we chase these Ivans away, we're goin' home. This is my last cruise and I want it to be a good one.'

The torpedomen appeared unconvinced, but none spoke. Lopez swore under his breath, cursing Springfield for not informing the crew that the Russian sub never sank. He was still muttering when the exchange between the captain and the radio operator came over the command intercom. As the torpedomen listened, they grew visibly concerned. Lopez lit a cigar.

'It's just routine,' he said, 'and you all know it. The trawler in the bay reports all ship movements to the picket. They're waiting for *Vallejo*, not for us.'

A moment later the ship began to submerge. As the hull compressed, the torpedomen gasped at every creak and groan. Every eye was on the new torpedo doors. Every weld had been X-rayed twice, and the tiger team had taken the ship for a brief sea trial, including a dive to eight hundred feet, but Lopez had sealed the hatch and prepared for the worst. When Springfield adjusted the trim and leveled the ship, all systems were functioning normally. The torpedomen's cheer sounded like a sigh of relief.

'You happy, Johnson?'

'We ain't here to fight the ocean, Chief.'

Lopez frowned and shook his head. 'Open the hatch. It's stuffy in here. Johnson, I want circuit tests on all the on-board computers in the fish. I'm going up to have a word with the skipper.'

The captain reduced speed to a crawl and began to circle. In the sonar room Sorensen closed his eyes and pressed his earphones tight against his ears, listening for the picket. When the circle closed, he spoke into his headset, 'Sonar to control. Negative contact.'

'Very well, sonar. If she's here, we'll have to wait until she tips her hand.'

Slowly *Barracuda* swung back toward the bay where *Vallejo* was due to emerge in ninety minutes.

Sorensen took off his headset and turned on the speakers. Fogarty watched the blank screen, giving a little start each time the brief sound of a distant surface ship flashed a target across one sector of his screen.

'What's the matter, Fogarty? You jumpy?'

'God, Sorensen, we steamed out here like a battleship. If there's a Russian picket, she's locked onto us.'

'I guess you are jumpy. Relax. This Russian isn't going to pull any dirty tricks. It's our turn.'

Fogarty rubbed his eyes and stretched. 'It's been a long day and I could use some sleep. Instead, I get more Russians.'

Sorensen glanced at the chronometer in his console. 'You'll have plenty of time to sleep when this cruise is over. Meanwhile, get Davic and Willie Joe in here. We have to try out the new down-searching passive array they installed in Rota. And get us some coffee. Let's stay awake.'

In the galley Fogarty found Cakes sipping tea with Stanley. Fogarty asked, 'What's shakin', Cakes?'

'Lopez just came through with a big mad on. Said he was goin' to shut down the rumor mill. You heard any good rumors lately, Fogarty?'

Stanley spoke up. 'I hear the Russians put out a contract on *Barracuda*. They want us bad. No shit, just like the Mafia.'

Cakes shook his head. 'What, like the Mafia?'

'Sure, man. This Mafia is all KGB. Same in Japan, this Yakuza, they all KGB, too. The Italians are just fall guys, get all the bad rep.'

Cakes laughed. 'Why put a contract on us, Stanley?'

Stanley put a finger to his lips and whispered. 'We sink their ship, kill their sailors. They want an eye for a tooth.'

Fogarty poured two cups of coffee and balancing them precariously returned to the sonar room where he found Davic and Willie Joe crowded around Sorensen's console. Sorensen had activated the new sonars.

Barracuda was at four hundred feet. A school of tuna passed under the ship at a thousand feet, turning the screen into a swirl of green dots. Sorensen took his coffee from Fogarty, punched a button, and most of the fish disappeared. 'This sonar is computer-enhanced. It compensates for the thermals,' he said. 'Not completely, not perfectly, but it helps.'

'What's the point?' Davic said. 'No sub goes that deep anyway.'

Sorensen said, 'I dunno, Davic. You never can tell. Go ahead and sit down. You're going to have to learn how to use this.'

Davic and Willie Joe each took a turn, and Fogarty was taking his when the overhead speakers came to life.

'Attention all hands. This is the captain. I'm sure you all recall Admiral Netts' visit to our ship in Naples. Now that we have put to sea, I am authorized to read you a communication from him. It is dated yesterday and addressed to all the officers and men of *Barracuda*, SSN five nine three. The message is as follows:

GENTLEMEN, I WISH TO COMMEND ALL OF YOU FOR AN OUTSTANDING PERFORMANCE DURING THE EXERCISE THAT RESULTED IN YOUR UNFORTUNATE COLLISION WITH A SOVIET SUBMARINE. AS MANY OF YOU KNOW, IT WAS BELIEVED AT THE TIME THAT THE SOVIET SUBMARINE SANK. I WISH FOR ALL OF YOU TO KNOW THAT, TO THE BEST OF OUR KNOWLEDGE, THIS WAS *NOT* THE CASE. THE SOVIET SUBMARINE DID NOT SINK, ALTHOUGH WE DO NOT KNOW WHETHER OR NOT HER CREW SUFFERED CASUALTIES. THE SOVIET NAVY HAS NOT ACKNOWLEDGED THE COLLISION. IT IS PROBABLE THAT THE SUBMARINE STILL IS OPERATING IN THE MEDITERRANEAN, BUT EVENTUALLY SHE MUST PASS THROUGH THE STRAIT OF GIBRALTAR AND INTO THE ATLANTIC. ONCE *VALLEJO* IS CLEAR OF A REPORTED RUSSIAN PICKET AND FREE TO BEGIN HER PATROL IN THE MEDITERRANEAN, *BARRACUDA*'S ORDERS ARE TO REMAIN ON–STATION ON THE ATLANTIC SIDE OF THE STRAIT OF GIBRALTAR AND WAIT FOR THE SOVIET SUBMARINE

TO ATTEMPT A TRANSIT WESTBOUND. YOU CANNOT STOP HER, BUT YOU WILL FOLLOW HER AND YOU WILL HAVE THE ASSISTANCE OF THE SOSUS DEEP-SUBMERGENCE SONARS IN THE ATLANTIC. USE EVERY MEANS AT YOUR DISPOSAL TO COLLECT AS MUCH INFORMATION ABOUT HER AS POSSIBLE. GOOD LUCK AND GOOD HUNTING. SIGNED, EDWARD P. NETTS.

'That is all.'

Stunned silence greeted the captain's speech. In every compartment each sailor was thinking the same thing, but in the torpedo room, Johnson, the mate, said it aloud. 'Holy shit, the ship that hit us is still alive. Alive and kicking and maybe after our ass.'

A rumble of assent issued from the other torpedomen.

Lopez looked hard at Johnson. 'Cool down, Johnson. We're going to find her, follow her, harass *her* ass from here to Leningrad, but that's it. Got it?'

Johnson nodded sullenly, but there was no doubt what he was thinking . . . get them before they get us . . .

In the sonar room Springfield's announcement interrupted the test of the new passive array.

Davic blanched. 'She is not sunk? Sorensen, what does this mean?'

'It means it was hit and run.'

'But the implosions . . .'

'Faked.'

'You *knew* about this.'

'What if I did? Now you know about it too. And I'll give you all something to think about. This is a new class of ship that can go down to at least four thousand feet, maybe deeper.'

'Four thousand feet!' Davic shook his head. 'What is it? A bathyscaph?'

'No, it's an attack boat, class name Alpha. She's a noisy devil. We have her signature. We got it just before the collision.'

'If it's so noisy,' Willie Joe asked, 'why can't anybody find it?'

'That's a good question. My guess is she's been running slow and deep, maybe on electric power, but she has to come up to pass through the Strait. She got in because we weren't looking for her.'

'How many do they have?' Davic asked.

'So far, we only know about this one.'

'Where is it?' Davic persisted. 'Is it coming after us?'

'Why would the Russians come after us?' Sorensen snapped.

'Because we have discovered their new ship, of course.'

'I don't think they'll do that, Davic. All we know is that they can go deep. We don't know how. I don't think they'll do anything so stupid. I figure all they want is to get that sub out of the Med and on its way home.' At least I hope that's all, he added to himself. And then, as much to reassure himself as the others, he said, 'Jesus Christ, we're not at war with these people.'

'We should nuke their shipyards,' Davic muttered.

'The next time I see Admiral Netts I'll tell him you say so, Davic. In the meantime let's get on with this test. This toy just might help us detect a deep-running sub.'

Exactly on schedule they heard the thrashing sounds of a submarine.

'Sonar to control. Contact bearing zero seven two degrees, speed twelve knots, course two eight eight, range eight miles. It's *Vallejo*, skipper.'

'Very well, sonar. All hands man maneuvering stations.'

Davic and Willie Joe took their asbestos suits and went forward to their damage-control stations.

'Control to navigation, set course zero seven two degrees.'

'Navigation, aye. Course zero seven two degrees.'

'All ahead half.'

'All ahead half, aye.'

Barracuda accelerated, her course parallel to that of the big missile ship emerging from the bay. The two subs swept past each other a hundred yards apart, frothing the sea like a pod of whales, then turned and steamed past one another again. They crisscrossed back and forth twice more.

Fogarty was shaking his head. 'Why don't we just send the Russians a telegram telling them where we are?'

'That's the idea.'

'But that's nuts. Can't they tell us apart?'

'No. Our signatures are almost identical. We have the same reactor, same reduction gears and the same prop as *Vallejo*. He has to get within a mile to tell the difference. For the moment, we're bait. We want this Russkie to come after us so *Vallejo* can escape. That's the name of the game, to help *Vallejo* shake her tail. Hang on. You'll see. HMS *Valiant* is just inside the Strait of Gibraltar, and some heavy-duty British ASW forces. No Russian captain has ever tried to run that gauntlet except the damned Alpha. We still don't know exactly how that son of a bitch got in there, but he did, and maybe this one will try it, too, if we can't juke him into coming after us.'

'Maybe the picket is the Alpha.'

Sorensen let his face fold slowly into a smile. 'And if it is? Is that what's making you nervous?'

Fogarty shrugged, trying to maintain a casual air. 'He rammed us once. I'd rather not give him a second chance.'

'You know what I think, Fogarty? I think you're pissed off at the Russians for fucking your head around. I think your high-minded ideals are out the window. I think you're ready to make war.'

'I'm not crazy, Sorensen.'

'I hope not.'

'Except this is a war now, Sorensen . . . an electronic war of nerves . . .'

'It's Cowboys and Cossacks, Fogarty. It's just a game. Believe it.'

Did he?

Half an hour into the exercise, at a precisely timed moment, both subs suddenly went quiet and drifted, their momentum carrying them in opposite directions.

Sorensen's fingers stabbed at his keyboard. In the abrupt silence that followed the shutdown of machinery he heard a faint mechanical rumble. An instant later, it stopped.

'Got her. That's it. Sonar to control. Contact bearing two three zero degrees. No range, but he's not too close. He's holding still, skipper. No identification yet.'

In the control room the bearing of the Soviet sub appeared on the navigation and weapons screens.

'Bingo,' said Lt Hoek.

'Where is *Vallejo*?' Springfield asked.

'Right here, skipper,' Pisaro answered, pointing to a blip on his chart.

Vallejo was making a wide turn to the right, away from *Barracuda*, and descending to one thousand feet.

Springfield spoke quietly into his microphone. 'Attention all hands. Prepare for quiet running. Quiet in the boat.'

In the sonar room the air conditioner stopped whirring. Sorensen switched off the overhead speakers and said quietly to Fogarty. 'We're going to try to make this Ivan think we're *Vallejo*. We're going to go north. If the Russian takes the bait and follows us, then *Vallejo* is clear.'

'And if she doesn't?'

'We'll have to wait and see.'

Sorensen played the brief tape of the picket, backed it

211

up and ran it through a series of filters that corrected the distortion and removed extraneous sound. Then he ran it through the signature program.

'Okay, Fogarty, what is it?'

'I'm not sure.'

'Is it Soviet?'

'Yes.'

'How do you know? That might be Her Majesty's Ship *Valiant*.'

'He moved when we moved, and stopped when we stopped. He's hostile. He's up above four hundred feet trying to listen to us, trying to decide which one to follow, and his prop cavitated just so. November class, even the computer knows that. It's not the Alpha.'

November was flashing on the screen.

'Very good, Fogarty. See, there's nothing so mysterious about these Russians and their noisy boats. Let's play the tape again. It *could* be the Alpha simulating a November.'

While the tape was running, Sorensen stood up and looked at the chart of Soviet subs. He tapped the drawing of the November class attack subs. 'Wait a minute, wait a minute, I recognize that boat. That's our old friend *Arkangel*. Jesus, they must've pulled that thing out of mothballs. Wow, we don't need sonars to pick up *Arkangel*. All we need is a Geiger counter.'

'What do you mean?'

'I mean, that is a hot boat. She's so radioactive I bet she glows in the dark. I sure wouldn't want to be on it. If you can feel sorry for any Russian sailors, think about that. Those suckers get more radiation in a month than we'll get in five hundred years. Just for them to come this far from Murmansk and then have to go back means every one of those guys has been zapped . . . Sonar to control, we have a signature. November class, it's *Arkangel*.'

'Very well, sonar. Control to communications.'

'Communications, aye.'

'Prepare to send up a radio buoy on my order. Message as follows: Hostile contact thirty-six degrees thirty-four minutes north, six degrees forty-one minutes west. Priority one.'

'Priority one, aye.'

They waited in silence, drifting slowly in the slight current. *Vallejo* was three miles south, six hundred feet deeper, and also drifting. The Russian was eight miles west and making no noise.

Sorensen hunched over his console, quietly humming and beeping along with the faint sounds of marine life that came through his earphones. Every few minutes he looked casually at Fogarty, noting the exhaustion beginning to etch deep lines under the young sailor's eyes.

After two hours Sorensen was ready to have Fogarty relieved. He whispered, 'You're through, kid. Hit the sack.'

Fogarty shook his head.

'That's an order. Get outta—'

'Attention all hands. General quarters, general quarters. Man battle stations. Man battle stations. Prepare for maneuvering.'

On the screen they could see *Vallejo* already moving.

'Okay, Fogarty, I guess you're going to stay put. You awake?'

'Never felt better in my life.'

'Control to navigation. Set course three three one.'

'Course three three one, aye.'

'All ahead slow.'

'All ahead slow, aye.'

The ship shuddered once and began to move. *Vallejo* was heading south and *Barracuda* north. The Russian hesitated, then moved toward *Vallejo*.

'Son of a bitch,' Sorensen said. 'She didn't take the bait.

This stupid fucker is in for it now.'

In the control room Springfield called communications. 'Send up the buoy.'

'Communications to control. Buoy away.'

From the top of the sail a small float detached itself from the ship and rose to the surface. A small, powerful radio beamed an encoded, enciphered, compressed and scrambled message to Rota. Thirty seconds later an alarm sounded on the Spanish aircraft carrier *Dédalo*, and helicopter rotors started churning up the night.

'Control to weapons.'

'Weapons, aye.'

'Lieutenant, load tubes three and six. Conventional warheads, wire-guided.'

Hoek could sense his blood pressure rising. He began to sweat. 'Conventional warheads, wire-guided, aye. Weapons to torpedo room.'

'Torpedo room, aye.'

'Chief, load tubes three and six with Mark thirty-sevens, Mod three. This is not a drill. Repeat, this is not a drill.'

Lopez pushed a button on his console and a red light began to blink in the torpedo room. The torpedomen jumped to attention.

'Johnson,' Lopez yelled across the room, 'load three and six. This . . . is . . . not . . . a . . . drill.'

The torpedomen unbolted two torpedoes from their bays and slipped them into tubes. When the inner doors were locked, the targeting computer began feeding data to the on-board computers behind the warheads.

'Control to weapons, lock on sonar.'

'Lock on sonar, aye.'

Hoek punched buttons on his console, and the signature of the November was fed into the torpedoes.

'Flood tubes.'

'Flood tubes, aye.'

214

Fogarty listening to the sound of seawater rushing into the torpedo tubes, thinking the war of nerves was about to become something else . . . 'We can't sink her,' he muttered, 'she's in international waters—'

'There is no way in hell the skipper is going to let *Arkangel* or any other Russian sub put a tail on a boomer,' Sorensen cut him off. 'Not allowed. No way. We know it, and the captain of *Arkangel* knows it. An attack submarine like that one, *or* this one, is still considered the most destabilizing military unit you can get. Suppose the Russians had a tail on every one of our boomers. They could sink all of them all at once. Result – no second strike, no deterrence. So we don't even give them a chance. Just like they wouldn't give us a chance—'

'Control to sonar. Echo range, maximum power, target-seeking frequency. Let him have it, Ace.'

Sorensen nodded, and Fogarty took a deep breath. The Russian on his screen had become much more than a blip. In a fraction of a second Fogarty remembered his first sonar lashing, the collision and Sorensen's tape. He was ready. His onetime concern for the Russians was gone. They hadn't sunk anyway, just faked it . . . Deliberately he locked the echo ranger on the Russian sub, turned it up to maximum power, and pushed the button. The echo came back with a resounding ping.

In the control room every screen came alive with incoming data from the target. Each man was holding his breath. They were alone, no longer a so-called 'instrument of national policy' but a state unto themselves in the open sea. In a matter of moments they might be infamous, or dead, or worse.

This time the Russians did not hesitate. The single ping from the target-seeking sonar meant the next thing they would hear would be a torpedo. *Arkangel* made an abrupt ninety-degree turn and suddenly the sea erupted with the roar of her machinery. She cut loose all her raw power, and in a matter of seconds she was heading due west at thirty knots, leaving *Vallejo* free to begin her patrol unmolested.

It happened so fast . . . no one had time to feel relief.

Fogarty's heart was banging his ribs hard enough to make his chest hurt. He could almost taste the adrenaline.

Sorensen was standing up, his face an inch from the screen. 'That was close,' he mumbled. 'That was awfully goddamn close.'

He sat down, with unsteady fingers lit a cigarette, took a long deep drag.

'Is it over?' Fogarty said.

'Yeah, it's over.'

'She sure hauled ass, didn't she?'

'It was, you might say, the prudent thing to do, under the circumstances. She was outnumbered, after all.' He grinned. 'You sure put the fear of God into them, Fogarty. Shit, you put the fear of God into me.'

Fogarty stood up and took off his earphones. He was flexing his hand muscles, snapping his fingers over and over from a fist into a straight edge. Sorensen saw the glint still flickering in his eyes. Maybe he had pushed the kid too hard. Fogarty's lifetime of self-control could blow up. He was like a volcano waiting to erupt . . .

Fogarty said, 'I scared the shit out of myself.'

'Take it easy, it's over.'

Fogarty shook his head. 'They'll come back, they'll always come back, and we'll chase 'em and—'

'*And* as long as we win the battles, we won't have to win the war.'

'You've got a smart answer for everything, Sorensen. Well why don't we follow her, chase her all the way to the ice—?'

'Jesus, next you'll ask me why we didn't blow her to hell. What did you do, take an upside-down pill?'

'Listen, Sorensen, you told me to shape up and do my job. So I'm doing it. Okay?'

'Sure, okay, killer.' He smiled when he said it. 'But don't turn into another Davic. Stay cool.'

'There's nothing *cool* about a target-seeking sonar. It's about as hot as you can get.'

'It's sure as hot as I ever want to see it . . . Listen, Fogarty, you scared yourself, you scared me. It's okay, sooner or later we all scare ourselves down here. We all feel like killers sometimes. You just got to put the beast back in his cage and keep him there . . . You're tired, you've had a busy day. Go get yourself some sleep.'

Fogarty reached for the door, smiled. 'Okay, cowboy, I'll try to belay the beast. Whatever you say.'

The quartermaster's voice came through the speakers just then. 'Secure from general quarters. Secure from general quarters. Midrats are now being served in the mess. That is all.'

Fogarty opened the door to find Pisaro about to move in from the control room.

'Pardon me, sir,' Fogarty said as he stepped past.

Pisaro shut the door and sat down next to Sorensen.

'Pretty hairy, wouldn't you say, Ace?'

'I'd say, Commander.'

'Did the kid do okay?'

'He's not ready to stand watch by himself. He got pretty excited, but he'll get used to it, as much as anybody ever does. This kind of thing can make you grow old quick.'

'Look, Ace, are you positive that was *Arkangel*?'

'Yes, sir. That was old dirty Ivan, in person, polluting the Atlantic. Must be a new crew. They're probably using the old one to light up Leningrad.'

'No more dirty tricks?'

'I don't think so, sir. Not this time.'

'All right. We're going to run a rear guard for *Vallejo* until she clears the Strait. You're relieved. Davic is on his way in here. Go get yourself some grub.'

22

GIBRALTAR

The longitude and latitude readouts on the navigation console stopped flickering and came to a rest. *Barracuda* hovered six hundred feet deep at the edge of the Atlantic. Above her, dozens of ships passed through one of the busiest waterways of the world, oblivious to her presence.

'Attention all hands, this is the captain. We are now on-station four miles west of the Strait of Gibraltar. Our orders are to monitor all westbound submarine traffic passing from the Mediterranean into the Atlantic. We might be here quite some time waiting for the Alpha. When she emerges, our orders are to track her into the Atlantic. Be advised that three more Soviet subs have been detected in the eastern North Atlantic. One of them is certainly *Arkangel*. Twelve hours ago they were reported approximately three hundred miles northwest of Rota. Prepare for combat drills. That is all.'

Some two hundred surface ships and several submarines passed through the Strait of Gibraltar every day, giving the crew plenty of targets for combat drills. At the moment twelve ships were on the sonar screens, eleven surface ships and a Turkish Navy relic from World War Two making a submerged passage eastbound through the strait.

Willie Joe was practicing for his qualifying exam for first class. While Davic and Fogarty watched, Willie Joe sat with Sorensen, tracking the old sub. They listened to the fixed arrays on the bottom ping off the Turkish hull. The sub was so old the computer had no record of her signature. Always thorough, Sorensen recorded her machinery and logged it into the signature program.

Willie Joe tracked the sub through the Strait, a difficult task because of the heavy surface traffic. At the extreme edge of his range, when he was about to lose it, the new sonars picked up another submerged contact. A sub was hovering near the eastern entrance to the Strait.

Willie Joe shouted, 'Sweet Jesus, it's a nuke. It's the Russkie—' He immediately punched the button on the console that turned on his intercom mike, but before he could speak, Sorensen stabbed at the keyboard and turned it off.

'Take it easy, Willie Joe. Check it out. Listen up, she's not going anywhere. Get a positive ID.'

Sorensen snapped on the overhead speakers. The sub was extremely quiet, but they could hear the freshwater still operating. 'If that was a Russian boat, they'd shut everything down, including their still. Anyone, identification?'

Fogarty replied instantly, 'HMS *Valiant*.'

'Correct. One brownie point for Fogarty. The Brits are on the job.'

'Dirty limeys,' said Davic, the all all-American.

Sorensen didn't bother to respond. What was the point? Their newest ethnic was the biggest bigot. Apparently he thought it made him more American to hate all non-Americans. Fuck him.

For two days Springfield ran the crew through repeated combat drills, using the endless stream of ships as simulated targets. As the third day began, Willie Joe was spending his watch tracking a giant container ship and feeding data to Hoek, who was sitting at the weapons console. Hoek thought he'd died and gone to weapons officers' heaven. In two days he had pretended to sink more tonnage than was sunk in all the wars of the twentieth century.

The container ship passed a mile away, the cavitation

of her giant screws and the whoosh of her bow wave obliterating every other sound for ten minutes. Hoek simulated her destruction, sending tens of thousands of Japanese televisions to the bottom.

The rest of the sonar gang were in the mess for dinner. They filed through the chow line, carried trays of roast chicken, giblet gravy, peas and mashed potatoes to one of the tables and squeezed in next to the torpedomen.

It was a lively mess. There was talk of home, of wives, and girlfriends and kids.

'Say, Fogarty,' Sorensen said, 'you have any plans for the thirty days' liberty we have coming up?'

'I thought I'd go home and see my dad.'

'You ever been to Japan?' Sorensen asked.

'Nope.'

'Ever think about going?'

'Nope. Too far away.'

'Hey, man, you're in the navy. You can hop a military flight anywhere, any time. I went to Tokyo and came back in two and a half days, no sweat. This time there's no hurry. Look, I want a new tape recorder. Wanna go with me?'

'Maybe. I'll think about it.'

'Well, you do that. Think about having a little fun. A woman walking on your back with tiny feet is very nice.'

'For chrissake, Sorensen, don't talk about women right now.'

Sorensen's eyes twinkled. 'Tell me, Fogarty, was the Brit a good lay?'

'Yes, sure. But why get people upset with talk about women? By the way, don't you ever go home, Sorensen?'

'Home?'

'Oakland.'

'This is home, Fogarty. I don't recommend it for everybody. But it's got its advantages . . . Most of these guys have families, or did. They all have trouble with

221

their wives and more than half get divorced. They have kids they never see and parents who don't know where they are. Home for them is mostly some tract house on a Navy base with a busted washing machine and a Pontiac that burns oil. Their heads are full of Russians but they can't talk about it to anybody. It drives a man bananas. I tried it and it didn't work. Up there I'm a misfit. Down here I'm at least a well-adjusted misfit.'

That drew a few knowing guffaws from the table. Sorensen went on to describe a night on Tokyo's Ginza that began in a massage parlor and ended in a sushi bar where the chef carved raw fish into erotic figures. Tunafish penis, octopus vagina. Everyone listened except Davic, who propped a Russian magazine against a water tumbler and methodically turned the pages, leaving greasy fingerprints on the paper and ink on his fingers.

Watching Davic, Fogarty picked at his chicken and let his curiosity grow. When Sorensen finished his story, Fogarty asked, 'What are you reading, Davic?'

'An article on Czechoslovakia.'

'That's interesting. What's it say?'

Sorensen now turned to listen.

'It says, "The Soviet cultural attache left the Spring Art Festival in Prague in indignation after he learned that the colorful abstractions presented by several artists could be interpreted as anti-Soviet propaganda."'

'My goodness, how rude,' cried Sorensen.

Fogarty clapped his hand to his forehead.

'What happened to the artists?'

'It doesn't say. But for them, the gulag.'

'Hey, Davic,' Sorensen asked, 'aren't you from New York?'

'I've lived there, why?'

'You ever been to Greenwich Village?'

'No.'

'How about Coney Island? You been there?'

'No.'

'You ever go to Yankee Stadium?'

Davic shook his head. 'No, no sports for me. Except once I saw Moscow Dynamo play ice hockey at Madison Square Garden.'

'Who'd they play?'

'Some Canadians, I think.'

'Who won?'

'I don't know. They made me leave.'

'For what?'

'I threw firecrackers at the Russians. Bang bang bang. It was wonderful.'

'Davic, you're a fucking nut case, you know that?' Sorensen laughed. 'Did you get arrested?'

'Sure, I've been arrested many times. At the UN, at the Russian consulate, at the Russian embassy in Washington. The KGB used to follow me home.'

'How do you know it was the KGB? Why would they bother with you?'

'It was them.'

'Davic,' Sorensen said, 'I know a lot of guys who don't like the Russians, but you, it's like an obsession with you.'

Davic folded up his magazine and leaned across the table.

'Does that bother you, Sorensen?'

'Yes.'

'Why?'

'We're supposed to be professionals. Too much emotion can foul up our decisions. You should know that.'

'You want to know why I hate them?'

'Shoot.'

'They killed my father in Budapest in nineteen fifty-six when I was twelve years old.'

'During the Hungarian uprising, the Freedom Fighters and all that?'

'Yes.'

'Well, I can understand that. What happened?'

'Do you really want to know or do you want to make some kind of joke?'

'You've got the floor, Davic.' Sorensen felt a little sheepish.

No one had ever heard Davic say much more than a couple of words at a time – usually a bitch of some kind. When he saw that all hands at the table were listening, he decided he'd go ahead and tell his story. He also decided he'd kill anyone who made fun of him . . .

'My family had a small grocery store on the ground floor of a new apartment building. It was a newly rebuilt part of Budapest. When the Russian tanks entered the city my father tried to keep me inside, but I wanted to watch the tanks and hear the roar of the guns. I was across the street when the first tank came down our block.

'A gang of boys attacked the tank with rocks. One threw a Molotov cocktail that just smashed against the tread of the huge tank and shattered. The gunner fired one shot over their heads to frighten them away.

'The shell landed in the store. Two soldiers climbed out of the tank and went in. When they came out, their arms were full of groceries, as much as they could carry. A ham, cans of fruit, jars of honey, bags of rice. I watched them go back again and again. When the tank finally left I went into the store. They didn't even move my father's body out of the way. They just pushed a few broken crates over him to get at the rest . . .'

Davic said these last words in a quavering voice.

'That's real bad, Davic,' Sorensen said quietly. 'But even for that you can't want to nuke all the people in Moscow—'

'*Yes*,' Davic said, 'and Leningrad and Kiev and Odessa too. The Russians have been doing the same thing for hundreds of years. The communists are no different from the czars. They rule through fear. They treat the whole

224

world like my father's grocery store.'

Sorensen now had to fight to keep his own temper under control. 'You want revenge, Davic, an eye for an eye? That's how we got into this bind in the first place.'

'The Russians understand revenge.'

'Everybody understands revenge, you peabrain. Look what we did to the Japanese. We nuked 'em. Twice. But if we attack the Russians, that makes us just like the Japs when they sneak-bombed Pearl Harbor. Besides, when we bombed Hiroshima and Nagasaki, we saved millions of American lives. Or at least so they said. And remember, ethics and shit aside, they didn't have any atomic bombs to throw back at us. The Russians do.' Sorensen took a deep breath, sort of pleased with his lecture. He hoped it got through to Davic and any others aboard who thought like he did.

Davic shook his head violently. 'You're *wrong*, Sorensen. They are very patient. They will wait for their moment, and when it comes they will recognize it and they will strike. If they think they can win, they will launch. What's the matter with you, Sorensen? Are you blind? We sit and watch their power grow every day. More ships, more weapons, more men. Like this new Alpha. The only way to save ourselves is to stop them now . . .'

Davic sat back and looked around the mess. All conversation had ceased. Every sailor was looking at him.

Johnson, sitting at the far end of the table among the torpedomen, leaned over and said, 'Right on, Davic.'

Davic nodded and smiled. It was the first show of approval since he'd been aboard and it was heady stuff. Sorensen thought he caught a couple of more heads nod, torpedomen. Fogarty stood up and was about to walk out of the mess.

'Stay put, kid. Look the old monster in the eye. It's the best way to put it back in its cage. Besides, Davic is doing us a favor, helping some of the guys face their worst nightmares and maybe get rid of them.'

Pisaro, passing through the galley, had overheard some of the exchange, then pushed through the hatch.

'Attention!' Sorensen ordered.

Pisaro smiled and rubbed his hands over his scalp. 'Gentlemen, let's try to keep it cool. You too, Davic.'

'Yes, sir. Aye aye, sir.'

'World War Three hasn't started yet. Our job is to see that it doesn't,' and he left the mess, shaking his head.

In sonar Willie Joe was chatting over the intercom with Hoek. 'How many is that, Lieutenant?'

'Let's see. That makes one eight eight. That's hulls, not tonnage. The last one was a big one.'

'When's the next sub scheduled to come through?'

'We've got an Italian due in three hours.'

'Okay, I've got a tanker on the screen. Big sucker. Let's take it.'

'My treat,' said the lieutenant, and three minutes later enough hypothetical crude was spilled to pollute the Strait for a hundred years.

As the noise from the tanker faded away, a bright streak flashed across Willie Joe's screen. He blinked and rechecked the list of submarines scheduled to pass through the Strait. Through his earphones he heard distinct propulsion noises. An unscheduled submarine was approaching the Strait from the west at high speed.

'Do you see him, Lieutenant?'

'I do.'

'That's not our Italian.'

'Agreed.'

'Sonar to control, we have a contact. Bearing two five five, course one two one, speed three zero knots, range ten miles and closing.'

'Control to sonar. Do you have identification?'

'Sonar to control. Soviet November class. It's *Arkangel*.'

'Control to sonar, we have him on the repeater. Attention all hands. Attention all hands. General quarters, general quarters. Man battle stations, man battle stations. Control to radio, send up a buoy.'

In ten seconds the mess was empty. Sorensen and Fogarty were in the sonar room.

Willie Joe stood up. 'She's all yours, Ace.'

'Who is it?' Sorensen asked, sitting down.

'Who else? *Arkangel*,' said Willie Joe on his way out. 'If she's after *Vallejo*, she's three days late.'

As Sorensen sat down, a second streak appeared on the screen, diverging at a slight angle.

'Sonar to control, we have another contact. Same bearing, same course, same speed.'

Then a third streak appeared. The sound of the three subs together was as loud as Niagara Falls.

Sorensen had never heard anything like it. 'This is a wolfpack assault on the Strait,' he said to Fogarty. 'The Russians are storming into the Mediterranean like—'

'Like Cossacks?' Said with a straight face.

'Yeah. Sonar to control.'

'Sonar, this is the captain, we see her. Thank you. We see all of them.'

The Russians were following the eastbound NATO beacon through the Strait, the lead ship, *Arkangel*, directly astride it, the others following on either side.

Sorensen sat back in his chair, staring at the screen as the subs passed from right to left three miles south. The Russians blew through the Strait and into the Mediterranean in a remarkable display of arrogance and power.

Fogarty hunched over and watched his screen. 'If this were chess,' he said, 'I'd say this looks like a sacrifice.'

'Could be, Fogarty. Could be. But this ain't chess. It's boys playing with boats. I don't know what's worse, Davic or those maniacs.'

227

They heard *Valiant* start her turbines and take off in pursuit.

Springfield sent up a radio buoy and made his report. Thirty seconds after it was received in Rota, the alarm sounded in the helicopter hangar on the Spanish carrier, *Dédalo*. An instant later the message was relayed to Gibraltar, and British ASW helicopters were in the air.

The helicopters quickly outdistanced the Russian subs. At one hundred fifty miles per hour, six British choppers raced over the sea and dropped a cordon of sonar buoys in their path. The hydrophones, dangling two hundred feet below the buoys, easily picked up the loud sound of the three subs. *Arkangel* plowed right through. The helicopters leapfrogged ahead, dropped a second cordon, located *Odessa*, and dropped two-dozen sonic depth charges. Within the hour the antisubmarine forces of the Sixth Fleet, still in Naples and still smarting from the humiliation by *Barracuda*, were brought to bear on the noisy Russian subs.

Barracuda remained on station west of the Strait.

'I'm no Davic,' Fogarty said, 'but I don't see why we don't track them instead of just sitting here and letting the blood pressure build.'

'If this is a sacrifice, as you say,' Sorensen said, 'there's no reason to make it. These old Russian subs are so noisy they won't be able to hide. The Brits will take care of tracking them, seeing they behave. We don't give a shit about *Arkangel* or these other boats. We want the Alpha, and we're going to sit here until she comes through.'

23

FIFTY KNOTS

The interior of *Potemkin* smelled like Lubyanka prison. Running slow and quiet since the collision, the freshwater still had been shut down so no one could shave or bathe. Despite snorkeling twice and flushing out the carbon dioxide, the problem with the scrubbers had resulted in an epidemic of headaches.

Potemkin now had been at sea eighty-four days, the longest submerged cruise in Soviet naval history. The men looked like shaggy, grimy albinos. Twelve days of running slow and deep, breathing poisoned air, had rubbed them raw. In the engineering compartment the reactor operators were decimated by virulent colds. Federov knew that their resistance to infection was crumbling because they were suffering from the first symptoms of radiation sickness. Only Federov's outward calm kept them under control.

Weeks before, when *Potemkin* had passed eastbound through the Strait, Federov had taken advantage of the tide and current conditions, plus the fortuitous passing of a huge tanker, and drifted in silence over the bottom-mounted sonars and past the British picket sub.

No such combination of circumstances would aid *Potemkin*'s escape into the Atlantic. The predominant currents were against her, and she would have to use her engines in the Strait. Any bottom sonars were certain to pick up her passage. Operators on shore would alert the ASW forces, and picket subs at either end of the Strait would tail her into the Atlantic.

Before *Potemkin* sailed from Murmansk, Admiral Gorshkov had foreseen the difficulty of *Potemkin*'s exit from the Mediterranean and had ordered the three subs, *Murmansk*, *Odessa* and *Arkangel*, to pass through the Strait at a prearranged time as a diversion to draw off the pickets. But who knew if it would work?

From time to time the ship's surgeon changed Kurnachov's bandage and emptied his chamber pot. Federov brought him meals, but no one spoke to him. Even in his own mind Kurnachov had become a nonperson. When he looked in the mirror, he saw a dead man.

The ship moved slowly, making wide turns and stopping frequently. Twice it seemed to rise almost to the surface, remain there for half an hour, then slide back down to a great depth. Each time the air improved, at least for a while. Noise was kept to a minimum. Kurnachov assumed that they were on course for Gibraltar and home.

After ten or eleven days – Kurnachov wasn't sure of the exact number – the ship halted and remained stationary for several hours.

When Federov brought him a meal he asked, 'Where are we?'

Federov told him, 'Thirty kilometers east of Gibraltar.'

'Are we waiting for *Arkangel* and the others?'

'Yes.'

Federov reached for the door.

'Please,' Kurnachov said. 'Don't go. Give me a moment. The silence is torture.'

Federov set down the tray and turned cold eyes on his prisoner. Listless, Kurnachov sat on his bunk and looked away. Federov took a chair.

'All right, what do you want to know?'

'After the collision, what happened to the American submarine?'

'You failed to sink it, Kurnachov. You only succeeded in making them angry.'

'How did we escape? Are the Americans searching for us?'

'We fired a decoy, Acoustical Reproduction Device Number Five, which confused them. At first, they were convinced we sank. However, I don't believe their conviction will remain firm. They're searching for a wreck that isn't there.'

There was a lingering silence. Finally Kurnachov said, 'Must I remain here alone?'

'Several men were injured during the collision and Zadecki died. If I let you out, the crew will attack you.'

'That might be preferable to what's waiting for me . . .'

After Federov left, Kurnachov prolonged his meal as if it were his last. Lifelong devotion to the party could not help him now. There would be a trial; then he would be shot. No military firing squad, no ceremony. In a cellar under Lubyanka, one bullet would be fired into the back of his head.

Kurnachov understood. He was not navy; he was Party.

On Popov's screen three streaks radiated from the west.

'Captain, I have a contact. They're right on schedule. *Murmansk*, *Odessa* and *Arkangel*.'

The trio of Soviet submarines roared past, followed at close quarters by *Valiant*.

'One more and we're home free,' said Alexis, the engineer who was now first officer.

For an hour they waited for the second NATO picket to come through, but the submarine west of the Strait remained on station. When it never arrived, Federov knew the gambit to draw off the subs guarding the Strait had failed.

'Take us up,' ordered Federov, 'we have to go through. We'll die here. Depth two hundred meters, all ahead slow.'

231

'All ahead slow,' Alexis repeated the order. 'Depth two hundred meters.'

For the first time since the collision, *Potemkin*'s great engines rumbled to life. Without Acoustical Reproduction Device Number Seven, the Alpha became the noisiest submarine in the sea.

The bottom sonars in the Strait immediately recorded her presence. British operators on Gibraltar heard the sub, but all their ASW forces were deployed to the east, chasing the three Russian decoys.

Halfway through the Strait Popov heard the first ping of active sonar. Others followed in rapid succession and seemed to come from all directions at once.

'They've locked onto us, Captain.'

'Make revolutions for thirty knots,' ordered Federov. 'There's no point in being coy.'

In the engine room the crewmen put cotton balls into their ears. The steam pumps began to hammer and the turbine wailed like a jet engine.

In the turbulent waters of the Strait, *Potemkin* pitched and bounced like a surface ship. When she reached thirty knots, Federov shouted above the racket, 'Increase speed. Thirty-five knots.'

Through the Strait, opposite the Bay of Tangiers, Federov ordered, 'Make revolutions for full speed. Fifty knots. Let him chase us all the way to the Azores.'

24

THE ART OF WAR

To Sorensen four miles away, *Potemkin* sounded like a tank division smashing through a forest. Alone, it was almost as noisy as the three subs that had passed through in the other direction.

'Listen up, Fogarty. Tell me what you hear.'

'An earthquake? World War Two and a half?'

'You're such a clever boy . . . Is this *Arkangel* coming back?'

Fogarty took off his headset and turned on the overhead speakers.

'No more games, Sorensen. It's the Alpha.'

'*Right*. Sonar to control, contact bearing zero niner two degrees, range seven five zero zero yards, course two seven zero, speed four four knots.'

'Control to sonar, say speed again.'

'Speed, four four knots, sir, and increasing. Four seven, four niner, five zero knots. Holding steady at *five zero knots*.'

'Jesus,' said Pisaro. 'I should have joined the Air Force. We need afterburners to catch that thing.'

'Control to sonar. Sorensen, do you have identification?'

'Yes, sir. It's our boy.'

Pisaro said, 'Well, what are we waiting for?'

'Quartermaster, run sonar through the intercom.'

'Aye aye, sir.'

A moment later every sailor on *Barracuda* could hear the roar of *Potemkin*.

'Attention all hands, this is the captain. Gentlemen, you all hear the sound of a submarine operating in close proximity to us. Listen good. That's the same submarine that collided with us. As you know, our orders are to track her, record every sound she makes and, if possible, surprise her on the surface and take her pretty picture. We're going to be up against subs like this one for the next twenty years, we need to know everything about her. She's fast, but we will have assistance from the SOSUS deep-submergence detection system which we tested during our transit from Norfolk to Gibraltar. That is all.'

Springfield saw Hoek, looking like some fat bird of prey, poised over his weapons console, trying without success to track the fast-moving target. 'Skipper,' he said, 'she's moving so fast the only way we could stop her would be to lay down a pattern of nukes in her path—'

'Secure intercom,' ordered the captain. 'Relax, Lieutenant. We're not going to nuke anyone, especially not in the Strait.'

As *Potemkin* swept across *Barracuda*'s bow, heading due west into the Atlantic, the roar of her machinery was audible directly through the hull without benefit of hydrophones.

'Control to engineering.'

'Engineering, aye.'

'Chief, give me one hundred percent. Let her rip. All ahead flank, course two seven zero. Right full rudder.

Barracuda nosed into *Potemkin*'s wake and accelerated after the speeding Russian. By the time *Barracuda* reached her flank speed of forty-seven knots, the distance between the subs had increased to nine miles.

At flank speed, every system in the ship was strained to the limit. In the engineering spaces the heat from the steam lines caused the temperature to rise to ninety degrees, but the sweating nucs hardly noticed until perspiration dropped onto their instruments. Stripped to the waist, Chief Wong methodically inspected very inch of every pipe, tested every gauge, checked every calculation to coax every ounce of power from the turbines. *Potemkin* still continued to pull away.

Hour after hour, the Alpha struck farther into the Atlantic, deepening the frustration of her pursuers. Sorensen stood in front of his console, arms folded, nodding as if in a trance. On the screen the Russian remained a solid blip in the west, a sun that refused to set. Finally he said, as much to himself as to Fogarty, 'I used to have bad dreams about this sub. I used to wake up with the sound of her engines clanging in my ears. The mystery sub. Well, it ain't a mystery anymore. This nightmare is reality.'

'You scared, Ace?'

'You're damned right. This Alpha is fast and goes deep, but maybe worst of all is if the Russians believe in it so much they'll think they can get over on us, and that it's worth anything to keep its secrets from us. That makes them doubly dangerous—'

'Control to sonar.'

Fogarty answered, 'Sonar, aye.'

'You're going to have some visitors in there, boys.'

One by one, the officers and chiefs found excuses to step inside the sonar room to listen. Chief Wong came up from engineering and sat for ten minutes with his chin in his hands, frowning. Finally he took off his earphones and said, 'I don't hear reduction gears.'

'That's right, Chief,' Sorensen said, nodding. 'I think she's got a direct electric drive. Very noisy turbogenerators and an unusual reactor. I don't hear ordinary high-pressure water pumps. I bet it's metal-cooled.'

'That's a strange boat, Sorensen.'

'She sure is. All power, no finesse but a bundle of acoustic tricks. I've got a question for you, Wong. How long can we run at flank speed before we shake something loose?'

'Forever.'

'C'mon.'

'Longer than any Russkie I ever heard of. 'Course, I never heard of these guys.'

When Lopez sat down to take his turn at the console, he waved away the earphones and turned on the speakers.

'It sounds weird, like there's an echo,' he said.

'That's because she's pulling away,' Sorensen told him.

'She's going how fast?'

'Fifty point three knots.'

'Holy Madonna, it'll outrun a Mark thirty-seven. You know what, Ace? I think this is a good time to retire. I've heard enough.'

As *Potemkin* raced ahead, steadily increasing her lead, the solid blip on *Barracuda*'s screens began to deteriorate. The thunder that came through the hydrophones started to fade.

After four hours, two hundred miles into the Atlantic, *Potemkin* began to descend. Without decreasing speed she went down to fifteen hundred feet, putting a thermal layer between herself and *Barracuda*.

'Sonar to control, contact is growing indistinct. He's going down, recommend descent to eight hundred feet.'

'Very well, sonar, if you think it'll help. Stern planes down four degrees. Take us down to eight hundred feet.'

Barracuda nosed over and descended another four hundred feet. Sorensen pursed his lips and watched his screen. When the ship leveled off, the resolution of the contact had not improved. 'Damn,' he swore. 'We're going to lose her.'

Fogarty asked, 'How can we lose her if she's making this much noise?'

'She's twenty-one miles ahead of us now, and we're getting echoes, reverberations and a deteriorating signal.

We may hear machinery noises, but we won't know exactly where the sounds are coming from. She can fire a decoy, go silent, go deep. If she continues at fifty knots she'll be completely out of range in four or five hours and we won't hear a damned thing except ourselves.'

'But what about the bottom sonars?'

Sorensen nodded. 'They'll track her all right, but they can only locate her within fifty miles. They can get an exact fix only when she passes over one of the cables.'

'She has to stop and clear baffles, doesn't she?'

'Why?'

'For safety.'

'Not a chance. She's hell-bent on running away from us. She isn't going to stop for anything, and I guess neither are we until we lose her. Sooner or later that Russian captain is going to learn that we are the boat he hit, and that, my friend, is going to put him right on the edge, if he isn't there already. Maybe we should let him take his Maserati submarine back to Murmansk. Where's Davic? He's supposed to be in here. I want to hit the beach.'

'You're not giving up, are you, Ace?'

Sorensen snapped his sunglasses over his eyes. 'What do *you* think we should do if we catch up with the son of a bitch? Make him say he's sorry?'

Potemkin continued west for another seven hours, during which time the distance between the two subs stretched to over forty miles. Davic stood his watch, eyes glued to the screen, then turned over the console to Willie Joe. During both watches enlisted men filed into the sonar room to listen to the Russian sub. The roar gradually deteriorated into a faint buzz, then an erratic hum. Finally, eleven hours and fifteen minutes after *Potemkin* broke into the Atlantic, she disappeared from the screens.

'Sonar to control,' said Willie Joe. 'She's gone.'

'Control to sonar. Very well. Prepare for slow speed.

Prepare to clear baffles. Prepare to send up a buoy.'

'Aye aye.'

Asleep in his bunk, Sorensen was having a nightmare. In a basin the size of a house, a pinhead of metal glowed blue in the dark. The basin was a giant aquarium. People stood outside, watching the bright blue speck as it shot off torpedoes and rockets. With a roar the water turned to fire, exploded the glass and showered the spectators with shards of uranium. In a thousand pieces the sub settled to the bottom and lobsters began to eat the debris. Just as one of the spindly monsters stepped on his face, he sensed the *Barracuda*'s abrupt change of speed and woke up.

His sweat felt like burning seawater. He pushed open the curtain and leaned into the passageway. On the opposite tier Fogarty was reading *The Art of War*, by Sun Tzu.

'She's gone?' Sorensen said.

Fogarty looked up for a moment, nodded, then read aloud, 'All warfare is based on deception. When near, make it appear that you are far away; when far away, that you are near. Pretend inferiority and encourage your enemy's arrogance.'

'Well, where'd you get that?'

'It was in the library. It's been around for a couple of thousand years.'

'That's a lot of blood in the sea. Seems like we haven't learned too much. All you have to do is get mad, and be willing. Even you, Fogarty. The Russians got under your skin, didn't they?'

'It wasn't them, it was you.'

'Me?'

'Yeah, you and your little tape machine.'

Barracuda slowly circled, cleared baffles and sent up a radio buoy. Springfield transmitted a position report and the last known location of *Potemkin*. A moment later Norfolk flashed a reply that Springfield and Pisaro took into the captain's cabin to decode.

The bottom sonars had successfully tracked both subs into the Atlantic. The Alpha was still heading due west at great speed, generating enough noise to make her easy to track as she passed over the sonar-seeded cables that radiated out from the Azores.

Springfield spread out a chart of the North Atlantic. A chain of marine mountains, the mid-Atlantic ridge, ran north and south, splitting the ocean in half. A deep-running submarine could hide indefinitely among the mountain peaks, and travel north and south through the deep valleys.

'This Russian skipper is heading straight for the ridge,' Pisaro said. 'He'll go north, try to break through the Iceland gap and go under the ice.'

'I'm not so sure, Leo. If he were heading for the ice pack he'd already be making a northerly course. There's no way he could have escaped the collision with no damage at all. He's got to be hurt. He can't go under the ice. Plus he's been at sea a long time. A normal cruise for them is twenty-one days tops. Their sailors get too much radiation if they stay out any longer. The Soviets have never built a boat that's properly shielded. My guess is that he has a radiation problem. Maybe he's got sailors with radiation sickness. They're probably tired, anemic, less than alert. He needs a new crew.'

Springfield tapped the chart in the region of the Caribbean. 'He isn't going north, Leo. He's going south. He's trying to make it to Cuba.'

Pisaro shook his head. 'Into their FBM base? They think we don't know about that. They have no idea that Havana harbor, the Caribbean and half the Atlantic Ocean are seeded with bottom sonars. He wouldn't lead us into it.'

'I agree. But he might try to rendezvous at sea with their missile boat coming out of the Puerto Rican trench. A year ago, when we discovered what they were doing down there, we were looking at another Cuban missile crisis. That FBM base is a clear violation of the agreement. It could have meant war. Netts claimed it was best to let them be, track their FBM every minute and keep them under the gun. If worst came to worst, we *could* blow it out of the water. Point is, if we throw it up in their faces, we've got another Cuban missile crisis on our hands.'

'Christ,' Pisaro said. 'Do you really think they would pull a missile sub off-station for a rendezvous?'

'This Alpha apparently means a great deal to them, and she's in trouble. They think they can bring the FBM out quietly, rendezvous with the Alpha and slip right back into the Puerto Rican trench. If we catch them red-handed, photograph the FBM on the surface and then follow it, it will never be able to return to the Caribbean. This way, we'll get them out of the Caribbean for good without provoking a crisis. The price will be that we'll have to reveal to them the new system in the Atlantic. Still, once they realize we can track them anywhere, maybe they'll pull back into their home waters. Whatever, I believe this Alpha is going to lead us right to the big boy. That's some bonus.'

25

FBM *DHERZINSKI*

Aboard *Potemkin* Federov stood before the reactor displays in the engineering room, his face impassive, his ears plugged with cotton balls. The sailors wore no radiation badges, but Federov had managed to acquire a US Navy dosimeter that he kept secret even from his friend Alexis. It verified what he knew already: he was expendable. He was condemned as surely as Kurnachov. He found the thought strangely comforting. Knowing was better than not knowing. The radiation would kill him slowly. It could take years, but eventually he would develop leukemia. A genuine patriot, Federov considered the loss of his life a proper sacrifice, but meaningful only if he returned his ship safely home. *Potemkin* was everything – the future of the Soviet Navy.

He moved to the atmosphere displays. The carbon dioxide concentration was an uncomfortable three-and-a-half percent. Half the crew had headaches miserably aggravated by the rattle and vibration of the racing turbines. Comfort was sacrificed to demonstrate *Potemkin*'s durability to the Americans.

Federov supposed eventually the US Navy would discover *Potemkin*'s titanium hull. Presumably *Potemkin*'s performance would force them to renew their efforts to build a titanium sub, a project they seemed to have postponed. But at least in this one his country had the lead. *Potemkin* mustn't be further exposed to them.

In the previous few years the Americans had focused on shielding their sailors from radiation, and making their boats quiet. It was a question of priorities, and who knew which was right? He did know that without Acoustical

Reproduction Device Number Seven *Potemkin* was too noisy. All the essential machinery – turbine, electric motor, steam condenser, saltwater pump and coolant pumps for her lead-bismuth reactor – was hard-bolted to the decks, and the decks themselves hard-bolted to the pressure hull without benefit of shock absorbers or acoustic insulation. Everything vibrated, turning the hull of *Potemkin* into a massive sonic beacon.

Federov was reasonably certain the American picket sub had followed him into the Atlantic, but for how long and how far he didn't know. After eight hours he decided it was safe to change course. *Potemkin* made a wide turn to the left and continued southeast another three hours. Finally he ordered, 'All stop.'

In the abrupt silence the men heard their own labored breathing.

'Clear baffles. We're going to snorkel.'

Potemkin made a full circle. 'No contact, Captain,' said Popov. 'We're clear.'

'Take us up, Alexis. Snorkel depth.'

For thirty minutes the snorkel projected above the water. The carbon dioxide-rich atmosphere inside the ship was pumped out and replaced with fresh ocean air. While the ventilation was taking place, Federov remained in his cabin with Alexis and studied charts of the Atlantic.

'We must have carbon dioxide filters if we are to make it to Murmansk,' he said. 'Once under the icepack we can't snorkel. *Potemkin* is many things, but an icebreaker she is not. The sail is not sufficiently hardened to crack through.'

'Who can help us? *Deflektor*?' Alexis named the surveillance ship stationed in the Bay of Cádiz.

'No. They don't carry stores for us, and even if they did, the Americans would follow her if she pulled off-station.'

'But we have no tenders in the Atlantic.'

'I know. We have better than a tender. As first officer you are entitled to learn a few secrets, my friend.'

Federov unlocked his safe and removed a sealed set of documents that contained the disposition of all Soviet Navy vessels throughout the world. He broke the seal, unfolded a chart of the Caribbean and put his thumb on Cuba.

'We can't go *there*—'

'You're right, but *Dherzinski* is operating from there, and he can meet us here, where the Americans least expect it.'

Federov moved his thumb to a spot five hundred miles southwest of the Azores.

Two thousand miles west, *Dherzinski*, a Soviet fleet ballistic missile submarine of the Hotel class, hunkered under a half mile of water in the Puerto Rican trench, the deepest part of the Caribbean. Inside her enlongated sail three huge Serb missiles, armed with hydrogen warheads, were aimed at Washington D.C., Norfolk, Virginia, and Charleston, South Carolina.

Hovering in silence in the Puerto Rican trench was not exciting. The sub drifted slightly in the current, requiring the constant attention of the junior officers to keep her on-station and thereby target her missiles accurately.

On this occasion Captain First Rank Felix Andreivitch Olonov had enjoyed nineteen days of a successful patrol without incident. A chess tournament engrossed the crew. In the engine room the engineers were constructing a model two meters long of the czarist battleship *Potemkin* at the moment of her famous mutiny in 1917. Detailed with czarist officers hanging from the rigging, maggots in the food and the blood of revolution, the model was nearing completion.

Olonov took no interest in the toy boat. Closer to his heart, First Officer Piznoshov had revealed a craving for

243

English spy novels, of which Olonov had a plentiful store. Occupied with the heroics of George Smiley, James Bond and Sidney Reilly, the commanders of *Dherzinski* scarcely gave a thought to the three missiles in the sail aimed at America, eight hundred miles northwest, or to the Americans themselves.

Dherzinski's presence so close to the American mainland and her supply base in Cuba were among the most carefully guarded secrets in the Soviet Navy, second only to the existence of *Potemkin*. For a year *Dherzinski* had operated regular twenty-one-day patrols out of Havana, moving in and out of the harbor by steaming directly under Soviet cargo vessels. The huge sub, 328 feet long, never surfaced, and the satellites which frequently passed over Cuba never photographed her. Submerged in the harbor, moored under a Soviet freighter with a false bottom, she took aboard supplies and new crewmen via a submersible elevator that clamped over her forward hatch. The sailors never went into Havana. When they left the ship, they were taken directly to an airstrip and flown to the Soviet Union.

Olonov had seen neither the sun nor the stars in over a year. Seventeen times, by his count, he had piloted his ship into the harbor, stopped under the freighter and watched his crewmen go through the hatch and into the watertight elevator. The lift went up, paused, then returned full of strangers, and *Dherzinski* went back on patrol.

Olonov was in his cabin reading *The Spy Who Came in from the Cold* when the nervous voice of the senior radio operator called him to the radio room.

Annoyed, Olonov demanded, 'What is it?'

'A very low frequency message is arriving from Leningrad.'

'Which code?'

'Priority one-time, book three.'

Olonov blinked and tried to swallow. His throat was dry. The code was the one to be used in the event of war. Only he or the first officer could decode the message. Olonov locked himself in his cabin and rendered the transmission into Russian.

OLONOV: DHERZINSKI: RENDEZVOUS ON SURFACE 52 WEST 33 NORTH. PLUS 36 HOURS. SONIC CODE 2. SUPPLY LITHIUM HYDROXIDE FILTERS FOR CO_2 SCRUBBER M7. TAKE EIGHT CASUALTIES. SUPPLY EIGHT REACTOR TECHNICIANS. GORSCHKOV.

Olonov's first reaction was relief. The message was not an order to launch missiles, but it was almost as bad. He summoned Piznoshov.

'A rendezvous on the surface? With one of our subs?' said the first officer.

'We're not going to rendezvous with *Nautilus*.'

'You can't be serious,' Piznoshov said vehemently. 'Gorshkov himself has ordered *Dherzinski* to surface? It's crazy.'

'I know,' Olonov said. 'Obviously the scrubber failed on this ship, and they have a reactor problem. It's happened before.'

'Yes, but Gorshkov has never pulled a missile sub off-station. Never. Right now *Dherzinski* is the most important ship in the Soviet Navy—'

'Perhaps not . . .'

Olonov was not officially aware of *Potemkin*'s existence, but he was a man of long experience, with many friends, and he had heard rumors of a titanium-hulled attack sub. This was not the kind of information he wished to share with a political officer.

'If the scrubber on this mysterious submarine has failed, why doesn't he simply snorkel back to Murmansk? Why compromise *Dherzinski*?' Piznoshov made an obscene gesture indicating what he thought Gorshkov should be doing with himself.

'Ours is not to reason why, Comrade First Officer, but I have a rather good idea of what this is all about. And there is no question we have an appointment thirty-five hours and twenty minutes from now. Prepare to make way.'

26

ZAPATA

Twenty-two hours had passed since contact was lost with *Potemkin*. *Barracuda* had continued southwest at full speed, stopping frequently to clear baffles, and now was one hundred miles south of the Azores.

'Prepare for all stop. We're going to transmit a position report.'

'Aye aye, sir.'

'Control to engineering, all stop.'

A moment later the roar of *Barracuda*'s propulsion plant slackened, and the ship rocked in its own turbulence.

'Control to sonar. Clear baffles.'

'Sonar to control. Clearing baffles, aye.'

Barracuda circled and Sorensen echo-ranged three hundred sixty degrees.

'Sonar to control. All clear.'

'Very well, sonar. Radio depth. Take us up, Leo.'

Above on the surface it was seven minutes after midnight, May 21. A new year greeted the ancient sky whose stars gleamed like pearls above the clean ocean air. To the west, America tossed and turned in troubled sleep. Much farther west, in southeast Asia, soldiers died in the noonday sun. To the east in the Soviet Union tank battalions prepared for the invasion of Czechoslovakia, scheduled for later in the summer. Much farther east, Red Guards burned books in the Great Square of Peking.

They were far into the Atlantic now, alone in the great ocean. Sorensen heard no ships, no whales, no sign of life. Alone. Fogarty was in the control room, learning from Hoek how to track a target on the weapons console.

Sorensen felt weary. He had sat through three consecutive watches and was an hour into a fourth, obstinately refusing to relinquish the console to less experienced hands while there was a possibility of *Barracuda* chancing on the Alpha. The cards, he thought, were in *Barracuda*'s favor. The North Atlantic was the US Navy's *mare nostrum*. They could track the Alpha just about all the way to Murmansk if they had to. Of course the closer they came to Mother Russia, the greater the risk. Not that the tracking itself wasn't a risk. But that was the order – track, observe, photograph. Aye aye, sir.

A moment later *Barracuda*'s radio antenna broke the surface and a message flashed the ship's position to Norfolk. A radio operator in Virginia immediately sent a reply. Springfield and Pisaro decoded the message in the captain's cabin.

COMSUBLANT: BARRACUDA SSN 593: SOVIET ALPHA CLASS SSN DETECTED BY SOSUS GMT 2200 HRS 052068 LAT LONG 30 W 56 N. COURSE TWO THREE ZERO. SPEED UNKNOWN. SPECTRO-GRAPHIC ANALYSIS OF BARRACUDA HULL FRAGMENTS SHOW TRACES OF TITANIUM. SOVIET FBM HOTEL CLASS DHERZINSKI DETECTED BY SOSUS GMT 2330 HOURS 052068 LAT 27 N LONG 53 W. SPEED THREE ZERO KNOTS, COURSE ZERO FIVE ZERO. PROCEED ON COURSE TWO THREE ZERO, INTERCEPT, PHOTOGRAPH, TRACK DHERZINSKI. IF SHE RETURNS TO CUBAN WATERS, NOTIFY COMSUBLANT IMMEDIATELY. NETTS

'We hit the bull's-eye! *Dherzinski*'s coming right at us. She must be going for a rendezvous with the Alpha. We're going to catch up with them both.'

Pisaro sounded more excited than any time Springfield could remember. He tried to sound especially calm as he said, 'Call the officers into the war room. We need to brief everyone. Meanwhile, set course two three zero. All ahead full. Let's not waste time.'

Lt Hoek went directly from the officers' briefing to the sonar room, where he found Sorensen mesmerized by the blank screen.

'You trying to set a world record for consecutive watches, Ace? You've been in here for thirteen hours.'

'What's the word from Norfolk, Lieutenant?'

'They picked up the Alpha three hours ago. She was two hundred twelve miles southwest of our present position.'

'That it?'

'No. They found traces of titanium in the hull sections cut out of the bow.'

'Titanium? Son of a bitch. That explains how they go so deep and how they survived the collision. Titanium, Jesus, that stuff is unbelievably hard. What else, Lieutenant?'

'They're tracking *Dherzinski*. She's coming this way.'

'*Dherzinski*? That's the Cuban boat. We put a tail on her for a couple of days last year. Lord, talk about out of the frying pan into the fire. Do you know what this means, Lieutenant?'

'Your goddamn right I know what it means.'

'The Russians aren't going to like this.'

'Well, tough shit for them. They've been throwing their weight around, it's time we get them to back down . . . Look, Ace, you're beat. Willie Joe is on his way in. Take a break, get outta here.'

'Aye aye, sir.'

'By the way, I heard a rumor about a new batch of plutonium wine back in engineering.'

'No shit? Is it any good?'

'Is what any good? I didn't say anything.'

Sorensen stood up, stretched, went out and shut the door and paused in the control room to watch Fogarty practice on the weapons console. In the center of the CRT a pulsing red blip simulated a target, a Soviet FBM. Red speckles danced in Fogarty's eyes as he jabbed a finger at his keyboard.

The red blip disappeared. 'Very good, Fogarty. Only, that time we nuked ourselves too. That gets you a posthumous Navy Cross and your kid can go to the Naval Academy.'

Unaware that Sorensen had been observing him, Fogarty swiveled around in his seat. 'If we ever get the order . . . well, there won't be a Naval Academy.'

'So, what are we now, kid? Kamikazes?'

'It's just the simulator, Sorensen. Like you like to say, cool it.'

'Yeah, right. In a few hours you won't need a simulator. You're going to have a real boomer on the screen. You'd better pull all the Soviet FBM tapes. You'll like the *Dherzinski* tape. I made it last year.'

Sorensen shuffled through the passageways to the engineroom, where Chief Wong gave him a Dixie cup of distilled grapefruit juice.

'Happy days, Chief. Thanks.'

'Don't mention it.'

Sorensen drained the cup and Wong gave him another. 'How come you're so jazzed on this Alpha, Sorensen? It ain't nothin' but another boat.'

'Maybe you're right, Chief. I hope you're right.'

'I mean, this is for officers, not for us. I know you're pals with that cherry admiral, what's his name?'

'Netts.'

'Yeah, him, Netts. I'll bet a dollar against your dime that he's never told you the whole story. And probably even Springfield isn't telling the whole story, although he's a good guy. Why sweat it? Sorensen, you been around for a long time. You know nothin' is what it looks like. You should follow your own advice. Leave your mind behind, Jack.'

Sorensen smiled. 'Just keep up a good head of steam, Chief. We may have to drive all the way to Murmansk.'

He continued aft to Sorensen's Beach, snapped on the sunlamps, put on his wraparound Italian sunglasses, stripped off his jumpsuit and began doing pushups in his red Bermudas.

'One two, one two, one two . . .'

He wanted to flush the Russians out his pores. After five minutes he stopped, opened the cabinet and pulled out the deck chair. Casually, he unfolded the chair, set it on the deck and dug into the stock of magazines.

As he was about to sit down he glanced down – and there was long lost Zapata.

The scorpion eyed him, tail acquiver.

'Jesus H. Christ, I almost sat on you.'

He didn't know whether to kill it, catch it or walk out and leave it. Before he could make up his mind, Zapata scrambled off the chair and disappeared under the pipes at the rear of the compartment.

Sorensen got down on hands and knees and searched the shadows under the machinery, but the little arachnid was invisible. Cautiously, he backed up to the chair and stretched out, keeping one eye on the pipes beyond his feet.

'I'll make a deal with you, bug. You stay out of sight and I won't step on you.'

The heat from the lamps felt good. After a few minutes of lying perfectly still, Sorensen noticed the scorpion crawling out of the shadow of a pipe. It came to rest in a pool of warm light.

'You little devil. I get it,' said Sorensen to Zapata. 'You found your way in here because it's warm. Those steam pipes are real cozy, aren't they? Like the desert. I bet you miss the desert. Hot sand, cactus, real rocks, lots of bugs to eat. Maybe I should take you down to Mexico and turn you loose on a pyramid. Would you like that, or would you rather go back and live with Lopez in the torpedo room? You don't have to make up your mind until we get back to Norfolk, but you can't stay on this boat. She's going into the yard. They're going to cut her into pieces, rip her guts out and use her for target practice. The only *Barracuda* left will be this one right here.' Sorensen tapped himself on his tattoo, and suddenly felt foolish. The scorpion must think he was a jerk. Don't rat on me, you scorpion. You do and you'll be a damn scorpion-rat. Now there's a combo for you . . .

He grabbed a magazine. *National Geographic*. Clean, slick. He flipped through it, knowing he would never find the article he wanted to read . . . 'Inside the Newest Soviet Submarine – the Alpha, a Marvel of the Deep.' He wondered what its name was. The Russians named their subs for cities or heroes of the People. They didn't have one named *Joseph Stalin*, so maybe that was it. After all, it had sounded like a tank division. Whatever had made it quiet at first had stopped working for good – he caught himself. He had hoped he could forget about the Russians for an hour but apparently he couldn't. Whenever he pushed them out of his mind for five minutes, one popped up again where he wasn't expected – sort of like old Zapata there.

It was, it seemed, finally getting to him. He had left his mind behind a long time ago, and it occurred to him that if he stayed underwater much longer he would damn well lose it forever. As a young man, hardly more than a boy, he had found a perfect niche for his talent. His temperament was suited to life underwater. He enjoyed it so much he never pulled back and questioned it. Now, for the first time in his life he was confused by doubts. By fears. Yes, the Ace was afraid. He began to speak again to Zapata.

'Listen up, bug. They want to make me chief of the boat. What do you make of that? If I was chief, for once things would get done right. No Muzak on my boat, no way. And no bullshit, definitely no bullshit. Better movies too. And *Star Trek* every day if I want it. Man, being chief is better than being captain. I would *own* the pharmacist's mate. the supply officer would be *mine*.

'Would you like to hear a secret? I'll tell you why I really joined the navy. When I was a kid in Oakland my dad used to take me to watch the Giants play in old Seals Stadium in San Francisco. We'd go to watch Willie Mays. Willie was different. He was the best. He never let up and never gave less than one hundred percent. When he stepped between the white lines he was *all* there, and I wanted to be like him. One day we drove across the bridge to watch the Giants and the Cardinals. Bob Gibson hung a curve ball and Willie sent it into the parking lot. After the game we found the ball lying on the front seat of our car. Willie had smashed the windshield five hundred feet from home plate. That busted windshield was like a monument to *true* greatness, and we drove downtown with the wind of Willie's bat in our faces.

'After the game we went downtown to eat. Market Street was always jammed with sailors from Hunter's Point. I thought they were pretty sharp in their uniforms and cocky hats. They all had Lucky Strikes stuffed into their jumper pockets, and they strutted up and down the sidewalk like recruiting posters. On the day that Willie hit that home run I knew I'd never be a ballplayer, so in the back of my mind I figured the next best thing was to be a sailor. So, here I am, and you want to know something? I'm the best at what I do. Like Willie. I ain't braggin', it's the truth. Anyway, there's no one here but you and me, right? . . . Except just what do I have to show for it? Ten years underwater, an ex-wife, string of dockside whores, binges, brawls and a bunch of stripes down my arm. Nothing fixed, no lady. In this life nothing matters except the ship, a set of earphones and the screen.

Well, they're taking the ship away and want to give me a new one. I've done my bit, just like *Barracuda*. Me and the ship, we're finishing together . . . That Netts, he's trying to jack me off with his line of baloney. He knows I can make thirty, forty grand a year in any sound studio in the world, so he wants to make me chief of the boat. Wang it, Netts. Chief of the boat and then what? Another five years of Cowboys and Cossacks? Making the world safe for World War Three? . . . Well, old buddy, I ain't gonna be no chief of no boat. Fuck no. I'll get my own studio somewhere. Sorensen Sound, three hundred dollars an hour. Not bad. Right on Market Street. No more chasing around. Besides, nobody in his right mind wants to live underwater. So why am I doing this?' He grinned. 'I know why, because I'm alive down here. I also love it. Well, I'd better learn to live topside, love something else.'

Sorensen noticed that Zapata was ignoring him. 'Listen up, bug. I'm *talking* to you. I've done my job, this kid Fogarty has talent, let him be the new Sorensen, ace of the fleet. The next ten years can be his. I don't need anymore Cowboys and Cossacks. You and me, Zapata, we're going to fade into the goddamn sunset . . .

Sorensen closed his eyes and for the first time in years slept without nightmares. Zapata basked silently in the light, observing him.

27

RENDEZVOUS

Eight hours later Sorensen and Fogarty mustered in the sonar room for their next watch. Sorensen had slept too long under the sunlamps and had sunburn.

As Willie Joe was logging out, Sorensen asked, 'You ready for your qualifying exam, Willie Joe?'

'The Lieutenant says I've got Fire Control down pat.'

'You're gonna make it, no sweat.'

'Thanks, Ace.'

'You got plans for the thirty day leave, Willie Joe?'

'Sure do. Me and and the old lady are takin' the kids to Baton Rouge. That's where her folks are. They got a nice place, a big back porch all screened in. Keeps the bugs out.'

'You going to buy that new Bonneville?'

'You said it. Gonna get me some high-class Detroit steel and cruise on down to Louisiana. You never went for cars, did you, Ace?'

'Never had much time to drive 'em.'

'You ain't got an old lady. Them bitches, all they wanna do is show off in the parking lot at the supermarket. I don't give a shit. If that's what she wants, well, it beats her banging the whole fleet while I'm on patrol.'

Sorensen nodded, keeping a straight face, and Willie Joe opened the door. 'I'm outta here. Maybe you'll get lucky and catch a Russian.'

Barracuda was running slow and quiet. Two more messages had been received from Norfolk. *Dherzinski* continued on the same course, but between the first and second messages the Alpha had disappeared five hundred miles southwest of the Azores.

Figuring the Alpha was waiting at the rendezvous point for *Dherzinski*, Springfield maintained a course five miles south and parallel to the projected track of *Dherzinski*. He knew it wouldn't be long before they intercepted the huge missile sub which he calculated was less than fifty miles away.

Between watches, Fogarty had spent four hours listening to tapes of Soviet FBMs. The tape of *Dherzinski*, collected as she entered Havana harbor, was clear and distinct, and he had listened to it several times.

'Say, Ace, how long has this boat been making patrols out of Cuba?'

'A year.'

'How did she get in there in the first place?'

'She must have crossed the Pacific from Vladivostok, passed around Cape Horn and come up through the South Atlantic. A British sub, *Conqueror*, picked her up off the Falklands and followed her all the way to Havana. The Russians never knew *Conqueror* was there, and they still think we don't know anything about *Dherzinski*.'

'I'm surprised the Brits or somebody didn't get crazy and blow her away.'

'Maybe they should have, but of course we've been trying to find a way to get her out of the Caribbean for good without firing a shot. Sinking a boomer under any circumstances is bad news. I'll tell you one thing. I bet her skipper is unhappy right now. I bet he'd like to put a fish into the Alpha himself for making him risk exposure.'

For three hours they listened and drank coffee. They heard a lone whale sing a mournful song, but no surface ships and no submarines. Fogarty listened to the tape of *Dherzinski* several more times.

Sorensen yawned and stretched.

'You sound tired, Ace.'

'Shit, Fogarty. They want to promote me to chief and put me on a new boat in the Pacific.'

'Congratulations. A lifer like you, what more could you ask for?'

'I'm going to turn it down.'

Fogarty was stunned. 'I don't believe it. Not you, not the great Sorensen.'

'Yeah, well, I'm going to be the former great.' He pointed to the speakers, which were churning out the signature of *Dherzinski*. 'I don't want to hear one of those things ever again.'

'What do you mean? This is what it's all about, isn't it?'

'It sure is, but this is it for me. I'm not going aboard *Guitarro*, you are. I talked to Pisaro about it. He's going to be the CO. Willie Joe is going too. You can look after the Russians, you're going to be the hotshot.'

'Me? Come on, Ace.'

'Look, Fogarty, number one, you're good enough. You've got it. Number two, you're hooked. You *want* to do it, whether you know it or not. Number three, you don't want a war but number four, you've come a long way, now you'll fight if you have to. You're gonna be bad, dude.'

Fogarty was embarrassed, partly for being pleased at Sorensen's words.

'Am I right or am I right?'

'We'll see . . . but what about you, Sorensen? If you're not going onto *Guitarro* what are you going to do?'

'Sorensen Sound Effects, three hundred an hour . . . But first we're going fishing for a big fish, and hope we don't get hooked.'

They were almost at the end of their watch when Fogarty saw the streak flash across his screen. He recognized it the instant he heard it.

'Contact, bearing two eight eight, range fourteen

thousand yards, course zero seven six, speed eighteen knots, identification, Soviet Hotel class FBM, *Dherzinski*.'

Sorensen barely glanced at the screen. 'Okay, champ, feed it to the skipper.'

'Don't you want to check it?'

'Nope.'

'Sonar to control,' said Fogarty, and repeated the data over the intercom.

'All stop. Quiet in the boat,' ordered Springfield.

The sonar screens immediately cleared as *Barracuda* glided to a stop. Fogarty closed his eyes and listened to the rumble of machinery gliding through the ocean. *Dherzinski*'s missiles, like *Vallejo*'s, represented Fogarty's worst nightmare. And it popped into his head that one way to get rid of them would be to sink *Dherzinski* right now – and that thought made him sweat. What was happening to him? . . .

Sorensen lit a cigarette and blew smoke at the air conditioner.

'Does she know we're here?' Fogarty asked him.

'I don't think so. We're too quiet. If she hears us, her commander will take evasive action, or threaten us.'

'What are we going to do?'

'Follow her. She'll lead us to the Alpha. In a few hours we're going to be on top of the two most secret ships in the Soviet Navy. *Dherzinski* must need something from the Alpha. Or vice-versa. Otherwise they'd never pull her off-station. I figure the last thing the Russians expect is for us to show up. If we're lucky we'll catch them together on the surface.'

'What will they do?'

'I don't read minds, kid. But I do know Springfield will do his job, which won't win us the Order of Lenin—'

'Control to sonar.'

'Sonar, aye.'

'We're going to play tag. Let's keep our range between ten thousand and twelve thousand yards.'

'Sonar to control, aye aye.'

Barracuda fell in behind *Dherzinski* and began to follow the huge missile sub at a distance of six miles. Steaming on an easterly course, *Dherzinski* rolled through the sea like Leviathan, her computers continuously tracking targets on the east coast of the United States fourteen hundred miles away. The noise from the boomer's engines was so loud that her sonar operators never heard the American sub.

Sorensen quietly listened to the sounds of machinery, then spoke up. 'You know, Fogarty, as of now we're tailing a part of the strategic deterrence of the Soviet Union. She's got the capacity to hit our coast cities, and she's in our sights. If she so much as floods a missile tube . . . well, we can't give her a chance to launch a missile. Shit like this gives me the jitters.'

Fogarty stared at the blip on his screen.

Fifty miles away *Potemkin* hovered six hundred feet down, waiting for *Dherzinski*. *Potemkin* had not moved from the rendezvous point in eighteen hours, and the atmosphere inside the sub was fetid, the crew anemic, weak and irritable. The seven reactor engineers with virulent colds grew steadily worse. The constant bombardment by neutron radiation was killing the marrow in their bones. They were going to be transferred to *Dherzinski* and replaced with engineers from the FBM, and it had better happen fast.

In the cramped crew quarters in the stern, Engineering Officer Lieutenant Third Rank Polokov lay dying of infection. He pleaded with Federov to make the sign of the cross over him.

Federov complied, dragging from his memory a child's prayer. Polokov stopped breathing. The surgeon pulled a sheet over his face. 'Shall we prepare for burial at sea, Captain?'

'Later.'

Popov's voice came through the intercom speakers. 'This is sonar calling the captain. We have made contact with *Dherzinski*.'

Federov rushed to the control room and stood over Popov at the sonar console. *Dherzinski* was beaming a sonic signal over the prearranged frequency that *Potemkin* was to use as a homing device.

'Prepare to surface. All ahead slow,' ordered Federov. 'Alexis, put life jackets on Bolinki and the others to be transferred. I'm sending along a sealed copy of the log with an account of Kurnachov's actions for Gorshkov's eyes only. I want your signature.'

'Yes, Captain.'

On *Barracuda* Sorensen and Fogarty heard *Dherzinski*'s signal.

'Sonar to control. *Dherzinski* is echo-ranging.'

'Very well, sonar. Slow speed. We must be near the Alpha. If *Dherzinski* starts to circle, we'll go around with her.'

Sorensen stood up. 'Any second now *Dherzinski*'s echo ranger will pick up the Alpha. When the echo bounces back, we should hear it. That's when one of them might pick us up. Cross your fingers. If they hear us they'll never surface. And we won't be able to see them. And that means we can't get the pretty pictures the admiral wants.'

Tension crept through the ship. In the control room Springfield studied the repeater.

'She's turning. Go left three degrees.' A second blip appeared on the screens. 'There it is. All stop.'

The two Russian subs were a mile apart, six miles from *Barracuda*. Slowly the two blips moved together.

'General quarters, general quarters. All hands prepare

for maneuvering. Control to weapons. Load tubes two and four with Mark thirty-sevens, acoustic homing.'

'Weapons to control, understand load two and four with Mark thirty-sevens, acoustic homing.'

'If they discover us right now,' said Pisaro, 'I think they'll shoot . . .'

Springfield silently agreed. 'Leo, if we hear a target-seeking sonar, we got to turn tail. Tell the quartermaster to load the camera. When we raise the scopes, you blow off your film in a hurry. As soon as you're done we back off and do our best to pick up *Dherzinski* later. We're not going to invite this Alpha driver to be a hero of the Soviet Union at our expense. All ahead slow.'

Barracuda inched toward the hovering subs. When the distance was reduced to a mile Sorensen heard strange garbled noises. The Russians were communicating on an underwater telephone.

'Sonar to control, they're talking on a gertrude.'

'Very well, sonar. We're sending Davic in.'

A moment later Davic pushed through the door into the sonar room. Sorensen greeted him with a big smile. 'You're on, Davic. Listen up.'

Davic squeezed into the third console, put on a headset and shook his head. 'It's breaking up. They're too far away. Wait a minute, wait a minute, I'm getting something – something about carbon dioxide . . . lithium . . . now I've lost it again.'

Fogarty said, 'One of them is blowing her tanks. It's *Dherzinski*, she's rising. Now the Alpha. They're both surfacing.'

Sorensen watched the screen. 'Okay, it seems they still don't know we're here. Sonar to control. They're surfacing. Holding steady at six thousand yards.'

'All ahead slow. Helm, take us in to one thousand yards. Periscope depth, gear for red,' ordered Springfield.

The lights in the control room switched from green

fluorescence to cherry red.

'Take her up. Quartermaster, rig the camera to number one scope.'

'Aye aye, sir. It's going to be dark up there.'

'Switch on light intensifiers.'

'Light intensifiers on.'

'Mr Pisaro, try standard film first. If we have time, we'll activate the infrared system.'

'Aye aye, skipper.'

'Control to engineering. Chief, increase steam to ninety percent. We may have to get out of here in a hurry.'

'Engineering to control. What's he going to do? Fire a broadside across our bow?'

'Not funny. Up scopes.'

Barracuda angled up, and at sixty feet the periscopes broke the surface. Springfield bent over the binocular eyepiece of the number two scope.

Olonov stood on the bridge on *Dherzinski*'s squat ugly sail, looking at the short, sleek sub rocking twenty meters away in the gentle sea. He shouted through a bullhorn, 'Who are you?'

'This is *Potemkin*,' came Federov's reply. 'Do you have the lithium hydroxide?'

Olonov's mood was dark. 'So you're Federov, Gorshkov's fair-haired boy. Prince of the Northern Fleet. Pleased to make your acquaintance.'

Federov did not appreciate the sarcasm. 'Send across the lifeline.'

It had been thirty years since Olonov last worked as a deckhand. Alone on the bridge of *Dherzinski*, he managed to fire the small rocket that catapulted the rope across the void. Federov secured the line to a cleat and spoke into his headset.

'Send Bolinki up. Get the others ready.'

Olonov secured the bag of crystals to the line and

Federov slowly pulled it across. When the precious chemical was safely aboard *Potemkin*, Federov tied the unconscious Bolinki into a litter, stuffed the copy of his log into the sailor's jacket, and Olonov began to pull the crewman toward *Dherzinski*.

Bolinki was suspended over the sea when Federov heard Popov's voice on the intercom. Radar had picked up periscopes at a distance of one kilometer.

Federov was furious at Olonov for letting himself be picked up and trailed, compromising *Potemkin*. He spoke to Popov again. 'Identification?'

'None, Captain. We never heard him . . . but now we have periscopes on radar—'

'Alexis, prepare to dive. Load torpedoes and flood tubes, *now*.' He shouted into the bullhorn, 'Olonov, get that man aboard. You dive first and proceed due north exactly five hundred kilometers. We'll rendezvous again in twenty-four hours to finish the transfers.'

Olonov was equally dismayed. He too was risking exposure, and possibly being cut off from retreating back to the Cuban lair. Through infrared binoculars he now could see the periscopes. *Dherzinski* was compromised.

It was three o'clock in the morning on a clear night. Through the binocular lenses of his periscope Springfield saw a mottled shape a half mile away rolling in the sea like a beached whale. *Dherzinski*. One man stood on top of her low stubby sail wrestling with a lifeline. As the big ship rocked in the waves, Springfield saw that the line stretched across to another much smaller submarine.

'Leo, start the camera. I think we've got our hit-and-run artist here.'

Pisaro put his eye to the Nikon's viewfinder and activated the motor-drive. The camera began taking rapid-fire pictures.

'We got a Hotel class boomer and what has to be the

Alpha,' said Pisaro. 'They're not acting like they know we're here.'

'Then they'll know any minute,' Springfield replied. 'Their radar will pick up the scopes. *Dherzinski* is sending a container across. They've got a man rigged to the lifeline. They're taking him off the Alpha and putting him on the missile sub—'

'Sonar to control. They're echo-ranging. They've got us.'

'Radar to control. They've picked up the periscopes. I've got two discrete frequencies.'

'They're cutting loose the lifeline,' Pisaro announced. 'They're closing the hatches.'

'Attention all hands. This is the captain. Prepare for steep angles and deep submergence. Control to radio, prepare a position report and the following message: Soviet Hotel Class FBM *Dherzinski* and Soviet Alpha class SSN photographed on surface. Will follow FBM according to orders.'

'Radio to control, aye aye.'

'Sonar to control. One sub is flooding his tanks, he's making way. It's *Dherzinski*.'

'Steady now,' said Springfield. 'We'll wait until the Alpha is down before we transmit. We don't want them to intercept our message. Control to sonar.'

'Sonar, aye.'

'Keep track of the boomer. We'll want to pick up its trail fast, as soon as we're sure the Alpha isn't on our tail. We've got to get free of him first.'

'Sonar to control, echo-ranging. *Dherzinski* is making six knots. She's not going down easily. The Alpha is holding steady on the surface.'

Through his periscope Springfield saw Federov staring back at him through infrared binoculars. He knew the Russian was waiting for him to transmit.

'Sonar to control. *Dherzinski* is still on the surface,

speed eight knots, course zero zero zero.'

'Mr Pisaro, shoot the infrared film.'

Pisaro changed film and fired off thirty-six exposures of *Potemkin*. He detached the film cartridge from the camera and called to the quartermaster. 'Chief, get Luther to process this film right away.'

'Sonar to control, the Alpha is flooding torpedo tubes.'

'Steady as she goes. He won't fire from the surface. That's suicide. Control to weapons. Flood tubes.'

'Weapons to control. Flooding tubes.'

'Mr Hoek, program your fish to home on the Alpha. Do you have her signature?'

'Yes, sir.'

'Easy on the trigger, Lieutenant. Very easy. Give him a chance to back off.'

In the sonar room Davic was yelling at the blip on his screen. 'Shoot him. Shoot him *now*—'

Fogarty turned on him. 'Shut up, Davic. Shut the hell up.'

'Chickenshit . . .'

Sorensen wheeled around, barely restraining himself. 'Get out of here, Davic. Take your white suit and go to your damage-control station. *Now*.'

Davic hesitated for a moment, then put on his asbestos suit and left, trailing an untranslatable curse.

28

FOUR THOUSAND FEET

Federov gazed through binoculars at the four thin vertical lines that poked out of the sea a half mile away – radar and radio antennae and two periscopes. He still had no positive identification but he felt certain it was *Barracuda* – who had a better motive? And of course by now they must have deduced or established that *Potemkin* had not sunk. Once more he realized what a self-serving game it was to assume the Americans were stupid or easily fooled. The acoustical device may have bought them time. The apparatchik had brought them a crisis.

He had outrun *Barracuda*, outdived it, outmaneuvered it, but he had not escaped it. They were good, damn them. The very stealth of the American submarine disturbed him. No, this was no chance encounter; the Americans had tracked him – precisely how, he wasn't certain, though a likely possibility was that they had managed to lay down a bottom sonar system, as rumor had had it. He also realized with a chill that the American sub could have sunk him. But they had observed him, and more . . . He had no doubt that the American commander was taking his picture, and he could not allow that film to be delivered to the Pentagon. His orders, which had always seemed to leave him too little room for discretion, even if he realized the reason for them, had been delivered in person by Gorshkov the day *Potemkin* had sailed – under no circumstances was he to permit discovery of this top-secret, most advanced submarine. Well, he had been discovered. Now he had to take the action necessary to offset the damage of that discovery.

But first he must do what he could to drive off

Barracuda to make possible *Dherzinski*'s escape, then using *Potemkin*'s depth and speed, try to recover his advantage. Both sides knew the rules, the FBMs of both navies were supposed to be untouchable. Yet now both sides had violated that unspoken understanding. His side had by dispatching *Dherzinski* from its hidden station to save his ship and its wounded, and the Americans had by persisting in tailing the FBM and even, no doubt, photographing it just as they had *Potemkin*. He had wondered when he sent his message to Gorshkov describing his condition whether the admiral would risk exposure and identification of *Dherzinski* to save *Potemkin*. He was glad he had, but wondered what he would have done in Gorshkov's place . . .

All of which was at best a momentary diversion from the action he knew he must take. *Barracuda* must be silenced. He would make a threatening gesture, then submerge . . . to attack from the surface would give the American an opportunity to shoot back, and possibly destroy the *Potemkin* . . . And the destruction of the *Potemkin* must not be allowed, it was not even thinkable – which thought helped him push from his consciousness what he was charged with doing . . . Secretly, in a corner of his mind, he wished the American would escape, save him from what he must do – and then quickly he shook his head, forcing himself to concentrate on his mission . . . Damn you, damn you, damn you was the inclusive litany reverberating in his brain, but nobody was listening, and now he no longer could.

He spoke into his headset. 'Radio, did the American transmit?'

'No, sir, not yet.'

He took a deep breath, wiped his eyes. 'Range to target.'

'Range one thousand meters.'

'Start torpedo guidance sonar.'

'Guidance on.'

And silently he screamed across the sea at the periscopes, at the American captain, at Gorshkov . . . This is madness . . .

In *Barracuda*'s sonar room Sorensen and Fogarty snatched away their earphones just in time. The screech of the Russian targeting sonar erupted from the loudspeakers.

'Sonar to control, she's activated her target frequency.'

'Down scopes. Retract antennae. Right full rudder. All ahead full. Stern planes down twenty degrees. Take us down to four hundred feet, Leo. All hands prepare for evasive maneuvers.'

In the maneuvering room Chief Wong opened the main steam valve all the way, and *Barracuda*'s prop suddenly turned the sea to foam. The helmsman pushed his joystick over to the right and tilted it forward. The ship banked, tilted forward, and shot down into the depths.

Springfield watched the depth gauge as *Barracuda* rapidly approached four hundred feet.

'We're going to come around and make sure there's no torpedo on our stern. Left full rudder.'

Still accelerating and descending, the ship wrenched to the left.

'Control to sonar, activate ultrasonic torpedo detection frequency.'

'Sonar to control, activating torpedo detection frequency.'

A burst of ultrasonic pulses searched the water for a hard, swiftly moving object. 'Sonar to control. No contact. He didn't shoot.'

'Very well. Secure echo ranger. Helm, make our course zero four five. Depth, eight hundred feet. We'll go under the thermal and give him a run for his money. We have positive proof of her existence, Leo. I tell you, she's going to come after us. We won't be able to pick up *Dherzinski* until we know the Alpha is on her way north.'

Pisaro was still holding the Nikon. 'We got the goods. Do you think *Dherzinski* will try to go back to Cuba?'

'Maybe. Maybe not. If she does try, she'll run into our blockade. Then she'll know for sure that we have the ability to track her. Eventually the Russians will discover SOSUS. When they do they'll know we can pinpoint *Dherzinski* wherever she goes, and that should be the end of her Caribbean patrols. The next time we have a chance to send up a buoy we'll get a SOSUS report on *Dherzinski*. Control to sonar, where's the boomer now?'

'Sonar to control. Five thousand, two hundred yards. Speed fifteen knots and increasing. She's submerging now, but I'm about to lose them both above the thermal. The Alpha is still on the surface.'

Barracuda descended to eight hundred feet, turned northeast, and began to move away from *Potemkin*.

Federov scrambled off the bridge, down the ladder and into the control room. One glance at the diving panel told him all the hatches were sealed.

'Identification, Popov.'

'It's *Barracuda*, Captain.'

As he thought. 'What's his course?'

'Zero four five. He's running away. I'm about to lose him under a thermal.'

'We must catch him.' To stop those pictures of *Potemkin* from being delivered, to insure *Dherzinski* getting safely back to its lair. Once again a litany, to keep *himself* on course . . . 'Belay torpedo guidance. We're going right down there with him. Engineering, this is the captain. Fast dive. Take us down to three hundred meters. Flood tanks, now.'

Alexis opened all the saltwater vents and *Potemkin* dropped like an anchor, an extremely dangerous maneuver. One hundred fifty meters down and rapidly descending, Federov ordered, 'Blow tanks. Neutral buoyancy. Alexis, stop us at three hundred meters.'

It took all of Alexis's engineering skill to slow *Potemkin*'s rate of descent without suddenly popping back to the surface or completely losing control and sliding down to crush depth and imploding. He shouted through the intercom.

'Captain, we must make way to get some lift on the planes.'

'All ahead slow.'

Potemkin moved forward and gradually stopped sinking. Alexis stopped her at exactly three hundred meters, a thousand feet down.

'Popov, is *Barracuda* back on your screen?'

'Yes, sir, we're under the thermal now – there he is, bearing zero four five. Speed estimated fifteen knots and increasing. And there's *Dherzinski*.' On Popov's screen *Dherzinski* was steaming due north, by now almost out of sonar range.

Alexis appeared in the control room. 'Captain,' he said quietly so as not to be overheard by the others, 'are we going to try to rendezvous with *Dherzinski* again? We have to get these sick men off the ship. They're too sick to work, and I need engineers. I can barely spare the men I need to crank the stern planes by hand.'

Federov spoke without looking at him. 'We must eliminate the American sub first. There is no other way.'

'Did he transmit?'

'No, and we will not give him a chance. You know our orders as well as I do. Don't think about it, Alexis. *Don't*. He would do the same thing if the situation were reversed.' He needed to believe that.

'This American is no fool, Nikolai, and his boat is very quiet . . .'

'All ahead two thirds,' was Federov's reply. 'Course zero four five. We're right on his stern now.'

*

In the control room of *Barracuda* each man felt both tension and exultation. The film was a success: seventy-two sharp photos of the Soviet subs. Luther had blown up one of the photos, and Springfield had a grainy eight-by-ten print of the Russian captain's face. High cheekbones, dark eyes and a peaked cap.

'He must be the CO,' said Pisaro, although there was no insignia of rank on the cap. Pisaro nervously lit a cigarette and rubbed his hands over his scalp. 'We're outnumbered here, Skipper.'

'Leo, all we can do about that is what we're doing, drawing the Alpha off and separating them. Control to sonar, where is *Dherzinski*?'

'Sonar to control. *Dherzinski*'s speed is holding at eighteen knots. Course holding steady at zero zero zero, but I'm not gettin' much of a signal, Skipper. She'll be out of range in a few seconds.'

'Very well. Control to engineering. Make revolutions for thirty knots. Go right ten degrees, course zero five five.'

As the ship banked to the right, the side-sweeping sonars picked up the sound of *Potemkin*'s flooding vents. 'Sonar to control. The Alpha is descending rapidly. Captain, she flooded her tanks and dropped straight down. She's going to be on our stern, right in our baffles.'

Sorensen switched off the intercom and swore at the screen. The Alpha was going down swiftly, using her titanium hull to best advantage. Thirty seconds later, she disappeared. 'Sonar to control, the Alpha is gone. Her last recorded depth on the down-searching scanner estimated one thousand feet. She's in our baffles.'

Springfield looked at Pisaro, then at the photograph of Federov. 'Leo, they're trying to intimidate us with the Alpha. He wants to scare us with his titanium boat. And if he does, he'll get bolder, figure he owns the damn ocean . . .'

Sorensen stared at his screen. 'The last time this bastard

disappeared from the screen he hit us,' he said to Fogarty. 'I've got a feeling . . . Sonar to control.'

'Go ahead, sonar.'

'Recommend we clear baffles, sir. I don't know where she is.'

'Very well, sonar. Control to engineering, prepare for slow speed. All ahead slow. Go right twenty degrees.'

Ninety seconds into the turn, the Alpha reappeared on the screen.

'I knew it,' said Sorensen. 'Sonar to control. Contact bearing one four eight. Range three two five zero yards and closing. Speed twenty-four knots, depth one thousand feet.'

'Very well, sonar. We have her on the repeater.'

Springfield crossed the control room to the weapons console and stood behind Hoek. 'We've got to threaten him, give him second thoughts. Make him back off . . . otherwise the bastard will try to finish us . . . Control to sonar. Prepare to activate target-seeking sonar.'

As Sorensen punched at his keyboard, Fogarty felt as if he were in suspended animation. The impossible was about to happen? No one was going to back down?'

The Alpha abruptly slowed and turned sharply to the right.

Sorensen reacted instantly, understanding that the Alpha's action meant he was about to shoot. 'Sonar to control, recommend evasive action.'

'Helm, left full rudder! All ahead full. Thirty degrees up angle! Sonar, activate torpedo detection frequency!'

Potemkin's torpedo room was portside amidships. Federov wheeled to the right, reversed his prop and stopped dead in the water. 'Fire acoustic-homing torpedo.'

Alexis hesitated, then stuck his thumb into the red button on his console. A gas turbine-propelled torpedo shot out of a tube. The projectile took off after *Barracuda* at forty knots, the on-board ultrasonic echo-ranging sonar probing the sea for its target. The instant the torpedo was away Federov ordered, 'Stern planes, maximum down angle, all ahead one third. Take us down to one thousand three hundred meters.' He must not give the *Barracuda* a chance to find him and shoot back. He must not think of the torpedo he had loosed. He must not think.

'Incoming! Torpedo, bearing one eight zero!'

Barracuda was racing upward at thirty degrees, trying to rise into a cooler layer of water. Springfield was counting on the torpedo's searching in a normal down-spiraling pattern. He calculated he had ten minutes before the torpedo either ran out of fuel or outpaced *Barracuda* and ran up her stern.

'Control to weapons, load chaff decoy.'

'Weapons to control, understand load chaff decoy. Weapons to torpedo room, get the decoy in the tube.'

'Torpedo room, aye aye.'

When *Barracuda* was at four hundred feet, Springfield ordered, 'Zero angle on the planes. Fire decoy.'

'Decoy away.'

A jet of compressed air pushed the chaff decoy out of the tube, and it promptly began to emit electronic pulses that imitated *Barracuda*'s target-frequency sonar. The decoy began to spiral down as *Barracuda* continued up.

The Russian torpedo had remained at eight hundred feet, its sonar confused by the reflecting nature of the ceiling of the thermal layer. When it heard the decoy it zeroed in.

Two minutes after the decoy was fired, Sorensen and Fogarty heard the explosion.

'Goddamn,' Sorensen exclaimed. 'It worked. Keep your eyes on the screen, kid. There may be another one.'

In the control room there was momentary relief. When the decoy destroyed the torpedo, even Springfield allowed himself a minor celebration. A moment later, however, it was replaced with a quiet fury. 'Go right thirty degrees, stern planes down ten degrees. Leo, take us down to fifteen hundred feet. We've got to get this son of a bitch before he gets us. He fired first.'

'One thousand three hundred meters and holding.'

Potemkin was steaming at twelve knots, 4,264 feet beneath the surface of the sea. At that tremendous depth she was in the deep sound channel, and Popov's sonars were subjected to a barrage of strange noises. Ordinarily sounds in the channel were trapped by a warm thermal layer above and a very cold thermal below. The only exception was a thundering source of noise such as *Potemkin* herself. *Potemkin* with her hard-bolted machinery produced sonic signals of many different frequencies, some of which were refracted into the layer above, revealing her presence, while at the same time rendering her own sonars ineffective. Popov could hear neither *Barracuda*, nor the torpedo, but he did hear the unmistakable sound of an explosion.

'Captain, we got him—'

Federov looked at the screen and at Alexis, who was shaking his head. 'Don't be too sure, Popov. We don't know what we hit. Go right six degrees. We'll make a wide circle.'

Sorensen was standing before his console, working the down-searching sonars. 'C'mon, Ivan, you shot your wad, come back and see what damage you did. C'mon . . .' And then to Springfield: 'Sonar to control. Recommend all stop and quiet in the boat.'

'Attention all hands. All stop. Quiet in the boat.'

Barracuda hovered at fifteen hundred feet. Fogarty expected another torpedo, Sorensen did not. The down-searching sonars were acutely sensitive to frequencies that refracted through the various thermal layers.

A fuzzy splash of illumination appeared on one side of the screen. 'There she is. Sonar to control. Contact, range six thousand yards, depth four thousand two hundred feet, bearing one one three, speed twelve knots. She's coming right at us, Captain, but she's deep.'

Fogarty slammed his fist on the console. 'But we can't shoot her that deep. A Mark thirty-seven will implode at twenty-five hundred feet.'

Sorensen nodded. 'You're right, Fogarty, but when this Alpha took a shot at us, I figure he bought himself a nuke. Our job is to survive . . . and his is to see we don't.'

Fogarty stared at the screen. 'We wouldn't . . . Springfield wouldn't . . . Jesus, we can't—'

'Fogarty, prepare to feed the guidance system on a Mark forty-five.'

Fogarty hesitated. Sorensen just stared at him, and Fogarty, numb, began punching buttons . . .

'Attention all hands. Battle stations, nuclear. Control to weapons, load tube six with a Mark forty-five.'

In the torpedo room Lopez bit through his cigar. He stood up and crossed himself. 'Johnson, cut loose a Mark forty-five. Open the door.'

Four torpedomen moved along the rack and unbolted the torpedo from its mooring. A fifth opened the torpedo door. Carefully, they slid it onto the guides, and pushed it into the tube. Lopez closed the electronic locks in the proper sequence and ran the circuit tests. 'Torpedo room to control,' he said into his headset, 'Mark forty-five loaded in tube six.'

'Control to weapons, arm warhead.'

Hoek was having trouble breathing. He responded in a scarcely audible whisper and pushed the coded numbers into his keyboard. 'Mark forty-five warhead armed and ready.'

'Flood tube.'

'Flooding tube, aye.'

In the sonar room Sorensen and Fogarty could only listen to the commands as they passed back and forth over the intercom.

29

NUCLEAR WARRIORS

The carbon dioxide scrubber on *Potemkin* was back in operation and the air was fresh. Federov watched the sonar console.

Barracuda was not on the screen. Federov didn't know if she was sunk or whether signal interference in the deep sound channel prevented him from hearing her. He had heard neither implosions nor a train of debris settling toward the bottom.

'Engineering, how go the stern planes?'

'This is engineering. We can move them.'

'All right. Prepare for maneuvering. Slow speed. Let's be quiet.'

On Sorensen's screen the Alpha decreased speed and became quieter.

'Sonar to control, range now four thousand yards and holding. He's looking for us. Depth three eight zero zero feet.'

'Control to sonar, activate target-seeking sonar.' And pray he comes to his senses and backs off . . .

Sorensen looked at Fogarty, punched the button and a wave of high-pitched sound pulsed out of *Barracuda*'s bow in a narrow sound ray directly at *Potemkin*.

Popov screamed in pain, his eardrums ruptured by *Barracuda*'s target-seeking sonar. Federov rushed to the sonar console. The pulse of sound that appeared as a bright streak on the screen was like a sharp jab in his guts. Their sonar had found him.

'All ahead full. Right full rudder.'

For thirty seconds *Potemkin*'s engines pushed her through a sharp turn. 'All stop,' commanded Federov. 'Level the planes.'

The American target-seeking sonar gave him an exact fix on *Barracuda*. *Potemkin* was gliding on her planes back toward the American's position. If a torpedo was coming right at him, he had a chance to evade by diving. The question rattling through his mind was whether or not the American torpedoes had an enhanced capability like their sonars. His choices were back off and run, or fight. If he ran, *Dherzinski* would never escape, the *Potemkin* would be fatally compromised by film and *Barracuda* would surface and report that *Potemkin* already had fired one torpedo. Which would bring out the whole damn United States Navy to hunt him down . . . He looked at Alexis, who had taken his position at the firing console. His friend was reading his mind, sharing his thoughts. He waited.

'Activate targeting sonar.'

The waiting was over. 'Targeting sonar activated. I'm getting one signal, Captain, from *Barracuda*. He hasn't fired.'

Federov moved to the weapons station. This was his to do. 'Alexis, take the helm.'

'Yes, sir . . .'

Federov pushed the button. 'Torpedo away.'

He steered the torpedo toward *Barracuda* at forty knots, trailing its guidewire behind.

Barracuda's sonar screens blazed with red blips. 'Sonar to control, he's fired a torpedo, wire-guided, speed forty knots. Torpedo range three seven zero zero yards and closing.'

No more hesitation. No more options. The Russian had not backed off. 'All stop. Prepare to fire Mark forty-five. Set detonation for maximum depth.'

Hoek watched on his screen as the single red blip that was *Potemkin* began to blink. His hand trembled over the keys, then a spike of pain shot down his left arm. He could barely whisper, 'Set detonation for maximum depth, aye.'

'Fire one.'

Hoek reached for the button, but his hand never made it. Clutching his chest, gasping for breath, he fell to the deck.

'Good God, I think he's had a heart attack,' Springfield shouted, and ran toward the weapons console.

Springfield punched the buttons. 'Chief, fire one.'

Lopez muttered a prayer and pushed the button. The Mark forty-five leaped out of the tube and immediately nosed over for a fast run to maximum depth.

'Evasive maneuvers. All ahead flank. Left full rudder.'

The warhead would explode in two minutes. By then *Barracuda* should be three miles away, and at that distance she should withstand the shockwave that would pass through the water like a nuclear-powered tidal wave – except the Russian torpedo was still coming at them at forty knots.

Springfield looked at Hoek lying behind the weapons station. Luther bent over the weapons officer, pumping his chest. *Barracuda* was coming around a tight turn at speed and they were leaning into the deck. Torpedo alarms were sounding, but to Springfield it was almost as if they were echoes from another ship in another ocean on another planet. Suddenly the door to the sonar room opened and Sorensen stood there, looking around the control room, eyes blazing. The torpedo was gaining on them, he said.

Popov had fainted from the acute pain of his ruptured eardrums. Federov snatched way his earphones and pressed them to this ears. On the screen he saw *Barracuda* fire a torpedo, turn one hundred eighty degrees, then begin to accelerate away. Could *Barracuda* outrun his torpedo? For a brief moment he continued to guide the missile, but then heard the active sonar in the Mark forty-five – it was unlike any sonar he had ever heard. And then he knew. The American torpedo was diving, was already below two thousand feet.

'Evasive action,' he ordered. 'Left full rudder. Dive! Dive! Flank speed! It's nuclear!'

Potemkin turned and accelerated, and though the stern planes failed to respond quickly, the forward motion was enough to snap the torpedo's guide wire. The fish was now on its own, he no longer had control of it.

'The wire's cut,' shouted Pisaro. 'It's running wild.' On the sonar screens the Russian torpedo went awry.

Barracuda's control room dared to hope.

Sorensen, standing in the control room door, turned back to Fogarty. His face said he was not ready to celebrate.

'Quiet on the boat,' Springfield ordered. 'Right full rudder. Engineering, give it all you've got.'

The echo ranger in the Mark forty-five torpedo immediately recognized *Potemkin*, ignoring the frequencies of *Barracuda* and the Russian torpedo.

The two torpedoes sped past each other, missing a collision by fifty yards. The Mark forty-five closed on *Potemkin*.

Inside the Russian torpedo a relay snapped and the guidance switched to an active sonar homing system. The transducer heard and recognized the surge of sound from *Barracuda*'s pumps, and the onboard computer smoothly turned the rudder to the left. The torpedo homed in on *Barracuda*'s engine room compartment.

*

Sorensen heard the torpedo's high-pitched homing sonar as it bounced off *Barracuda*'s hull. *Barracuda*'s speed was now up to twenty knots, but the torpedo was rapidly closing the gap. Three minutes, four? . . . He stood up, took off his earphones and turned off the overhead speakers.

'I guess I'll be going back to the beach. What say, kid, join me in a few rays?'

Fogarty was unable to speak. Found himself rising like a zombie to follow Sorensen. He felt nothing as he and Sorensen moved through the control room, barely heard Springfield order in a curiously bland voice. 'Flank speed, stern planes down twenty degrees, sail planes down twenty degrees.'

The planesman was staring at the sonar repeater, not able to accept what he saw. The helmsman wet his pants. Springfield stepped quickly across the control room to the helmsman's station, and pushed over the joystick himself.

The radiomen were trying to send up a communications buoy. Pisaro looked as though he had swallowed his tongue. Cakes was frozen in a hatchway, a tray of coffee in his hands. The tray slipped out of his grasp and crashed to the deck. He stayed immobile.

Sorensen and Fogarty proceeded aft.

In the maneuvering room there was silence. The nucs monitored their instruments with undistracted attention. After all, the system had never been pushed to the limit. A technician's dream come true.

In the engine room Sorensen peeled off his jumpsuit and entered Sorensen's Beach in his red Bermuda shorts. He snapped on the sunlamps and put on his sunglasses.

Fogarty came in. They pulled out the mat and sat there. Zapata crawled out of the shadows and looked at them.

The Mark forty-five reached its maximum depth six hundred feet above *Potemkin*. A spherical shell of high explosive ignited, imploding a perfect sphere of plutonium that instantly reached critical mass.

The warhead exploded.

In a millionth of a second a fireball thirty yards in diameter erupted into a mass of superheated steam. The sudden impulse of energy pushed out a shock wave that slammed into *Potemkin* with the force of a freight train. Her titanium hull was not designed to withstand that much asymmetric overpressure and ruptured in a dozen places. At four thousand feet the pressure of one hundred twenty-two atmospheres killed *Potemkin* in eight seconds.

Federov's last thought was of the hand of God grabbing his ship and crushing it in His fist.

The giant bubble of highly radioactive water vapor continued to expand, pushing above it a waterspout that rose one hundred feet into the air. The bubble rose swiftly to the surface, where it erupted over an area the size of a football field. A large wave radiated over the surface, and the steam was slowly diluted and dispersed in the atmosphere. When the waterspout fell back into the sea after a few seconds, all visible traces of a nuclear explosion vanished. All that remained was the sonic record heard by SOSUS and the sonar operators on *Dherzinski* twenty miles away.

Sorensen and Fogarty heard the explosion at the same time that the shock wave rolled through *Barracuda*.

Sorensen said only, 'He didn't move after he shot his wad. He thought he was too deep to get hurt.'

Fogarty sat perfectly still, his mind numbed, seeing only a picture of his toy submarine diving into Lake Minnetonka.

The Russian torpedo did not function perfectly. It struck *Barracuda* twenty feet forward of the reactor.

Exploding on impact, the warhead punched a hole six feet in diameter in the pressure hull, directly into the control room. The full, lethal force of the explosion struck Springfield, Pisaro, Hoek, Cakes and the others in the control room. Cracks radiating from the rupture opened around the circumference of the hull.

Barracuda broke in half.

The blast expended itself against the forward bulkhead, which caved into the officers' quarters and galley. The after bulkhead resisted the blast, and the stern broke away and began to sink.

Eight thousandths of a second after the explosion ripped *Barracuda* in two, the sea and the laws of physics finished her.

In the bow, only the new steel installed at Rota failed to shatter in the succession of implosions. Lopez, the torpedo gang and the damage-control team of Davic and Willie Joe died in the last implosion.

In the stern, water poured into the reactor compartment, instantly cooling the reactor vessel, which became brittle and split open. The primary coolant water, saturated with radioactive isotopes and pressurised to sixteen hundred pounds per square inch, exploded into the flooding compartment and became mingled with the sea.

Water poured into the engineering spaces, squeezing the atmosphere in the compartment into a smaller and smaller pocket until the air itself exploded, destroying the turbines and reduction gears.

An electrical fire ignited a tank of light lubrication oil that exploded and destroyed Sorensen's Beach. Fogarty burned up.

As *Barracuda* sank to the bottom, twelve thousand feet below, Sorensen lived long enough to drown.

30

GORSHKOV

A plain, unmarked Mercedes was waiting for Netts when he stepped off the plane at the airstrip near Hamburg. Three days had passed since *Barracuda* and *Potemkin* had destroyed one another.

A young lieutenant stood on the tarmac, holding open the rear door. The admiral waved the lieutenant aside, slid into the driver's seat and drove south along the west bank of the Elbe.

It was a fine spring morning and the river was wide and beautiful. In that part of central Germany the Elbe is the border between East and West. Thirty miles east of Hamburg fields of rye stretched ripe and green, and on both sides of the river farmers on their tractors looked busy, but there was one difference. In the East, a hundred yards from the river, a chain of high guardtowers marched along the Elbe, guns trained on the open fields.

Netts drove through Lauenberg an der Elbe, an ancient town of long slate roofs, and stopped when he reached a single-lane bridge that crossed the river. Two West German border patrolmen, whose usual station was at the foot of the bridge, sat in a jeep a discreet distance away.

On the other side of the river another Mercedes was parked behind a lowered crossing gate. In the middle of the bridge, alone, stood Sergei Gorshkov, admiral of the fleet of the Soviet Union.

They had never met before. Netts looked at him, not trusting himself to speak. He waited for the Russian to start it.

Gorshkov was a tall, heavy man dressed in a dark well-made suit. His face was bland. He watched the river barges for several minutes, as though admiring the hard-working rivermen. Finally he spoke in heavily accented but otherwise good English. 'I am pleased you agreed to meet.'

'I thought it prudent. Tell me what you have to say.'

'You will not inform your press agencies of what has happened?'

'Of course not.' No need to get such an assurance in return. Everything *Potemkin* had done was to keep the secret of its existence and of *Dherzinski*'s presence in the Caribbean.

'*Dherzinski* is returning to Murmansk. She is no longer in position to—'

'We know. She passed through the Iceland gap this morning . . . Admiral, your captain sank my ship.'

'He died for it.'

'He committed an unprovoked act of war. You were responsible—'

'It was not unprovoked. Your ship came within a kilometer of *Dherzinski*—'

'*Dherzinski* was in our waters.' Like medieval popes, the two admirals were dividing up the world . . . 'Admiral, I don't think you were so concerned about *Dherzinski*. In any case, you now know your attempt to violate our Cuban agreement is ended. Your patrols in the Caribbean have been terminated. But you were trying to protect your new class of attack submarines. What was the name of the ship that sank *Barracuda*?'

'*Potemkin*.'

'How apt. Named for a czarist prince. You Russians never forget who you are. Why are you so anxious to protect *Potemkin*?'

Gorshkov smiled. 'Admiral Netts. I am sure you would not ask such a question unless you knew the answer. Your technicians have spectroscopes. By now they will have examined the sections of the bow removed from

Barracuda in Rota after the collision and found traces of titanium.' Gorshkov added, 'We do not want to sink your ships. We want to put a stop to this before it gets out of control.'

'You're buying time, Admiral. You want to delay until you have a fleet of deep-diving titanium subs.'

Gorshkov's face was still bland, almost affable. 'You're a gambler, Admiral Netts. I would enjoy playing poker with you. But, as it is, we have each lost a submarine, and neither of us wishes to lose another. Or be provoked into a war.'

They both turned to the river. Gorshkov said, 'And so, once again, it is agreed neither of us will speak of what has happened, or of this meeting.'

Netts nodded curtly. 'I have already said so. *Barracuda* disappeared, causes unknown.'

'For us, it is simple. *Potemkin* never existed.'

They did not shake hands on the bargain. Self-interest sealed it. For now. They would have no war today.

Below them a barge whistle shrilled. They faced each other for a moment, then turned and walked off in opposite directions.

Fontana Paperbacks
Fiction

Fontana is a leading paperback publisher of both non-fiction, popular and academic, and fiction. Below are some recent fiction titles.

☐ FIRST LADY Erin Pizzey £3.95
☐ A WOMAN INVOLVED John Gordon Davis £3.95
☐ COLD NEW DAWN Ian St James £3.95
☐ A CLASS APART Susan Lewis £3.95
☐ WEEP NO MORE, MY LADY Mary Higgins Clark £2.95
☐ COP OUT R.W. Jones £2.95
☐ WOLF'S HEAD J.K. Mayo £2.95
☐ GARDEN OF SHADOWS Virginia Andrews £3.50
☐ WINGS OF THE WIND Ronald Hardy £3.50
☐ SWEET SONGBIRD Teresa Crane £3.95
☐ EMMERDALE FARM BOOK 23 James Ferguson £2.95
☐ ARMADA Charles Gidley £3.95

You can buy Fontana paperbacks at your local bookshop or newsagent. Or you can order them from Fontana Paperbacks, Cash Sales Department, Box 29, Douglas, Isle of Man. Please send a cheque, postal or money order (not currency) worth the purchase price plus 22p per book for postage (maximum postage required is £3.00 for orders within the UK).

NAME (Block letters) _____

ADDRESS _____

_____

_____